"Can I help

Cassie Lynn blin... ...rself, and quickly nodded. "... ...' Hoping there was no visible sign of th... ...th she felt climbing in her cheeks, she held out her hand.

He took it in his larger, work-callused one and placed his other hand behind her back. With surprisingly little effort the green-eyed stranger had her on her feet in no time. He stepped away once he was certain she was steady, and she found herself missing the gentle strength of his touch.

He continued to eye her cautiously. "Are you sure you're okay?"

Cassie Lynn nodded as she busied herself dusting her skirt. It wasn't often she found herself flustered this way. "Please don't worry. I've taken worse falls tripping over my own feet."

She studied him while trying not to appear to be nosy. There was something about the man that intrigued her. It wasn't his vivid eyes, or his appearance, though that was appealing enough in a rugged, well-muscled sort of way.

No, it was something about his demeanor and bearing that commanded her attention.

Winnie Griggs is the multipublished, award-winning author of historical (and occasionally contemporary) romances that focus on small towns, big hearts and amazing grace. She is also a list-maker and a lover of dragonflies, and holds an advanced degree in the art of procrastination. Winnie loves to hear from readers—you can connect with her on Facebook at Facebook.com/winniegriggs.author or email her at winnie@winniegriggs.com.

Books by Winnie Griggs

Love Inspired Historical

Texas Grooms

Handpicked Husband
The Bride Next Door
A Family for Christmas
Lone Star Heiress
Her Holiday Family
Second Chance Hero
The Holiday Courtship
Texas Cinderella

Visit the Author Profile page
at Harlequin.com for more titles.

WINNIE GRIGGS

Texas Cinderella

HARLEQUIN® LOVE INSPIRED® HISTORICAL

Recycling programs
for this product may
not exist in your area.

 LOVE INSPIRED BOOKS

ISBN-13: 978-0-373-28375-0

Texas Cinderella

Copyright © 2016 by Winnie Griggs

www.Harlequin.com

Printed in U.S.A.

Live in harmony with one another; be sympathetic, love as brothers, be compassionate and humble.
—*1 Peter* 3:8

Dedicated to my fabulous agent, Michelle Grajkowski,
who is always there for me
and who never loses faith in me.

And to my wonderful writer friends who are always
willing to help me brainstorm my way out of sticky
plot scenarios—Amy, Christopher, Dustin and Renee.

Chapter One

Turnabout, Texas
August 1898

Cassie Lynn Vickers stopped at the doorway to the parlor and smiled at the woman seated in her wheelchair. "Mrs. Flanagan, I'm about to head out for my afternoon walk. I left a pitcher of lemonade and a slice of pie on the kitchen table. Is there anything else you need before I go?"

Her employer waved a hand dismissively. "Go on with you. You know I hate being fussed over."

Cassie Lynn hid a smile. Mrs. Flanagan detested any reminder that she could no longer do for herself, at least not for the near future. She'd injured her leg in a fall two weeks ago and had been confined to a wheelchair ever since. That's when the cantankerous widow had hired Cassie Lynn to act as her housekeeper and personal attendant.

"Yes, ma'am," she said meekly. "And I'll try not to tarry today. I have extra baking to do tonight."

Cheered by the thought of her new enterprise, Cassie Lynn gave a final wave and headed for the front door.

But as soon as she stepped out on the porch and closed the door behind her, she paused. There was someone striding up the walk. That was odd—Mrs. Flanagan rarely received callers.

Cassie Lynn's eyes widened in recognition. She'd know that slight limp and stiff-backed posture anywhere. It was her father. What was he doing here?

Although she'd seen him from time to time since she'd moved to town last December, it was the first time he'd deliberately sought her out. Fearing something was wrong, she quickly descended the porch steps, meeting her father halfway down the front walk.

"Hello, Pa." She was breathless and tried to calm herself. "Is something the matter? Did something happen to one of the boys?" She had four brothers, three of them younger than her, and all still living with her father out on the remote farm.

He frowned disapprovingly. "Goodness, girl, there's no need to get all in a fret. Your brothers are just fine."

She let out a relieved breath, then gave her father a smile. Perhaps he'd come especially to check on her, after all. She set her market basket down and gave him a quick hug. "You're looking well," she said as she stepped back.

He hooked a thumb under his suspenders. "Comes from living a simple life filled with honest labor."

"Yes, sir." He'd always been a no-nonsense, unsentimental sort of man. Trying to ignore the little pinch of yearning for a softer greeting, she offered him a tentative smile. "I have some news."

His brow went up at that and he gave her a keen glance. "And what might that be?"

To her surprise he seemed truly interested. Buoyed by that, she rushed to explain. "I'm going to start a bakery business. Mrs. Fulton over at the restaurant and Mrs. Dawson over at the sweet shop are both going to try my wares. And Mrs. Flanagan here is talking about partnering with me." It was a modest start, but if things worked out, by the time Mrs. Flanagan no longer needed her help, Cassie Lynn might actually be able to make a go of this bakery idea. And then she would truly have established herself as part of the town, something she'd been striving for since she'd escaped her father's farm nine months ago.

Her father was no longer smiling, though, and she found herself almost apologizing. "I know it's not a lot, but in time it could grow to something big enough for me to make a good living from."

Her voice trailed off as she saw the disappointment deepen on his face.

"I thought you might be wanting to tell me you'd found yourself a beau." His tone made it clear she'd failed in some significant way. "I figured that was why you left home in the first place. After things didn't work out with Hank Chandler, I assumed you were setting your sights on some other bachelor."

When Verne, Cassie Lynn's oldest brother, had married and brought his bride home to take over as lady of the house, Cassie Lynn had made her escape from the isolation and drudgery of her father's farm and moved to town. At the time, Hank Chandler had been looking for a wife to help him raise the two children in his charge. For a while it had looked like she might just be that woman, but then she realized Mr. Chandler had fallen in love with the schoolteacher, and Cassie Lynn had pulled herself out of the running.

Not that she had really minded. Finding a husband had never been her reason for leaving the farm.

"I didn't move to town to find a husband, Pa." She struggled to keep her tone matter-of-fact. "I moved here to be around other people and to make a new life for myself."

Her father dismissed her statement with an impatient wave of his hand. "And just what kind of life can a girl make for herself without a husband and young'uns?"

Cassie Lynn's chest tightened as she realized that trying to explain her dreams to him was useless, that he would never understand. So instead of responding to his statement, she changed the subject. "Was there something you came here to see me about?"

Her father nodded. "Verne bought himself some land of his own to farm, and he and Dinah are planning to build a house on it and move out."

Cassie Lynn smiled, genuinely pleased for her older brother. "Verne always loved working the land. He'll do well."

"That he will. But once he and his wife move away, that leaves me and your other brothers on our own."

Her stomach clenched. She knew what was coming next, and she frantically searched her mind for a way to stave it off.

But her father pressed on. "I want you to come back home and take your place as lady of the house. Since it doesn't look like you're going to have a home and family of your own to care for anytime soon, that shouldn't be a problem."

No! She'd already escaped that life. She couldn't return to that lonely drudgery. "I've made a commitment to take care of Mrs. Flanagan," she protested, "and I can't go back on my word. Surely you wouldn't expect me to."

"No, I suppose not. A Vickers's word is never given lightly." Her father rubbed his chin thoughtfully. "How long does Doc Pratt say she's gonna be stuck in that chair?"

"Probably another four or five weeks."

He nodded in satisfaction. "Well then, that shouldn't be a problem. Even if Verne is ready to move out sooner, I'm sure I can convince him to stay that long."

Cassie Lynn steeled herself to take a stand. Her father couldn't *force* her to return to the farm. "I didn't say I would come home when I'm done here. I told you, I'm starting a bakery business."

He frowned. "Of course you'll come home. This town doesn't need a baker—any housewife worth her salt can do her own baking. So there's nothing here in town to hold you." He eyed her sternly. "Me and your brothers work hard keeping that farm going—sunup to sundown most days. You don't want us to have to cook our own meals and do all the housework, too, do you?"

"No, of course not. But—"

He gave a decisive nod. "Good. Then it's agreed. I'll expect you back when your work here is done." And with a quick pat to her shoulder, her father departed, apparently assuming the subject was closed.

Cassie Lynn's fists tightened at her sides as she watched him walk away. If her father had his way, she'd have only four or five weeks before her world drew in once more to the narrow confines of the isolated farm—

the world she thought she'd escaped for good. She *couldn't* let that happen.

How could her father expect her to meekly return home, as if she had no ambitions for her life? So what if she didn't yet have a husband? She was only twenty-two! It wasn't as if she was past marriageable age. Besides, what chance did she ever have of finding a man if she returned to the farm?

But how could she refuse her father when he was so determined? Especially when it was her fault that her mother was no longer around to fill that role.

Cassie Lynn picked up the basket and began to slowly walk down the sidewalk, trying to tamp down her panic and focus on finding a solution to this problem. She'd tried to reason with her father and she'd tried to stand against him, and neither tactic had been very effective. What did that leave?

The Good Lord commanded that children should honor their parents, and she certainly didn't want to *dishonor* her father, but surely there was a way out of this without having to outright stand against him.

She wasn't surprised that her father thought a woman's only goal should be to look after the men in her life. It was how he'd treated her mother, after all. Cassie Lynn had never heard him, or her brothers, for that matter, utter a word of thanks for all her mother had done. And they'd certainly never extended her that courtesy, either, after her mother had passed.

She paused as an idea occurred to her. According to her father's own words, if she had a husband, or at least a serious suitor, he wouldn't have asked her to come home. So, perhaps that was her answer.

She just had to get herself a beau before her commitment to Mrs. Flanagan was completed.

Riley Walker stepped out of the Turnabout train depot, ushering his niece and nephew before him. This hadn't been a planned stop, but the kids had gotten restless and a bit cranky after three days of travel, so he figured it wouldn't hurt to lay over here for a few days. After all, the meeting in Tyler wasn't until next Wednesday morning, a whole week away.

Besides, his horse, River, was no doubt ready to escape the livestock car and have a chance to get some freedom to move about, as well. A quick look to his left showed Riley that the gray gelding was already being led off the train.

He turned to the kids and pointed to a bench near the depot door. "Sit over there while I see to River. Don't move from this spot, understand?"

Ten-year-old Pru nodded and took her seven-year-old brother's hand. Riley watched until she and Noah were seated, once again feeling his own inadequacy as guardian to these children. But they'd needed a protector when their mother died and so they'd been stuck with him.

He turned and quickly took possession of his horse, checking the animal carefully for any injuries he might have sustained on the trip. Satisfied, Riley led him to where the kids were seated.

"Ready? Let's get River settled at the livery and then we'll head over to the hotel." He'd gotten directions to both establishments when he'd stepped inside the depot to make arrangements for their bags to be delivered to the hotel.

"How long can we stay here, Uncle Riley?" Noah asked.

Riley heard the hopeful note in the boy's voice, and made a quick decision. "What do you say we stay through Sunday so we can all attend church service here? Would you like that?"

Noah nodded enthusiastically.

Riley turned to his niece. "What about you, Pru?"

She nodded, as well, though with more reserve than her brother. Pru was normally quiet and shy, but this listlessness was unusual. Was all the traveling they were doing starting to wear on her?

Fortunately, the livery stable was near the train station so they reached it quickly.

Cassie Lynn placed her now full shopping basket at her feet and leaned against the corral fence behind the livery stable.

She dug the apple slices from her pocket. Already the two resident horses were trotting over to see what she'd brought them today.

"Here you go, Duchess," she crooned as she held out her hand and let the black mare lip two slices from her palm.

She laughed as a reddish brown mare tried to push Duchess aside. "Mind your manners, Scarlett, I have some for you, too."

She gave Scarlett her treat. "I've had some excitement today, both good and bad," she confided to the two mares as she stroked Scarlett's muzzle. "The good news is that I'm moving forward on my bakery business."

Cassie Lynn shifted to give Duchess her share of attention. "The bad news is that Pa wants me to go back to the farm and take care of him and my brothers." She breathed a sigh. "I don't want to do that, of course. So now I need to find me a husband."

She gave both horses a final pat, then crossed her arms on the top rail and leaned into it. "I sure wish you gals could speak. I bet you'd be able to give me some good insights. I figure the way a man treats his animals is a good measure of his character."

"Are you talking to the horses?"

Cassie Lynn turned her head to see a freckle-faced boy of six or seven eyeing her curiously.

"Of course. They're friends of mine." Then she smiled and stepped back from the corral fence. "I don't think we've met before, have we?"

The boy shook his head. "We just got to town a little while ago. I'm Noah." As he stepped out of the shade of the livery, the sun highlighted a bit of copper mixed in with his blond hair.

"Glad to meet you, Noah. I'm Cassie Lynn."

"My uncle Riley likes to talk to horses, too."

"Sounds like a smart man." She held out her last few apple slices and nodded toward the two mares. "Would you like to feed them?"

The boy smiled, displaying a gap where one of his front teeth should be, and took the slices. He eagerly stepped up on the second-from-the-bottom board of the fence so he could lean over the top rail. Fearlessly holding his hand out just as she had, Noah smiled as the black mare happily took the offering. "What's her name?" he asked.

"Duchess." Cassie Lynn moved beside the boy and propped a foot on the bottom board, concerned by his precarious perch. She rubbed the other mare's neck. "And this here is Scarlett."

She smiled as the boy stroked the mare's muzzle. "I see you've done this before," she said.

The boy nodded. "Uncle Riley has a real fine horse— a gray named River. He's inside right now talking to Mr. Humphries about stabling him here."

Well, at least she knew the boy wasn't alone. Cassie Lynn patted Scarlett's muzzle so the animal wouldn't feel left out, then she leaned her elbows on the top rail again. "Are you visiting someone here or do you and your folks plan to settle down in Turnabout?"

The boy shook his head. "We don't know anyone here. And I don't have folks anymore. It's just me, Pru and Uncle Riley."

She absorbed the words, as well as his matter-of-fact tone. Before she could form a response, though, they were interrupted.

"Noah, what are you doing out here?"

At the sharply uttered question, Noah quickly turned, and in the process lost his footing. Cassie Lynn moved swiftly to stop his fall and ended up landing in the dirt on her backside with Noah on her lap.

"Are you all right?"

She looked up to see a man she didn't know helping Noah stand up. But the concerned frown on his face was focused on her.

"I'm a bit dusty, but otherwise fine," she said with a rueful smile.

He stooped down, studying her as if he didn't quite believe her reassurances.

She met his gaze and found herself looking into the deepest, greenest eyes she'd ever seen.

Chapter Two

Cassie Lynn found herself entranced by the genuine concern and intelligence reflected in the newcomer's expression. It made her temporarily forget that she was sitting in the dust and dirt of the livery yard.

"Can I help you up?"

She blinked, coming back to herself, and quickly nodded. "Yes, thank you." Hoping there was no visible sign of the warmth she felt climbing in her cheeks, Cassie Lynn held out her hand.

He took it in his larger, work-callused one and she had the strangest feeling that she could hold on to that hand forever.

Then he placed his other hand behind her back, and with surprisingly little effort, the green-eyed stranger had her on her feet in no time. He stepped away once he was certain she was steady, and she found herself missing the protective strength of his touch.

He continued to eye her cautiously. "Are you sure you're okay?"

Cassie Lynn nodded as she busied herself dusting off her skirt.

What was wrong with her? It wasn't often she found herself flustered this way. "Please, don't worry. I've taken worse falls tripping over my own feet." She quickly turned to Noah. "How about you? Are you all right?"

"Yes, ma'am. Thanks for catching me."

She ruffled his hair. "Glad to help." For the first time she noticed a young girl standing slightly behind the man, chewing her lip as if she didn't want to be here. Before Cassie Lynn could introduce herself, however, the man spoke up again.

"I've told you before not to wander off without telling me." His tone was stern.

Noah's expression turned defensive. "I just wanted to get out in the sunshine. We've been cooped up *forever*." The boy scuffed the ground with the toe of his shoe. "Besides, you were right inside, and I didn't go far."

The man didn't seem the least bit appeased. "That's no excuse."

Noah's shoulders slumped. Then he gave his uncle a hopeful look. "But you found me right away. And I knew Pru saw where I was going."

Watching the interplay between the two of them, Cassie Lynn could detect genuine concern behind the man's scolding. This, of course, must be the Uncle Riley that Noah had mentioned.

She studied the boy's uncle while trying not to appear to be nosy. There was something about the man that intrigued her. It wasn't just his vivid eyes, or his appearance, though that was appealing enough in a rugged, well-muscled sort of way. No, it was something about his bearing that commanded her attention, an air of self-confidence and strength, balanced with a concern for his nephew, which lent just a hint of vulnerability. It all came together in a way that she found compelling.

The man gave his nephew a final exasperated look, then turned to face her.

She quickly schooled her features, hoping she hadn't given away any hint of her rather inappropriate thoughts. To her relief, his expression was merely polite.

"My apologies, miss, for any trouble Noah might have caused you."

"No need to apologize." She gave the boy a companionable smile, then held out her hand to the man beside him. "I'm Cassie Lynn Vickers, by the way."

He took her hand and gave it a perfunctory shake before releasing it. "Glad to meet you, Miss Vickers. I'm Riley Walker. And I appreciate you coming to Noah's rescue the way you did."

She dipped her head in acknowledgment. "Glad to help." Then she turned to the little girl. "And I assume you are Noah's sister, Pru?"

The girl, who looked to be no older than ten or eleven, nodded.

Cassie Lynn turned to the children's uncle. "I understand you folks are new to town. I hope you enjoy your stay here."

"I'm sure we will." Mr. Walker touched the brim of his hat, and she thought for a moment he would make his exit. But instead he hesitated a moment and then nodded toward the corral. "Which one of these horses is yours?"

"None, I'm afraid. We're just good friends." She rested an arm on the fence. "I understand from Noah you've brought your own horse to town with you."

He nodded. "River goes everywhere I do." He waved toward the livery end of the corral, where Mr. Humphries was leading what was presumably Mr. Walker's horse through the gate. "That's him now."

She heard the pride in his voice and turned to study the animal more closely. His coat was silvery-gray with a few darker flecks on his flank and a charcoal colored mane and tail. The animal appeared spirited and well cared for.

"He looks to be a fine horse."

Mr. Walker's smile had a touch of affection in it. "He is that." Then he turned serious again. "It was nice meeting you, Miss Vickers, but if you'll excuse us, I need to get us checked in at the hotel."

"Of course." As he moved away, she called out to them. "Mr. Walker?"

He paused and turned back, his expression one of polite inquiry. "Ma'am?"

She felt foolish for her impulsive act. "I just wanted to say if you have questions about any of the local establishments, or need directions of any sort, I'd be glad to help you."

"That's very kind of you, but not necessary at the moment."

They resumed their exit and this time she let them. But she overheard another snippet of their conversation before they moved out of hearing range.

"Are you really going to work here, Uncle Riley?" Noah asked.

His uncle nodded. "I am. But just for a few hours each day."

Were the Walkers going to settle here then? She certainly hoped so. It would give her a chance to see that sweet little Noah again.

And his uncle.

She watched them until they disappeared around the corner of the livery. Then she dusted the back of her skirt with her hands and turned to the horses. "Well, now, wasn't that an interesting little encounter? I must say, I found Mr. Walker and his charges to be quite fascinating." She stroked Scarlett's muzzle again. Given that Cassie Lynn was looking for a husband, she couldn't help but think that Mr. Walker would be a not unpleasant choice.

Ridiculous, of course, since she didn't really know him. Then again, she didn't know any of the local gents very well, either. It certainly couldn't hurt to put the newcomer on her list while she tried to learn more about him. For instance, learning if he was even planning to settle down in Turnabout or was just passing through.

She grinned at her own silliness. Then the reminder of just why she was making her husband candidate list came flooding back, and she no longer had any desire to smile.

It was time to stop her foolish daydreaming and get down to business. Cassie Lynn picked up her shopping basket and walked away from the corral.

Finding a husband wouldn't be easy, but it wasn't altogether impossible.

Please, God, if this plan be in Your will, prepare the man You have in mind for me so that he is open to my proposal.

Feeling somewhat better now that she had a direction, Cassie Lynn straightened and moved forward with a lighter step.

But there was one big problem with her plan. She didn't know the men in town well enough to evaluate them against her requirements. Which meant she needed an advisor, someone who could help her make those comparisons and who would perhaps think of candidates she might not be aware of. There were only a few people she felt comfortable turning to for that kind of assistance.

There was Janell Chandler, the former schoolteacher who had eventually won the hand of Hank Chandler.

Then there was Daisy Fulton, the restaurant owner Cassie Lynn had worked for for six months.

And of course there was her current employer, Mrs. Flanagan. Daisy and Janell were closer to her own age, and both had moved to Turnabout from elsewhere, so they would know something of her situation. On the other hand, Mrs. Flanagan had grown up here and knew just about everything there was to know about her fellow townsfolk.

But did she really want her employer involved in her dilemma that way?

Better to turn her thoughts to what she would prepare for Mrs. Flanagan's evening meal and let the other matter simmer a bit.

A simple vegetable soup, perhaps, or a potpie could be prepared with very little thought and would leave her mind free to ponder her situation…

What would Mr. Walker and his two charges be doing for supper tonight? Maybe she could convince Mrs. Flanagan to invite the Walker family to dine with them one night soon. Having company to ease the monotony of the widow's days would be good for her, whether she would be willing to admit it or not.

And it would, after all, be the neighborly thing to do.

Riley hurried Pru and Noah along. There were several things he still had to do this afternoon, and the sooner he settled the children at the hotel the better.

The most pressing matter was to get a telegraph off to Mr. Claypool. He always made a point of letting the Pinkerton detective know where to reach him when he arrived in a new town.

Then he wanted to take River for a run. The horse had been cooped up in that train car for much too long and would be ready for some exercise. And truth to tell, Riley was, too. He missed being on horseback—there hadn't been nearly enough opportunity for him to turn loose and ride lately.

His mind drifted back to Miss Vickers. She was an interesting lady. At first glance he'd thought her a tomboyish adolescent. The way she'd stood so casually at the corral fence, elbows on the top rail, laughing with Noah—no wonder he'd gotten the wrong idea. And her slight build had only reinforced that impression.

Rushing to Noah's aid with such disregard for her own well-being or dignity as she had, and then taking her fall with a touch of humor rather than dismay—there weren't many grown ladies who would have done such a thing.

It was only when he'd stooped down to check on her that he'd realized his mistake. That engagingly rueful smile had most definitely belonged to a woman, not a child.

It was when their gazes first met, though, that he'd found himself thrown off balance. He'd never encountered quite that combination of innocence and humor before, especially mixed as it was with an air of maturity and resolve.

It was such a curious mix he wondered if he'd really seen all that in one quick glance. Still, the impression had remained with him. Of course, her cheery smile, and the dimple that kept appearing near the left corner of her lip, had contributed to the unexpected air that seemed to surround her. It bestowed on her a kind of unconventional attractiveness, even when she was sitting in the dust with a chagrinned look on her face. He hadn't been so taken by a woman in quite some time. For just a heartbeat he'd been tempted to linger, to get to know her better.

And that had brought him up short. Because he couldn't afford to let himself be diverted by such fetching distractions now, no matter how intriguing. Especially when there was no chance it could go anywhere. In another few days he and the kids would be moving on again.

"Uncle Riley?"

Noah's words brought his thoughts back to the present. "Yes?"

"That Miss Vickers lady seems nice, don't you think?"

It appeared he and Noah were thinking along similar lines. "I suppose." Actually, "nice" seemed inadequate. Not everyone would have gone to such lengths to come to the aid of a stranger and then brushed off his thanks so modestly.

"And there are probably lots of other nice folks in this town, too, don't you think?" Noah's tone had taken on a cajoling quality.

"Could be." Riley had an idea where this was headed and tried to cut it off. "But there are nice people everywhere." He gave his nephew a little nudge. "Besides, who wouldn't be nice to a great kid like you?"

Noah grinned up at him, then pressed on. "Anyway, since there are such nice folks here, don't you think it would be okay for us to stay longer than a few days?"

There it was. "We've talked about this before. We

don't stay very long in small towns. Big towns are better for long stays." Places where it was easier to disappear and not stand out so starkly. The only reason he'd stopped here in the first place was because the kids, especially Pru, had seemed unusually restless. It would do them good to get out and move around and get some fresh air and sunshine. "Besides, I have to be in Tyler for a meeting by Wednesday morning."

Riley could tell Noah wasn't satisfied with his answer. "I promise I'll find us a nice big town to spend some time in real soon. Maybe you two could even go to school for a while." He gave his niece's shoulder a nudge. "You'd like that, wouldn't you, Pru?"

The girl nodded. "I miss going to school."

"That's settled then. By the time school starts next month, we'll be someplace where we can stay put for a while." Assuming they could keep their relentless pursuer off their trail.

To Riley's relief, they'd reached the hotel by this time and it ended the need for further conversation.

This whole business of moving from town to town, never staying in one place for long, was taking its toll on all of them. If only there was some other way. But he couldn't afford the luxury of letting them set down permanent roots anywhere.

The well-being of the children depended on his keeping them several steps ahead of Guy.

His stepbrother.

The kids' father.

Chapter Three

Cassie Lynn pushed open the door to Mrs. Flanagan's home, her mood considerably different from the cheery one she'd had when she'd left here just one short hour ago. So much had happened in such a short period of time.

Dapple sat just inside the door, tail swishing impatiently. Seeming to sense her mood, the normally imperious tortoiseshell cat stropped against Cassie Lynn's legs with a sympathetic purr.

She bent down and stroked the animal's back. "Thanks, Dapple. You can be really sweet sometimes."

That was apparently too much for the feline. He gave Cassie Lynn a baleful look, then turned and stalked down the hall, the very picture of affronted dignity.

With a smile, Cassie Lynn headed for the kitchen. "I'm back," she called out as she set her shopping basket on the kitchen table. "Sorry I took so long."

Mrs. Flanagan wheeled her chair into the kitchen. "Rather than apologizing," the widow said acerbically, "tell me what that father of yours wanted."

Cassie Lynn should have realized her employer had

known he was there. How much should she say? "He wanted to give me some news about Verne and Dinah."

Mrs. Flanagan raised a brow. "They're expecting a new young'un, are they?"

"No, at least not that I know of." She started putting away the items she'd purchased at the mercantile. "But they *are* moving out and planning to set up their own place."

There was a moment of silence, but even with her back turned, Cassie Lynn could feel the keen stare the widow had focused on her.

"I've known Alvin Vickers most of his life," Mrs. Flanagan finally said, "so I know he didn't come all the way into town just to deliver news like that. He wants you to move back to his place and take care of him, doesn't he?"

Cassie Lynn reluctantly glanced back over her shoulder and nodded.

"You didn't agree to go, did you?"

"Not exactly."

The widow's eyes narrowed. "What does *not exactly* mean?"

Rather than give a direct answer, she hedged. "He was very insistent."

"You mean he tried to roll right over your objections!"

Cassie Lynn gave her a tight smile that was part grimace. "I appreciate you're concerned about me, but—"

"Ha! Who said I was concerned about you?"

When she'd first come to work here, Cassie Lynn had been taken aback by Mrs. Flanagan's vinegary tongue, but it hadn't taken her long to see behind the woman's facade to the soft heart beneath. So she didn't take offense at the words.

The woman settled back in her chair with a determined frown. "I've got a stake in that bakery business you're trying to start, remember? And you can't run it from that back-of-beyond farm."

Cassie Lynn felt compelled to defend her father. "He's my pa. I owe him—"

Mrs. Flanagan actually wagged a finger at her. "Cassie Lynn Vickers, you're twenty-two years old, a grown woman by anyone's reckoning. You need to grow some backbone and make that father of yours listen to you."

Cassie Lynn grimaced, then turned away. Mrs. Flanagan might not say that if she knew the whole story. "At any rate, I told him I wasn't leaving here as long as you needed my help."

"Well, that's something." The widow gave a decisive snort. "And I have a feeling that I may need your help for much longer than we first expected."

Startled, Cassie Lynn shot her a quick glance. Then, making up her mind, she decided to share her plan. "I do have an idea about how I might get around this."

Mrs. Flanagan straightened. "Well, bless my soul, you do have some gumption, after all." She leaned back with a satisfied nod. "Let's hear it."

Cassie Lynn took a deep breath. "It appears the only excuse my father will accept is if I was spoken for. So that's what I intend to do—find a man to marry."

The widow's brow went up. "Just like that, you're going to go out and find yourself a suitor?"

"I didn't say it would be easy." Cassie Lynn tried to keep the defensiveness from her tone. "And it's not as if I expect anything romantic." She didn't have any notions of finding a fairy-tale prince who would look at her, fall instantly in love and whisk her away.

After all, she'd already contemplated a businesslike marriage with Mr. Chandler when she'd first come to town. So she'd already come to terms with that kind of arrangement.

But Mrs. Flanagan was frowning at her. "You're much too young to be giving up on love. Don't you want at least a touch of romance in your life?"

"Romance is no guarantee of happiness. And even if that was something I wanted, in this case there's no time for such schoolgirl notions. So a more practical approach is called for."

"I see." Mrs. Flanagan crossed her arms, clearly not in agreement with Cassie Lynn's argument, but willing to move on. "Is there a particular bachelor you've set your sights on?"

"I've been pondering on that and I have a couple of ideas. The main thing, though, is I've decided what requirements the gents need to meet." She'd given that a lot of thought on her walk home.

"And those are?"

"Well, for one, since I want to continue pursuing my goal of opening a bakery, the candidate will need to be okay with having a wife who does more than just keep his house. And it would also require that he live here in town so I can be close to my customers, for delivery purposes."

"Surely you also want to consider his character."

"Of course. He should be honest, kind and God-fearing." She didn't expect affection—after all, this would be a businesslike arrangement—but she did hope for mutual respect.

"And his appearance?"

Cassie Lynn shrugged. "That's of less importance.

Though naturally, I wouldn't mind if he's pleasant to look at." Like Mr. Walker, for example.

She shook off that thought and returned to the discussion at hand. "But none of that matters unless I can find someone who's also open to my proposal."

"And you've thought of someone who meets this list of qualifications?"

"Two. But I don't really know the men here very well, so I was hoping that perhaps you could give me some suggestions."

"Humph! I've always thought of matchmakers as busybodies, so I never aspired to become one."

"Oh, I don't want a matchmaker—I intend to make up my own mind on who I marry. I'd just like to have the benefit of advice from someone who knows the townsfolk better than I do. And who has experienced what a marriage involves."

"Well, then, much as I'm not sure I approve of this plan of yours, I don't suppose I can just let you go through it without guidance of some sort."

"Thank you so much, Mrs. Flanagan. I can't tell you what a relief that is."

"Now don't go getting all emotional on me. I said I'd help and I will. Tell me who these two gents are that you're considering."

"The first name that occurred to me was Morris Hilburn."

"The butcher?"

Cassie Lynn nodded. "From what I can tell, he meets most of my criteria. Of course, I won't know how he feels about having a wife who runs a bakery until I talk to him."

"Morris Hilburn is a God-fearing man with a good

heart, all right. But he is not the smartest of men and he's not much of a talker."

"Book learning and good conversation are not requirements."

"Think about that before you rule them out. Do you *really* want to spend the rest of your life with a man whose idea of conversation is single syllable responses?"

Cassie Lynn paused. Then she remembered the fate her father had in mind for her. "There are worse things." She moved on before her employer could comment. "The other gentleman I thought of was Mr. Gilbert Drummond."

"The undertaker? Well, I suppose he might be someone to look at. Then again, he strikes me as being a bit finicky."

"There are worse qualities one could find in a man. Besides, a woman in my position doesn't have the luxury of being choosy." More's the pity. "But I'm open to other suggestions if you have any."

"I'll need to ponder on this awhile."

"Unfortunately, my time is short." She hesitated a heartbeat, then spoke up again, keeping her voice oh-so-casual. "There's actually a third candidate I'm considering."

"And who might that be?"

"I met a newcomer to town while I was at the livery. He just arrived on today's train."

"A newcomer? And you're just now telling me about this? You know good and well part of the reason I hired you is to have someone to bring me the latest bits of news."

Cassie Lynn laughed. "And here I thought it was for my cooking."

"Don't be impertinent. I want to hear everything. How did you meet him? Is he a young man or more mature? Is he handsome? Is he traveling alone." She waved impatiently. "Come on, girl, answer me."

She decided to respond to the last question first. "He's traveling with two children, a niece and nephew. I met the little boy first. Noah is about seven and such an endearing child—intelligent, curious, outgoing. The little girl, Pru, seems shy and quiet." Cassie Lynn searched her memory for all the little descriptive details, relating these tidbits as vividly as she could, knowing Mrs. Flanagan loved getting these glimpses of the outside world she was missing.

After a few minutes of that, however, her employer interrupted her. "Enough of the kids," she said with a grumpy frown. "Tell me about the uncle."

Cassie Lynn paused a moment to pull up Mr. Walker's image in her mind. "He has hair the color of coffee with a dash of cream stirred in, and his eyes are a piercing green." A glorious shamrock-green that she could still picture quite vividly. "He's lean but muscular, if you know what I mean, like he's used to doing hard work."

"And his age?"

"I didn't ask."

Mrs. Flanagan made a disapproving noise. "Don't be coy with me, Cassie Lynn. Take a guess."

She hid her grin. "I suppose I'd put him around twenty-four or twenty-five." Though there was something about the look in his eyes that spoke of experience beyond his years.

"How did you come to meet him?"

Cassie Lynn explained the circumstances as she

crossed the room to retrieve an apron that hung on a peg near the stove.

"I can see the man has obviously impressed you."

Cassie Lynn stopped midstep and glanced over at her employer.

"Don't look so surprised, girl, I'm no simpleton. If he hadn't caught your eye, you wouldn't have put him on your list." Then she leaned back. "So what was it about him that made you decide after only ten minutes in his company that he might be the husband you're looking for?"

"I only said he might be worth considering." Then, under Mrs. Flanagan's steady gaze, she shrugged. "I suppose it was the fact that he had two young children in his care—it made me think he might be a man in need of a woman's help. And it was also the way he interacted with them. He obviously cares about them."

It made her think about her relationship with her own father. He'd never been very affectionate, but when she'd been Pru's age she felt he'd had a little more time for her.

"I agree with you there," Mrs. Flanagan said. "A single man in charge of two young'uns sounds like a gentleman in need of a wife if there ever was one." Dapple had wandered into the kitchen and, with a graceful motion, leaped into Mrs. Flanagan's lap. The woman stroked the cat's back, her eyes remaining fixed on Cassie Lynn. "So tell me about these newcomers. Who'd they come here to visit?"

"According to Noah, they don't know anyone in Turnabout."

"Humph. That's strange. Not many folks come to Turnabout unless they have some purpose."

"I'm sure they *have* a purpose, it's just not to visit

someone they know." Cassie Lynn hadn't given the reason for their visit much thought until now. She hoped that, whatever it was that had brought them to Turnabout, it would keep them here for a while. Mr. Walker *had* taken a job, after all.

"If I am to advise you, then I think it's important that I meet this young man and his charges."

Cassie Lynn nodded in agreement, pleased that Mrs. Flanagan had given her the opening she wanted. "We could invite them to have supper with us tomorrow evening. Sort of as a neighborly gesture, welcoming them to town."

"Excellent idea." She stroked Dapple's head absently "In the meantime I'll think on what other men might also meet your requirements."

Cassie Lynn smiled as she pulled the cast-iron pot from its hook above the stove. Having the Walkers over for supper would do more than give her an opportunity to get to know them better.

It had surprised her that Mrs. Flanagan never had anyone, other than Dr. Pratt or Reverend Harper, drop in to see her since her accident. The woman apparently didn't have any close friends.

Cassie Lynn had been trying to come up with a way to remedy that. But how did she invite people to come by and visit a flinty widow who'd never made any effort to make friends with her neighbors?

And now she would be able to do just that. Having Mrs. Flanagan help her find a suitor wouldn't just benefit her, it would give the widow purpose, as well.

And wouldn't it be nice if Mr. Walker turned out to be *the one*.

From a purely expedient perspective, of course.

Chapter Four

Cassie Lynn exited the Blue Bottle Sweet Shop the next afternoon with a spring in her step. Eve Dawson had sold all four fruit tarts she'd delivered to her this morning, and was very happy with her customers' reactions to them. It had been the same story with Daisy Fulton over at the restaurant. Both of them had placed additional orders for her goods.

If the worst happened and Cassie Lynn ended up back at her father's farm—though she still wasn't ready to surrender to that possibility—she would have the pleasure of knowing that folks enjoyed her baked goods well enough to pay for them.

Of course, if she was being entirely honest with herself, part of the reason for the lightness of her mood was her current destination, the livery. She was looking forward to visiting Scarlett and Duchess again, of course. But she was hoping she might also run into Mr. Walker. He was working there, after all.

When Cassie Lynn arrived at the corral she saw Scarlett and Mr. Walker's horse, River, penned there. But Duchess wasn't anywhere in sight.

Scarlett trotted over to the fence, nickered and tossed her head.

"And hello to you, too," Cassie Lynn said as she reached into her basket for one of the carrots she'd brought for just that purpose.

To her delight, River wasn't far behind. "Well hello, boy. Ready to be friends." She held out a carrot and the horse took it as if it was nothing out of the ordinary.

"So where is our friend Duchess?" she asked as she rubbed the horse's neck. "Did she get the chance to leave the livery today?"

"She did indeed."

At the sound of the male voice, Cassie Lynn turned to see Mr. Walker leading the mare into the corral. Her pulse immediately kicked up a notch.

"She and the buckboard were rented out to a Mr. Hendricks to transport a load of lumber." Mr. Walker gave Duchess a final pat before removing the lead and closing the gate to the corral.

Cassie Lynn smiled. "I understand you're working here now?"

"I am. A few hours a day, just to pay for River's upkeep." He moved around to where the trough was situated, checked the water level and began working the pump. "So, do you stop by here every day?"

She nodded. "Most days, anyway. It's my favorite part of the day." She held out another carrot as Duchess pranced up to her. "These two ladies and I are good friends." Then she reached out to touch River's muzzle. "And I hope this handsome gent and I soon will be."

"River likes you." Mr. Walker sounded surprised. "He's pretty discerning when it comes to who he lets get close to him."

"I believe the carrot might have had something to do with it," she said drily. Then she turned to face him fully. "Actually, though, I was hoping I'd run into you."

He raised a brow. "Were you now?"

Her cheeks warmed as she realized how that had sounded, and she rushed to clarify. "I mean, I told Mrs. Flanagan, the lady I work for, about meeting you and the children. And she thought it might be good to have the three of you over for supper, just as a neighborly gesture, you being new to town and all. Anyway, she asked me to invite you to join us this evening. If you're free and you'd like to come, that is." Cassie Lynn mentally winced. She wasn't normally one to babble, but felt that's exactly what she'd just been doing.

He kept working the pump. "That's mighty nice of you ladies, but please don't feel obliged."

Was he going to refuse? "We're not inviting you because we feel obliged. It's something we want to do."

"Still, I wouldn't want to take advantage."

Why did he seem so reluctant? "Actually, you'd be doing me a favor," she said diffidently.

He looked up from his task. "How's that?"

"Mrs. Flanagan is currently confined to a wheelchair. That's why I'm working for her, to take care of her and do the things around the house that she can't do for herself from that chair."

He finished pumping the water and leaned against the fence, facing her. "Sorry to hear that, but I don't understand where the favor comes in."

"With her being confined to the house the way she is, I think it would really cheer her up to have some new folks to talk to."

He studied her face for a long moment, as if mentally

weighing some issue. Had she pressed too hard? Did he really *not* want to be their guest for some reason?

She was trying to steel herself to accept his refusal when he finally spoke up. "All right then. The kids and I would be pleased to accept your generous invitation. What time should we be there?"

Relieved, she gave him a bright smile. "We normally eat supper around six o'clock."

His lips twisted in a wry grin. "And I guess I should also ask just where *there* is."

Cassie Lynn gave him the directions, then looked around. "Where are Noah and Pru?"

His expression immediately closed off. "They're back at the hotel." He straightened and gave a short nod. "If you'll excuse me, I need to get back to work." And with that he turned and headed toward the stable.

Cassie Lynn stared at his back for a moment, wondering at his abrupt change in mood. Had he been put off by her question?

She turned and slowly headed back to Mrs. Flanagan's, replaying the conversation in her mind. He said he'd left the children at the hotel. Were they alone? She could see why that would embarrass him. But he was new to town, so it was understandable that he hadn't found a caretaker for them. If she wasn't already committed to Mrs. Flanagan, she would have been happy to take that position herself.

But she would make a point of giving him some recommendations this evening.

Not only was she happy to help, but she wanted to do anything she could to make it easy for him to settle in here.

If that's what he wanted to do.

* * *

Riley went about his tasks at the livery automatically. It was the kind of work he knew well and was comfortable with. He didn't mind working with and around horses, even when he was asked to muck out the stalls. It was good, honest labor.

But what he really itched to do right now was saddle up River and take him out for a long run. Riding across wide-open spaces was something he craved, the way a hawk craved skimming the air currents. It made him feel free and alive. It also cleared his mind and helped him see things more clearly.

And the ability to think clearly was something he definitely needed right now.

He wasn't sure why he'd just accepted Miss Vickers's invitation. Ever since he'd taken the kids from their home in Wyoming and set out on this never-ending journey, he'd made it a practice to keep the three of them to themselves as much as possible. All things considered, it was best if they not draw any attention to themselves. It also made it easier to slip away when the time came to move on.

And it always came.

He'd had every intention of following that same course of action here by politely refusing her invitation.

But somehow, when he'd opened his mouth, *yes* came out instead of *no*. He still wasn't certain how that had happened. Maybe it was because he was getting travel-weary, or that the constant worry over whether Guy would catch up with them was wearing on him.

Because it certainly couldn't have anything to do with Miss Vickers herself. After all, in other towns, there'd been other ladies, some equally as pretty, some equally as interesting, who'd tried to claim his attention, and he'd never faltered from his course.

Then again, none had been pretty and interesting in quite the same way as Miss Vickers. A way that tugged at something inside him.

Riley gave his head a mental shake, pushing aside that totally irrational thought. It was more likely that he'd slipped up because he was just tired.

Her question about the kids had brought him up short, though. Brought him back to his senses. It was probably innocent, but he'd been put in tough spots by nosy, well-meaning folks before, folks who wanted explanations about where they'd come from, where they were going, what had happened to the kids' parents. Trust had never come easy to Riley and nothing that had happened the last couple of years had changed that.

He toyed a moment with the idea of finding a plausible excuse to cancel on her. Then he discarded it. Doing that would call as much if not more attention to themselves than if he just followed through. Besides, reneging on a promise, even one as minor as this, didn't sit well with him.

It was just one meal, after all. And once he'd fulfilled his obligation to attend, he could insert some distance, put up some walls. Which shouldn't be difficult since he and the kids weren't going to be here more than a few days anyway.

Grabbing a pitchfork, Riley headed for the hay stall, but before he could get to work, he heard someone step inside the livery from the street.

A new customer? Riley quickly looked around for Mr. Humphries, but when he didn't spot the owner, moved forward himself. "Hello. Is there something I can do for you?"

The man gave him an easy smile. "Actually, I heard Fred had hired someone new and thought I'd come around and introduce myself. I'm Ward Gleason, the sheriff around these parts."

Riley hoped his expression didn't give anything away. "Good to meet you, Sheriff." He pulled off his work gloves and extended his hand. "I'm Riley Walker."

"Mr. Walker." The lawman shook his hand and gave a short nod. Then he released it and eyed Riley with a casual glance that didn't fool him one bit. "Mind if I ask what brings you to our little town?"

He's only doing his job, Riley told himself. Surely there wasn't anything more to it than that. "Not at all. I've got my niece and nephew with me and we're making our way to California. But since we're not in a hurry and they *are* kids, I'm making frequent stops along the way to give them a chance to get out and about and see other parts of the country." That was true, as far as it went.

"Any particular reason you chose to stop *here*?"

Riley shrugged, keeping his demeanor open and casual. "I make it a point of never traveling more than a few days at a time. My niece was getting restless and this just happened to be a good stopping off point."

"Just the luck of the draw, is that it?"

"I guess you could say that." How much longer would this thinly disguised interrogation last?

But the lawman didn't seem to be in a hurry to take his leave. He crossed his arms and leaned against a support post. "So this isn't a permanent stop for you?"

"Nope." Riley placed his hands on top of the pitchfork handle and leaned his weight against it, trying to emulate the sheriff's relaxed pose. "Don't plan to be here more than a few days." Maybe shorter if the sheriff took too keen an interest in them.

"And where are your niece and nephew right now?"

Keep it casual. "They're resting at your town's fine hotel."

"Hi there, Sheriff." Mr. Humphries's hail turned both men's heads toward the side office. "You looking to rent a buggy?"

Riley tried not to let his relief at the interruption show.

The sheriff straightened. "Hello, Fred. No, I'm just getting acquainted with Mr. Walker here."

Fred Humphries gave Riley a smile. "Well, he's a good worker, at least so far. And he seems to know his way around horses, too."

Uncomfortable with standing there while he was being talked about, Riley cleared his throat. "I think that's my cue to get back to work." He nodded to both men and headed toward the hay stall once more.

Riley jabbed the pitchfork into the hay with a little more force than was necessary. Did every newcomer to town come under such scrutiny or was there something about him and the kids that had brought them to Sheriff Gleason's notice?

Now that he *had* come to the sheriff's notice, though, he'd need to be more careful than ever. Not that he'd done anything illegal, but getting certain matters untangled if they came to light could prove tricky.

It seemed the sooner he and the kids left Turnabout, the better.

Later that afternoon, Riley exited the hotel with Noah and Pru, feeling unsettled. For one thing, he hadn't had the chance to saddle up River and go for a ride as he'd hoped. Mr. Humphries had asked for his help repairing one of the stall gates and he'd felt obliged to agree. By the time that was done he'd had to get back to the hotel and check on the kids. Riley didn't like to leave them alone for more than a couple hours at a time. But they'd be boarding the train again in a few days, and he had hoped to get a lot of riding in while they were here.

The other reason for his unsettled mood was that he found himself wondering for the hundredth time why he was going through with this. He'd let down his guard when Miss Vickers looked at him with such entreaty in her gaze, thinking that one meal with her and her employer couldn't hurt anything.

But it was better to remember that he couldn't afford to have someone look too deeply into their situation, than to keep pondering over the way he felt when he was with her.

It was probably just as well that this was only a temporary stop along their unending journey.

Noah all but skipped along the sidewalk, seeming hardly able to contain his excitement. "I like Miss Vickers. She's really nice."

Pru cut her uncle a quizzical look. "Uncle Riley must think so, too, if he's letting us go to her house."

Riley mentally winced that his distrust of everyone they met was rubbing off on the kids. "It's only for supper," he said, feeling strangely defensive. "Besides, she helped Noah at the livery yesterday, so it would have been impolite to turn down her invitation."

"It doesn't matter why we're going, Pru," Noah said. "This is gonna be a whole lot better than eating in our room or in the hotel restaurant."

"Just don't get used to it," Riley warned. "Like I said, this is a one-time thing." He felt a small pang of regret as he said that. Which was odd. How had the woman, after only two brief encounters, gotten under his skin this way?

As they approached the house Miss Vickers had directed him to, Riley studied it with an objective eye. It was a modest white, one-story structure with a high roof, a porch in front that stretched the entire width, and a large swing hanging on one end. Turning onto the front walk, he realized this would be the first time he and the kids would enter a family home since they'd left Pru and Noah's own home in Long Straw, Wyoming.

Riley ushered them up the porch steps, making certain to rein in some of Noah's exuberance. Knocking at the front door, he steeled himself. They would visit, share the meal and that would be that. In three or four days they'd board the train and resume their journey.

Miss Vickers opened the door almost immediately and smiled warmly. "Welcome. Please come in."

"Good evening." He nodded to her as they entered.

She returned his greeting, then smiled down at the children. "Hello, Noah, Pru. It's so nice to see you again."

Pru nodded shyly, while Noah looked around with eager curiosity. She led them into the parlor, where an older woman with faded blond hair sat waiting for them, commanding the room as if she sat on a throne rather than a wheelchair.

Miss Vickers quickly made the introductions. Then she waved to the sofa. "Please, sit down. We have a few minutes before supper is ready."

Riley waited until she herself had taken a seat near her employer before ushering the kids to the sofa.

Mrs. Flanagan leaned back, with the air of a queen granting an audience. "Well now, Cassie Lynn tells me you all just arrived in town yesterday. What brings you to Turnabout?"

Riley repeated the answer he'd given the sheriff.

Their hostess frowned. "So you're not planning to be here very long."

"No, ma'am, not more than a few days." Was it his imagination or was there a shadow of disappointment in Miss Vickers's expression? If so, she covered it quickly.

Still, the thought that she might wish he would stay longer bolstered his spirits in a way that made no sense at all.

It was a good thing this would be a one-time visit and that they would be leaving town in a few days' time. It appeared the kids weren't the only ones who felt the pull of this taste of family home warmth.

Which was strange, because even before he'd had to go on the run with the kids, he'd led a less-than-settled life.

Well, there was no way he'd let one look from a young lady, no matter how winsome, further complicate his life.

Which meant he should do whatever he could, short of being impolite, to speed up this little outing.

He leaned forward looking for an opening to move things along.

Chapter Five

Cassie Lynn felt a stab of disappointment at Mr. Walker's announcement of his intent to leave Turnabout soon. Because he'd taken a job at the livery, she'd just assumed his move here was more or less permanent. Wishful thinking on her part, it seemed.

She hadn't realized until now just how much she'd been hoping Mr. Walker would be the man who would become her marriage partner. Then again, perhaps it was better this way. She'd already decided it would be best to marry someone she had no emotional ties to.

It was a setback, but not a major one. She'd just have to turn her attention to finding another candidate for her husband.

"Why are you in that wheelchair?"

Noah's artless question pulled Cassie Lynn back to the present.

"Noah!" Mr. Walker's sharply uttered reprimand was met with a confused look from the boy.

But Mrs. Flanagan flapped her hand at the boy's uncle. "Let him be." Then she turned to Noah. "Because I injured my leg, that's why."

He stood and moved closer. "Does it still hurt?"

The widow responded as if it had been a perfectly sensible question. "It aches a bit."

He tilted his head to study the wheels. "Can you get around in that thing yourself or does someone have to push you?"

She drew herself up. "I'll have you know, young man, that I manage quite well on my own."

Cassie Lynn hid a smile as she watched the exchange. Noah didn't seem at all put off by Mrs. Flanagan's manner. And for her part, the widow seemed to actually be enjoying the give-and-take.

A moment later Cassie Lynn noticed Pru, who was seated at her uncle's side, sit up straighter and stare at something across the room. Following the girl's gaze, she saw Dapple stretched out near the fireplace. The cat was watching them with half-closed eyes while his tail swished lazily back and forth.

While Noah and Mrs. Flanagan continued their spirited but unorthodox conversation, Cassie Lynn leaned toward the little girl. "I see you've spotted Dapple. Do you like cats?"

Pru nodded. "Yes, ma'am."

"I'm afraid Dapple's a little wary of strangers, but perhaps if I introduce you, you can make friends with him. Would you like that?"

Pru nodded more enthusiastically this time.

Cassie Lynn caught Mr. Walker's gaze for a moment. The approval in his expression caught her off guard and she felt warmth climb in her cheeks.

Quickly turning back to Pru, she stood and held out her hand. After only a moment's hesitation, the girl grasped it and let herself be led across the room.

As Cassie Lynn eased the way for Pru and Dapple to get acquainted, she imagined she could feel Mr. Walker's gaze on her. But that was foolish. He was no doubt just keeping an eye on his niece.

When she turned to escort Pru, who now held Dapple, back to her seat, Mr. Walker was once more focused on Noah and Mrs. Flanagan.

"If you'll excuse me," Cassie Lynn said to the room at large, "I'll go check on supper. We should be ready to eat in just a few minutes."

Mr. Walker stood as she made her way across the room. "Is there something I can help you with?"

He sounded almost eager, but she shook her head. "Thank you, but you're a guest here. I can manage."

"Nonsense. I hope you won't stand on ceremony with me. My ma taught me to help out in the kitchen rather than expect to be waited on. And helping is the least I can do to repay you ladies for your generous dinner invitation." He turned to Mrs. Flanagan. "That is, if you don't mind me leaving the kids here with you for a few minutes?"

The widow waved her hand. "Go on ahead, we'll be fine."

With a smile, Mr. Walker turned back to Cassie Lynn. "Lead the way."

She wasn't quite sure what to make of his offer. Her father and brothers had certainly never felt obliged to help her with what they considered women's work. She'd just assumed all men felt that way.

"Have you worked for Mrs. Flanagan very long?" he asked as they moved toward the kitchen.

His question brought her thoughts back to the present. "Just a little over two weeks. That's when she hurt her leg."

He nodded. "She seems like a feisty woman."

Cassie Lynn gave a smile at that understatement. "She is that. It's chafing at her not to be able to do for herself."

They'd arrived at the kitchen and Mr. Walker inhaled appreciatively, his expression blissful. "That sure does smell good."

"Thank you. It's a venison roast, one of Mrs. Flanagan's favorite dishes."

He rubbed his hands together. "All right now, what can I do to help?"

Cassie Lynn gave him a challenging look. "How are you at setting the table?"

He drew himself up with mock pride. "I'm an expert. It's a skill my mother insisted I master before I turned ten."

"Smart lady." She moved to the counter where the dishes were already stacked and waiting. "Mrs. Flanagan wants to eat in the dining room this evening rather than here in the kitchen, so I need to carry all the place settings down the hall. If you'll grab the plates and cutlery, I'll grab the glasses and napkins and you can follow me."

He gave a short bow. "I'm yours to command."

Taking him at his word, she led the way toward the dining room. Once there he helped her arrange the plates and flatware around the table, then returned with her to the kitchen and helped her transport all the food to the dining room, as well.

As they worked, they chatted about his horse, which she learned he'd raised from a colt and had a deep affection for. Just from some of the things he let fall in conversation, she could tell he thought of River as much more than a pack animal or means of transportation.

He seemed quite comfortable and at ease working beside her, as if he enjoyed her company. It was a novel feeling, interacting with a man this way. To be honest, she felt flattered and at the same time a little flustered by it all. The more she was around Mr. Walker, the more deeply Cassie Lynn regretted having to scratch his name off her husband-candidate list. She felt that they would have formed a very companionable partnership.

Were there other men who would as readily share her load, share their time and attention with her?

Is this what married life would be like? She was beginning to understand what Mrs. Flanagan had meant by not giving up on the thought of romance. Then she gave her head a mental shake. The man was leaving town in a few days. This was no time to be acting like a schoolgirl.

At last, the table was ready. Cassie Lynn returned to the parlor, with Mr. Walker ambling along at her side.

"Dinner is served," she announced.

Her companion crossed the room and stepped behind Mrs. Flanagan. "May I?" he asked gallantly as he put his hands on the back of her chair.

The widow sat up straighter, a delighted smile crossing her face before she schooled her expression into its normal disapproving lines. She gave a regal nod and waved a hand.

Cassie Lynn had already removed the chair that normally sat at the head of the table, so it was easy for Mr. Walker to wheel his hostess into position there. Once Mrs. Flanagan was properly situated, Cassie Lynn pointed him to the spot across from the widow, while she took a seat facing Noah and next to Pru.

Once they'd all taken their places, Mrs. Flanagan looked across at Mr. Walker. "Would you offer the blessing, sir?"

"Of course." He immediately bowed his head.

"Thank you, Jesus, for the meal we have before us and for the effort and skill of the one who prepared it. We newcomers are grateful that You have brought us to this place and for the generosity of the ladies who have welcomed us into their company. Bless this meal to the health and nourishment of we Your servants, and we ask especially that You provide a healing grace to Mrs. Flanagan. Amen."

Cassie Lynn echoed the amen, pleased to learn that Mr. Walker had what sounded like a familiar relationship with the Lord.

As the plates of food were passed around, Mrs. Flanagan took charge of the conversation. "So might I ask how you make your living, Mr. Walker?"

"I grew up on a ranch, and working with horses is about the only real skill I have."

"Uncle Riley is the best horse trainer around," Noah said proudly.

Mr. Walker leaned over and gave his nephew a mock punch in the shoulder. "At least the best you ever met," he said with a teasing grin.

"And is that where you all are headed, someplace where you can work with horses?"

Mr. Walker hesitated a moment as he shifted in his seat. It might have merely been irritation at the intrusive question, but Cassie Lynn got the distinct impression there was more to it than that.

"I do hope to one day have a horse ranch of my own,

but that's something I've put on hold for the time being. In the meantime, I get work where I can."

She noticed he hadn't really answered Mrs. Flanagan's question. But before the widow could press further, he turned to Cassie Lynn. "This roast is mighty fine eating. My compliments to the cook."

She felt her cheeks warm as she smiled at his compliment. "Thank you."

"If you think this is good, just wait until we get to dessert," Mrs. Flanagan declared. "Baking is where Cassie Lynn really shines."

Cassie was surprised by the compliment. She didn't often get praise from her employer.

Mr. Walker pointed a fork at her. "I look forward to it."

The conversation moved on to safe, mundane topics for a few minutes, then Mrs. Flanagan circled back around to her probing questions. "Seems to me, if raising horses is something you aim to work at, that there's lots of good places around here just perfect for a horse ranch."

Cassie Lynn cringed at the woman's continued probing. Was this her fault? Was Mrs. Flanagan trying to convince the man to stay in town because she'd shown an interest in him?

She saw a small tic at the corner of Mr. Walker's jaw, but when he spoke his tone was controlled. "Thank you, but as I said, I've put those plans on hold for now."

Then he turned the tables on her. "Mind if I ask how you hurt your leg?"

Cassie Lynn paused midbite. Mrs. Flanagan hated when anyone pointed out her infirmity. And Cassie Lynn had a feeling Mr. Walker knew that.

There was a tense moment of silence as the two at either end of the table stared each other down.

Then Mrs. Flanagan gave a nod, acknowledging Mr. Walker's point, and answered his question. "I fell off a ladder when I was trying to prune a tree out back." Then she turned to Noah. "Tell me, young man, are you as fond of horses as your uncle?"

Cassie saw the self-satisfied glint in Mr. Walker's eye. Apparently he'd figured out something she'd learned, as well. The best way to deal with Mrs. Flanagan's pushy manner was to meet it head-on.

When he turned her way, he seemed abashed to find her watching him. Her nod of approval a heartbeat later also seemed to momentarily startle him. Then he returned her smile with a conspiratorial one of his own, and her breath caught as she once more felt that connection with him, as if they were longtime friends. His smile deepened as he apparently noted her reaction and she felt the warmth rise in her cheeks. She quickly turned away, busying herself with passing another piece of bread to Noah.

As the conversation flowed around the table, Cassie Lynn suddenly realized Pru wasn't participating. Hoping to find a way to draw the girl in, she turned to her and only then noticed that Pru was picking at her food without really eating much of anything. Was there something more than shyness at work here?

Concerned, she leaned closer and asked quietly, "Are you all right, Pru?"

Pru gave her an embarrassed look and nodded. "I'm just not very hungry," she said softly.

Cassie Lynn patted the child's leg. "That's fine. You don't have to eat if you don't want to."

The girl nodded and broke off a small piece of bread to nibble on, as if to prove she was all right.

But apparently Mr. Walker had noticed. His expression concerned, he leaned toward his niece. "What's the matter, Pru?"

"I'm just not very hungry," she said again.

Cassie Lynn frowned. There seemed to be more than a lack of appetite going on with the girl. She was pale and her eyes had a slightly glazed look.

Placing her hand on Pru's forehead, Cassie Lynn shot Mr. Walker a worried glance. "She's running a fever."

He immediately pushed away from the table. "If you ladies will excuse our early departure, I should take her back to the hotel, where she can lay down."

Cassie Lynn moved her hand to the girl's shoulder and stood. "Perhaps it would be better to have Doc Pratt take a look at her first."

"Absolutely." Mrs. Flanagan's tone brooked no argument. "Let her rest on the bed in the spare room while Cassie Lynn fetches the doctor."

Mr. Walker's brows drew down. "I don't want to put Miss Vickers out—"

She gave him a smile. "Doc Pratt lives right next door, so it's no trouble at all. It won't take me but a few minutes to fetch him." She stood and pointed to the doorway. "The spare room is down that hall, third door on the left. Why don't you help Pru get comfortable and lie down, and I'll be back faster than a squirrel can climb a tree."

Mr. Walker hesitated and she saw the worry in his expression. The poor man likely had very little experience with childhood illnesses. She impulsively touched his arm. "Children seem to get these fevers with vexing regularity. I'm sure it's nothing to worry about, but it's always best to get a doctor to check it out if you can."

He nodded. "Very well. Thank you."

Riley picked Pru up and carried her down the hall to the room Miss Vickers had indicated. The little girl snuggled up against his chest with touching trust. Why hadn't he realized sooner that she was sick? Some guardian he was.

He gave her a squeeze that he hoped was comforting. Comforting the way Miss Vickers's touch on his arm had been.

Shaking off that stray thought, he looked down at his niece. "Don't worry, kitten, the doctor is going to come and fix you right up."

At least he sincerely hoped so.

Riley set Pru on one of the two narrow beds in the room and helped her remove her shoes.

His thoughts turned back to that fleeting touch Miss Vickers had given him. For just a moment there in the dining room, as she'd taken a moment to try to reassure him, he'd had a sense of what it would be like not to have to face all this on his own, to have someone at his side willing to support him in difficult times, willing to shoulder some of the responsibility.

It had felt good.

But it wasn't real. That kind of relationship didn't really exist, at least not for him.

As promised, Miss Vickers was ushering the doctor into the room in a matter of minutes. The introductions were made quickly, then the white-haired physician turned to Pru with an avuncular smile.

"Well now, young lady, I understand you're not feeling well."

"No, sir."

"Let me just have a look at you and see if we can do something to make you feel better." He turned to Riley. "Why don't you wait in the parlor? Miss Vickers here will assist me."

Riley started to protest, but Miss Vickers took his arm and gently led him to the door. "Don't worry, Doc Pratt knows what he's doing. He's been looking out for kids in this town since before I was born."

A moment later Riley found himself on the other side of a closed bedroom door. Shoving his hands in his pockets, he headed back down the hall.

He found Noah and Mrs. Flanagan in the parlor.

His nephew immediately popped up and rushed to him. "What did the doctor say? Is Pru gonna be okay?"

Realizing Noah was remembering his mother's illness and death, Riley placed a comforting hand on the boy's shoulder. "Of course she is. You heard Miss Vickers—kids get sick all the time."

Noah seemed only partially reassured.

Mrs. Flanagan spoke up then. "Your uncle is correct. I remember when my own two boys were little, they would get fevers and chills so often I near wore a path to Dr. Pratt's place. And my John has grown up to be a fine soldier in the army."

"Your son's a soldier?" Noah crossed back to Mrs. Flanagan.

She nodded. "A lieutenant, actually."

"I have some tin soldiers."

"Do you now. John had a set, as well."

As Mrs. Flanagan began to regale Noah with stories

of some of her sons' exploits, Riley caught her eye and mouthed a heartfelt thank-you. The woman's expression softened for a moment as she nodded, then she resumed her conversation with his nephew.

While the two talked, Riley moved to the window and stared out into the shadowy dusk, trying to fight off panic. He should have been paying closer attention, should have noticed sooner that something was wrong. He'd promised the children's mother he'd look after them and keep them safe. What if there was something seriously wrong with Pru?

Father above, please keep Pru safe. She's just a little girl and she's already been through so much. I know dragging them from town to town is not good for them and it might even be what caused this illness she has. But I'm doing the best that I can to keep 'em safe. If there's another way, please show it to me. But please, don't take her from us.

It occurred to him it was providence that he'd been here tonight. He would have managed on his own, of course—got the hotel clerk to send for the doctor. But the way the two women had immediately taken charge— seeing that Pru was made comfortable, fetching the doctor, keeping Noah entertained and distracted—had been a true blessing.

Miss Vickers, especially, had a comforting presence, a way of calming the children and setting them at ease.

Dr. Pratt finally stepped into the room, with Miss Vickers at his side, and Riley immediately came to attention, moving toward them. "How is she?"

He spied Miss Vickers's sympathetic expression, but

something in her eyes communicated that it would all be okay.

A heartbeat later, the doctor gave him the diagnosis. "She has chicken pox."

Chapter Six

Riley grabbed the arm of the chair beside him and blindly sat down. Chicken pox! He vaguely remembered having that himself as a kid. He'd pulled through just fine. And neither Dr. Pratt nor Miss Vickers seemed unduly concerned, so that was a good sign.

A number of emotions washed over him—relief that it wasn't something worse, panic over the thought of nursing a sick child, worry over what this would do to his plans to move on quickly.

He looked up at the doctor, trying to pull his thoughts together. Then, mindful of Noah, he stood and crossed to the hall. To his relief, Mrs. Flanagan said something to his nephew, pulling the boy's attention from the doctor.

"How serious is it?" Riley asked.

"Most children get chicken pox at some point and come though unscathed, except for a few scars as souvenirs."

Relieved for at least this glimmer of good news, he let out a long breath. "And you're sure that's what it is?"

Dr. Pratt nodded. "I've seen this countless times before. Besides, there are a few spots already forming on her back and neck." He gave Riley a penetrating look. "You *will* need to make certain your niece is closely cared for until she recovers. And you should be prepared for your nephew to start exhibiting signs in a few days, as well. The disease is easily spread from child to child. Which also means you should keep the children isolated as much as possible."

Riley jammed his fists in his pockets, feeling as if he was in way over his head. He didn't know anything about caring for sick kids. So far he'd only had to contend with sniffles and cuts and scrapes.

The doctor continued. "Your niece is a very sick little girl right now, but don't worry. In a week or so, she'll be good as new."

"A week!"

"Actually, it'll probably be a little longer. It usually takes ten days to two weeks for chicken pox to run its course." He eyed Riley sympathetically. "And then there is your nephew."

Riley felt the panic tighten in his chest. Caring for two sick kids, for at least two weeks—how in the world was he going to manage that?

Dr. Pratt glanced Mrs. Flanagan's way and raised his voice to carry across the room. "How are you doing, Irene? Is that leg giving you any more trouble?"

The widow flapped a hand irritably. "I'm fine. If I need you fussing around me, Grover Pratt, I'll let you know."

The doctor gave her a long-suffering look, then turned back to Riley. "I've left instructions with Cassie Lynn on how to care for your niece, as well as a lotion to relieve some of the itching, and something for fever.

I'm afraid that's all we can do for now. If there's anything else you need me for, you know where to find me."

"Yes, sir. And thank you." Then Riley straightened. "How much do I owe you for the visit and the medicines?"

"We can discuss that later. Right now you have sick children to see to."

Miss Vickers gave the doctor a smile. "Thank you for coming so quickly, Dr. Pratt. Sorry I had to interrupt your supper. Please let me make it up to you by sending some pie home for you and Mrs. Pratt."

The doctor gave her an appreciative smile. "You certainly don't have to twist my arm."

Riley followed them down the hall, wanting to ask the doctor another question. "Is there any chance at all we'll be ready to travel in less than two weeks?"

The doctor gave him a pointed look. "I'm sorry if it messes up your plans, son, but I wouldn't recommend taking those kids out in public until the blisters are gone. You don't want to be spreading it to others, do you?"

"No, of course not." So that was that. But if he missed the meeting with Claypool and Dixon in Tyler on Wednesday, he might not get another chance. And Dixon could hold the key to getting Guy put away for good.

Riley waited while Miss Vickers served up a generous portion of pie for the physician and escorted him out the back door.

Then she turned back to Riley with a bracing smile. "I know this seems overwhelming right now, but I assure you, you'll get through it okay."

"I appreciate your faith in my abilities." He hadn't been able to keep the sarcasm out of his voice, which wasn't fair to her. "And thank you, too, for all you've done." This time his tone was much more sincere.

Miss Vickers waved a hand dismissively. "All I did was fetch the doctor." She eyed him thoughtfully. "It seems you'll be spending more time here in Turnabout than you'd planned. I hope it's not too inconvenient."

It was, but that wasn't her fault. He shrugged. "No point in railing against what can't be changed."

"That's a very practical attitude."

If she only knew how badly he wanted to kick and scream over this setback right now. "I'm just thankful that, if it had to happen, it happened here where we'd already made such gracious friends. I don't like to think what might have happened if we'd still been aboard the train or had stopped in a town where we didn't know anyone."

By this time they'd made it back to the parlor, and he turned to Noah. "We'd better be heading to the hotel. You say your goodbyes while I fetch Pru."

He saw Miss Vickers open her mouth to protest, but Mrs. Flanagan beat her to the punch.

"Absolutely not," the woman said forcefully. "There is no sense in disturbing that child, especially when she needs her rest. She will spend the night right where she is."

That he couldn't allow. "But—"

"Mrs. Flanagan is correct," Miss Vickers said in a milder tone. "Dr. Pratt gave her a liquid for her fever that also made her drowsy. She was half-asleep by the time he finished his examination." She glanced toward his nephew. "In fact, since Noah's already been exposed, he could take the second bed in that room and sleep here tonight, as well." She gave Riley a be-reasonable look. "Dr. Pratt *did* say to keep them both isolated."

Riley rubbed his jaw while he thought over the offer. It was downright embarrassing just how tempted he was to let them take this responsibility from him, even if it was just for one night. But he had promises to keep. "I appreciate what you ladies are offering, but I think it's best I keep the kids with me."

Cassie Lynn admired the man's sense of responsibility, but one could carry that a little too far. "Have you ever nursed children through something like this?"

He grimaced, but his stubborn demeanor didn't soften. "No, but I reckon this won't be the last time I find myself in this situation. Best I go ahead and figure it out now while I have some folks I can count on to help me if I get in a bind."

"That's very admirable and responsible of you. But it will be a whole lot easier for us to help you if the kids are here. They'll be closer to Doc Pratt, too, if you should need his services." When Mr. Walker still didn't look convinced, she played her trump card. "Unless you don't trust us with the children?"

It wasn't a fair question, and she knew it. After all, what could he say?

"No, of course I trust you." He rubbed his jaw. "It's just—"

Mrs. Flanagan didn't let him finish that thought. "That's settled then." She shifted in her chair. "The children will stay here while you get some rest back at the hotel—believe me, you'll need it. We'll discuss long-term arrangements in the morning."

"Long-term—"

Cassie Lynn saw the concern on his face and intervened by changing the subject. "By the way, Pru mentioned something about a Bitsy. Does that mean something to you?"

He nodded. "It's her doll. She never goes to bed without her." He seemed to gather his thoughts as he turned to his nephew. "What do you say, buddy? Are you okay with staying here tonight and keeping Pru company?"

Cassie Lynn was pleased. As much as he seemed to be uncomfortable with being separated from the children, he was doing a good job of not letting that show to his nephew.

Noah nodded. "Don't worry, Uncle Riley, I'll look out for her tonight."

Mr. Walker gave his shoulder a light squeeze. "I know you will."

Then he turned back to her. "I'll go check in on Pru and then head back to the hotel to fetch Bitsy and a few other things they'll need tonight."

Once Mr. Walker made his exit, Cassie Lynn glanced back at the boy and saw a confused look on his face. "Is something the matter, Noah?"

He nodded, his nose wrinkling in puzzlement. "I was just wondering… The doctor said Pru has chicken pox, but we haven't been around any chickens lately."

Cassie Lynn gave him a grin. "You don't get chicken pox from being around chickens." Then she lifted her hands in an it-makes-no-sense gesture. "I don't know why it's called that. It *is* kind of a silly name for an illness, isn't it?"

She suddenly snapped her fingers. "You know what? I just realized that with all this excitement, we never had dessert. How about I fix you and Mrs. Flanagan each a piece of that cherry pie I baked earlier, and you can eat it while I'm cleaning up the supper dishes. Would you like that?"

"Yes, ma'am." Then Noah turned serious. "But if you need help with the dishes, I can do that first."

It appeared the boy had been taught his manners. "Thank you, Noah, that's very kind. But you're our guest, and it would hurt my feelings if you didn't try out that pie I baked just for you and your family."

With a nod, the boy happily moved to the table.

As Cassie Lynn carried a load of dishes to the kitchen, she pondered what impact this unexpected situation would have on her plans.

First she'd learned Mr. Walker was not going to settle in Turnabout, which took him out of the running for a potential husband. Then, in a twist, it turned out that he and his charges were not only going to remain in Turnabout for a couple weeks, but they were most likely going to be spending most of that time here at Mrs. Flanagan's place.

Of course, Mr. Walker still wasn't a candidate. Problem was, could Cassie Lynn effectively look for another man with the extra workload she now had? Not to mention the extra distraction, no matter how pleasant that distraction might be...

On the other hand, it seemed Mr. Walker's plans were rather loose. Could he perhaps develop a fondness for Turnabout during the time he was here?

Then she grimaced. Why did her wayward mind keep trying to add Mr. Walker to her husband list? She needed to accept he wasn't a candidate and move on.

Didn't she?

Riley stepped into his hotel room and began gathering up the few things the kids would need for an overnight stay. The first thing he grabbed was Bitsy. He studied the cloth doll and winced over how bedraggled it had become since his sister-in-law's death. Just one more sign that he was not as observant about the kids' everyday needs as he should be.

Then he found the few items of clothing they'd need and stuffed them all in a carpetbag.

He didn't like this arrangement, not one bit. The kids were his responsibility, not that of the ladies. And while they seemed nice enough, what did he really know about them? Other than that Miss Vickers was pretty and sweet and could cook better than his ma? And that Mrs. Flanagan had a sharp manner but seemed well-meaning at heart.

Of course, one could never count on outward appearances and first impressions. He just had to look to his stepfather and stepbrother to learn the truth of that.

Then there was the lady in Kansas City he'd hired to look after the kids while he worked. She'd seemed responsible enough, but she'd ended up not only neglecting her charges, but absconding with a necklace that had belonged to Pru's mother.

No, trust was something he didn't give lightly.

On the other hand, even he didn't think the kids would be in any real danger with the ladies for one night. Apparently, unlike him, they'd both dealt with sick kids before and knew how to take care of them. And it was unlikely Guy would show up in the middle of the night.

Riley had to admit he wasn't opposed to seeing more of Miss Vickers. Not that it could go anywhere, but still, it was nice spending time in her company.

He shook his head, trying to clear it of such dangerous thoughts. He couldn't afford to make connections of that sort, not while he and the children were still on the run.

Perhaps a good night's sleep would help him see matters more clearly in the morning.

Chapter Seven

Cassie awoke earlier than normal the next morning. As she took extra care brushing and pinning her hair, she told herself it was definitely *not* because she'd see Mr. Walker soon. Last night, when he'd delivered the children's things, she'd told him that he was welcome to join them for breakfast this morning, and he'd told her to expect him bright and early.

Her room was right next to the one the children were in and she quietly peeked inside to check on them. To her relief they were both still asleep, though Pru rolled over restlessly as Cassie watched.

She left the door slightly ajar as she stepped out, then headed for the kitchen. Her first order of business would be to set a nice hearty vegetable and bone broth simmering on the stove for Pru, and then she'd get breakfast started for the rest of them.

Mrs. Flanagan's hens usually produced five to six eggs a day. With four people to feed she'd have to use every one of them for the meal. Any eggs she needed for her baking would have to be purchased from the mercantile. But she supposed that was only right—she shouldn't be counting on Mrs. Flanagan to provide her with ingredients, anyway. After all, her employer was providing the kitchen and the baking pans she needed.

As Cassie Lynn neared the kitchen, she wrinkled her nose in confusion. Was that coffee she smelled?

She hurried forward and saw Mr. Walker sitting at the kitchen table, a cup of coffee wrapped in his hands, a look of worry furrowing his brow.

He stood as soon as she entered the room. "Good morning. I hope you don't mind that I let myself in."

She gave him a sympathetic smile. "Couldn't sleep?"

He shook his head ruefully. "How did Pru and Noah do last night?"

"Pru was a bit restless, but for the most part they slept through the night. I imagine today is going to be rougher for Pru, though, as the blisters form and start itching. I remember what an ordeal it was to keep my brothers from scratching themselves raw when they had it."

He winced at that. "I vaguely remember having it myself, but not any of the particulars."

She raised a brow as she crossed the room to fetch an apron from the peg by the door. "You must have been mighty young." She tied the apron strings behind her back. "Taking care of Pru and Noah is going to require lots of patience, as well as a bit of creativity in finding ways to distract them."

He grimaced. "Right now two weeks sounds like an excessively long time."

"About that." Cassie Lynn crossed her arms. "Mrs. Flanagan and I spoke about your situation last night. We'd like to offer to help you care for the children for as long as they're sick. Both of us have dealt with this before—me with my brothers, she with her sons. But that means letting them stay here with us while they get through this."

As she'd expected, his jaw set in that stubborn line again. "That's a generous offer, but—"

She held up a hand. "I understand your hesitation at being separated from them for so long, but all the reasons we discussed for not moving them last night still apply today. Besides, we've come up with a solution that should make this easier on everyone—you can stay here, too."

He raised a brow at that, his lips twisting wryly. "You're inviting me to, what—camp out on the sofa in the parlor for two weeks?"

She fetched her large stockpot and started filling it with water. "Well, you could do that," she said, as she transferred the pot to the stove. "Or you could use the attic. I'm afraid there's no bed up there, but it's roomy and will provide you with some privacy. Mrs. Flanagan has lots of extra quilts you can use to make yourself a passably comfortable pallet, if you don't mind bedding down on the floor."

Mr. Walker shook his head. "Believe me, I've bunked down in far less comfortable accommodations." Then he rubbed his jaw, his expression indicating he still wasn't convinced.

Did he have that much trouble letting go of his notions of how things should go?

Cassie Lynn began cutting up carrots, holding her peace, giving him time to make up his mind.

"I'll admit," he said slowly, "I'm not sure how good a nursemaid I'd make to a pair of sick children." He gave her a speculative look. "If you're sure you and Mrs. Flanagan are okay with me moving in, then I guess I have no real choice but to take you up on your generous offer."

It sounded as if he still wasn't convinced. Some folks just didn't like to admit they couldn't do it all. "Very sensible of you."

"But I do have one condition."

"And what's that?"

"That the kids are my responsibility and I'll help with their care."

"Good." Cassie Lynn couldn't stop the happy bubble rising inside her. It would be nice to have some new faces around here—for both her and Mrs. Flanagan. "Just give me a little time to get some things moved around in the attic, and do a bit of sweeping and dusting, and it'll be all ready for you to move in."

He shook his head. "You have enough to do around here, especially with all of us moving in on you. I can do any rearranging that's needed up there."

Again she was surprised by his willingness to jump in and help her with her chores. "Very well. But first I need to collect the eggs from the henhouse and get breakfast started. Then get Mrs. Flanagan up and ready to face the day. *Then* we can tackle the attic together."

He stood. "I can gather the eggs while you take care of breakfast and Mrs. Flanagan. But first I want to look in on the kids."

Cassie Lynn nodded, figuring he needed to reassure himself that they were okay. "Thank you. Just try not to wake them. The more sleep they get, the better." She moved toward the cupboard, then looked back at him. "And the newspaper should be on the front porch by the time you collect the eggs, if you don't mind bringing it in."

With a nod, he moved toward the hall.

She still couldn't get over how eager he was to do his part, no matter that most of this was women's work. Perhaps if her pa and brothers had had more of that attitude, she wouldn't be so dead set against moving back home.

Thirty minutes later Mrs. Flanagan was seated at one end of the kitchen table, while Cassie Lynn worked on breakfast at the stove. Riley sat at the other end of the table, sipping his second cup of coffee.

Mrs. Flanagan ignored the coffee in front of her as she rested her arms on the sides of her chair. "Cassie Lynn tells me you agreed to let the kids stay here and to move into the attic yourself."

"Yes, ma'am. And I'm very grateful for the offer. I can pay you the same rate the hotel charges, if that's agreeable."

The woman stiffened. "Young man, I invited you and those two young'uns to stay here out of the goodness of my heart. It is an insult for you to offer me money as if I were nothing more than an innkeeper."

Cassie Lynn did her best to hide a grin. No one could do righteous indignation better than Irene Flanagan.

"I meant no disrespect," Mr. Walker said quickly. "I just—"

"Apology accepted." Mrs. Flanagan appeared to unbend. "So we're agreed that you all will stay here as my guests and we'll hear no more about payments."

Apparently considering the matter closed, the widow turned to Cassie Lynn. "I suppose you're okay with cooking and cleaning for our guests."

Before she could answer, Mr. Walker spoke up. "That won't be necessary, at least not the cleaning part. I can take care of my own cleaning—don't want to make extra work for anyone." He gave her a boyish grin. "The cooking, on the other hand…"

Cassie Lynn returned his smile. "Don't worry. It's not any more work to cook for five than for four."

He lifted his coffee cup in salute.

Just then, Noah came padding into the kitchen, rubbing his eyes. "Is it time for breakfast yet?"

Mrs. Flanagan gave him a stern look. "And good morning to you, too, young man."

"Good morning." Noah didn't appear at all intimidated by her tone. He turned back to Cassie. "Pru's hungry, too. But she says she doesn't feel like eating." He shrugged. "That don't make no sense to me."

Cassie Lynn smiled. "I think she means her mouth hurts—Dr. Pratt warned me that might be the case. Don't worry, I have some broth simmering on the stove for her. And as for you, breakfast will be on the table in just a few minutes."

Mr. Walker stood. "I'll go check in on her."

"Good idea." Cassie Lynn moved to the pantry and retrieved a jar. "Why don't you bring her a bowl of applesauce. The broth is not quite ready and this shouldn't be too difficult for her to eat."

He nodded, then glanced at his nephew. "And you come along, as well. Time to get you out of that nightshirt and into your day clothes."

As Riley walked down the hall with Noah, he wondered if he was doing the right thing, moving in here. Not that he'd had much choice. Still, it was going to be difficult for the kids to not start forming relationships with these two women.

Because motherly influences were something they were sorely missing in their lives.

He was glad to find Pru awake now. She'd been asleep when he left last night. "Good morning, kitten. How are you feeling?"

The girl pushed herself into a sitting position, her doll clutched in her arms. "I'm sorry, Uncle Riley."

Pru's softly uttered apology tugged at something protective and guilt-laden inside Riley.

Had his own distraction and worry made her feel guilty about anything she perceived would cause him trouble? That wasn't a burden he wanted the little girl to feel, especially over something she couldn't help, like this.

He smiled down at her reassuringly. "No need to apologize, Pru. This isn't your fault. Everyone gets sick occasionally." He drew himself up with a deliberately solemn expression. "Why, one of these days I'll get sick myself and then you'll have to nurse me."

She gave him the smile he'd hoped for, and he used his free hand to pat her knee through the blanket. "The important thing right now is that we do what we can to get you well."

Pru nodded. "I'm sure I'll be better soon." She held up her doll. "Thanks for fetching Bitsy for me."

From her tone and appearance, Riley could tell she was still feeling down. "Bitsy was lonesome without you." He lifted the bowl he carried. "I brought you some applesauce. Want to try and eat some?"

Her face brightened somewhat. "Yes, sir."

Across the room, Noah had already shed his nightshirt and was slipping his arms into the sleeves of a faded blue shirt. "I like it here, Uncle Riley," he said. "Can we stay?"

The eagerness on the boy's face drove home to Riley again just how much they all hated living in hotel rooms and boardinghouses. Having grown up on a farm, these kids were used to having plenty of room to run around and play out in the open. They missed that freedom and he couldn't blame them. Before he could answer, though, the boy continued to make his case.

"Mrs. Flanagan said it was all right with her." Noah's voice took on a pleading quality. "They seem like nice ladies and this place is so much better than any ole hotel room. Besides, you said Pru needs some looking after."

"That's true."

Noah nodded, then gave Riley an earnest look. "And I promise I won't say anything about Pa or where we came from."

"I know you won't." Hopefully, the boy had learned his lesson last time. "Even if we do stay here, it'll only be for a little while, just until Pru gets better. Understand?"

Grinning widely, Noah nodded. "Yes, sir."

Knowing that Noah didn't truly understand how difficult it would be to go back to their previous life when they left here, Riley stood. "Very well. The ladies have offered to let me sleep upstairs, so I've agreed to stay here, but just until Pru is better." No point in letting the boy know he'd probably be sick for most of their stay, as well. Time enough when he actually started showing symptoms.

Riley patted his niece's shoulder. "Enjoy your applesauce. Miss Vickers has some broth cooking that you can have later. I'll be back to check on you in a bit."

He turned to his nephew. "Noah, you can join us in the kitchen as soon as you're dressed."

Riley paused in the doorway. "I'll leave this open so we can hear you call out if you need anything," he told Pru.

As he headed back to the kitchen it occurred to him that in less than twenty-four hours, this place had begun to feel like home.

Once they were finished with breakfast, Cassie Lynn opened the oven to check on the fruit tarts. Pleased with the golden color of the crust, she began carefully transferring them to the counter.

"Those look really good," Noah said, an appreciative gleam in his eye.

"Thank you." She set the last of them on the cooling rack. "But I'm afraid they aren't for us. I baked them to sell to the lady who runs the tea shop."

"Oh."

Cassie Lynn smiled at his crestfallen expression. "Don't worry, I plan to do some more baking this afternoon. We'll be having pie with our supper tonight."

She moved to the table and began clearing the dishes.

Mr. Walker immediately stood to help, instructing Noah to do likewise. When the last of the dishes had been transported to the sink, the man rolled up his sleeves. "Do you prefer to wash or dry?"

Cassie Lynn started to wave away his offer, then changed her mind. He likely wanted to contribute and she was becoming accustomed to his unexpected offers to help with the housework. "Wash."

"While she gets started on that," Mrs. Flanagan said to Mr. Walker, "you can push my chair into the parlor."

She turned to Noah. "If you will come along, I have something to show you."

As Cassie Lynn watched Mr. Walker obediently push her wheelchair from the room, she smiled. She'd been right about how having company would be good for her employer. The woman was more alert and spirited than Cassie had seen her in all the time she'd been here. And she seemed to have taken a shine to Noah especially.

Riley accepted a clean plate from Miss Vickers and set about drying it. "Mind if I ask what all those pies and tarts are for?"

"I'm trying to start up a bakery business. Those have been ordered by the restaurant and the tea shop."

Impressive. "That's very enterprising of you."

She gave him a challenging look. "Women are capable of more than housework, you know."

He lifted a hand as if to ward off a blow. "You'll get no argument from me on that. I just meant with all you do around here that I'm surprised you have time to work on this, too."

That seemed to mollify her. "I baked the pies after everyone else went to bed last night. And while they were baking I made the filling for the tarts. This morning I just needed to make the crusts and stick them in the oven."

"So do you plan to go into baking full-time when your work here for Mrs. Flanagan is done?"

He saw some emotion flash in Miss Vickers's face. It was there and gone too quickly for him to read, but he got the distinct impression his question had touched on a sore spot for her.

"I hope to." Her tone gave nothing away. "But I'll have to wait and see how things go."

He wondered idly why such a pretty, clever, ambitious woman didn't have a husband or at least a beau. Was there a story there?

Not that it was any of his business.

"By the way," she said, handing him another plate, "do you mind if I ask what your work schedule is?"

"Mr. Humphries asked me to work for an hour or so in the mornings, and again in the afternoon during his busy times. I also told him I'd meet the trains when they pulled into the depot, to see if anyone needed to rent a horse or buggy." He shrugged. "But now that the kids are sick, I'm going to talk to him about cutting back—"

She raised a wet hand to stop him. "No need. In fact, it's probably good for you to get out some. I just wanted to know what to expect." She gave him an earnest look. "I'd like to make certain you and I aren't gone at the same time, so Mrs. Flanagan isn't left alone with the kids. I mean, she'd probably be able to handle whatever came up, but just in case—"

It was his turn to interrupt her. "No need to say more. I agree completely."

"Then, if you don't need to be at the livery right away, I'd like to deliver these baked goods as soon as we finish here. I promise it won't take me long."

After she'd gone, Riley went to check on the kids. Pru was sleeping again and Noah was in the parlor playing with the cat, while Mrs. Flanagan watched them.

Feeling at loose ends, Riley stepped out on the back porch and stared at nothing in particular. Already, this place was weaving a spell on him. It was a real honest-to-goodness home, and moreover it felt like one.

And it was such a seductive feeling, one that made it easy to forget the danger they were in.

Of course, if his meeting with Detective Claypool and the informant he'd tracked down actually resulted in the break they were hoping for, perhaps he and the kids would actually have a chance to lead a normal life again.

But that was a big if.

He bowed his head.

Please, Father Almighty, let this meeting on Wednesday lead to something solid. I'm not certain how much more of this me and the kids can take.

Chapter Eight

"I take it your deliveries went well."

Cassie Lynn nodded in response to Mrs. Flanagan as she set her hamper on the counter. Mr. Walker had headed out the door almost as soon as she'd walked in, stating that he needed to stop at the hotel to have their things sent over before he went to work at the livery. Apparently, Pru had a book among her things that she'd been asking after.

"Daisy put the pies on her menu," Cassie Lynn said in answer to the question, "and Mrs. Dawson told me the choir was meeting there for tea this afternoon and she was sure they'd want the tarts."

Mrs. Flanagan nodded in satisfaction. "This bakery business is going to do well, just you wait and see."

Cassie Lynn smiled, then looked around. "Where's Noah?"

"With his sister. I got out my sons' old checker game and suggested he play with her to keep her mind off of her chicken pox."

Cassie Lynn nodded. "That's good. I don't suppose he's showing symptoms yet?"

"Not yet. But I expect he will in the next day or so."
Then her employer turned serious. "You and I need to
talk."

Puzzled, Cassie Lynn walked to the table and took
a seat across from her. "Of course. Is there something
you need me to do?"

"What I need is to know whether or not you're still
interested in pursuing a marriage partner."

Cassie Lynn felt an unexpected twinge of guilt at the
question. But she tamped it down. "Of course I'm still
interested. Why wouldn't I be?"

"I've seen the way you look at Mr. Walker. It's going
to be difficult for you to find yourself a husband if you're
already smitten with another man."

"Smitten! That's absurd. I hardly know Mr. Walker."
But even as she protested, she felt a flush warm her
cheeks.

Mrs. Flanagan didn't say anything, just continued to
stare pointedly at her.

Cassie Lynn felt compelled to break the silence. "Besides, even if it were true, that doesn't change anything.
You heard Mr. Walker. He plans to leave town just as
soon as Pru and Noah are well and able to travel."

"But that doesn't change the fact that you *are* attracted to him."

"I barely know the man," she protested. "And as I've
said all along, my selection of a man to marry will have
nothing to do with emotional entanglements."

"Easier said than done. And don't forget, you'll be
living under the same roof with Mr. Walker and sharing
your meals with him for the next two weeks."

"That won't make any difference." Cassie Lynn stood.
"But you're right about how busy my days are going to

be for a while. Perhaps I'll limit my search for the time being to developing a strong list of candidates and to figuring out my approach. Then, once Mr. Walker and his charges leave, I'll be prepared to act." Or as prepared as she could be. "After all, the goal wasn't necessarily to be married in five weeks, just to have a committed suitor by then."

Cassie Lynn tied her apron behind her back. "That being said, have you thought of any additional men I should consider?"

Mrs. Flanagan had apparently been ready for that question. "What do you think of Jarvis Edmondson?"

"Mr. Edmondson, the blacksmith?"

Her employer nodded. "He's a widower, going on five years now. He and Mary Ann had a happy marriage, as far as I could tell. He lives here in town, no one's ever complained about his honesty, and he attends church every Sunday. And Mary Ann made beautiful tatted lace that she sold to Hazel at the dress shop, so I don't think he'd have a problem with a wife who wanted to sell baked goods. Sounds to me as if he meets all the requirements you laid out."

"But he must be close to fifty years old."

"He's forty-eight." Mrs. Flanagan raised a brow. "And you never mentioned having an age requirement. I thought this was to be a businesslike arrangement."

"Yes, of course, but…" Cassie Lynn's voice trailed off, since she couldn't think of a good way to end that sentence.

"But he's not Mr. Walker."

She moved to the pantry, feeling the need for action. "Mr. Edmondson sounds like a very good candidate.

I'll add him to the list along with Mr. Drummond and Mr. Morris."

"Have you given any thought to how you'll approach these gentlemen? After all, it's not very often a woman proposes to a man."

That, of course, was the most difficult part of her plan. "I believe the direct approach will be best. Explain my situation and how a marriage based on practicality rather than emotion could be a mutually beneficial arrangement."

"I see. Well, I suggest you practice exactly what you plan to say before you approach one of your candidates. And if you could practice with a trusted male friend, that would be best."

Cassie Lynn couldn't hold back a quick grimace. Problem was, she didn't have any male friends, trusted or otherwise. Mr. Chandler was the closest thing, but even though he'd been in a similar situation not too long ago, she couldn't picture herself confiding in him.

Then, she straightened. The stakes were too high for her to let pride stand in her way. When the time came, she would do what needed to be done.

But now was not that time. "I think I'll go check on the children and see if I can talk Pru into another bowl of broth. The more we can get her to eat, the better."

Cassie Lynn walked down the hall, her mood sober. She was afraid. There, she'd admitted it. As much as she talked about just being direct and matter-of-fact, she wasn't certain she could pull it off. She'd been praying about it, and as much as she knew she should leave this all in God's hands, a part of her kept pulling the problem back into her own lap to worry over. The idea of approaching a man she didn't know and laying her unorthodox plan out before him left her shaking.

But she really didn't have any other choice.

Or did she?

Before she reached the kids' room, there was a loud buzz that indicated someone was at the front door. Cassie Lynn changed course and discovered Calvin Hendricks standing on the porch.

The youth doffed his hat and gave her a smile. "Morning, Miss Vickers. A Mr. Walker asked me to bring these here." He waved to a handcart at the foot of the steps that contained a trunk and a large leather satchel. "Would you like me to carry them in?"

She nodded and stepped outside. "It looks like you might need a hand with that trunk." Calvin stacked the satchel on top of the well-used trunk and they each grabbed an end. Within minutes they had the luggage situated in the parlor. She'd leave it there until Mr. Walker returned and decided what he wanted to do with them.

After Calvin had gone, Cassie Lynn studied the two pieces. The trio was apparently traveling light. Was this everything they owned or had they shipped the rest of their things to their ultimate destination?

She wondered again at this strange sort of nomadic lifestyle Mr. Walker was living with the children. He seemed to care so much about them, she would've thought he would want to give them more of a settled home life.

He must have his reasons, and it really wasn't any of her business.

Except that she was beginning to care a great deal about these three travelers, a lot more than seemed possible for folks she'd known for such a short time.

* * *

When Riley returned to Mrs. Flanagan's home at the end of his morning shift at the livery, he went around to the back without letting himself ponder why he wanted to enter through the kitchen. He paused before climbing the porch steps. Though he was anxious to check on the kids, he figured the ladies would probably appreciate it if he washed up from his work before entering the house.

He dipped some water from the rain barrel near the back porch and quickly washed. Feeling more presentable, he climbed the steps and knocked on the screen door before stepping inside without waiting for a response.

Miss Vickers looked up from her work at the stove and gave him a welcoming smile. "Hello. How was your morning at the livery?"

He leaned against the doorjamb. "It was busy, but I enjoy the work. How's Pru doing?"

"Itchy and uncomfortable, but she's resting right now."

"And Noah?"

"He hasn't shown signs of coming down with chicken pox yet, but it could be as long as a week or two. He and Mrs. Flanagan are in the parlor entertaining each other."

Riley cast a quick look in that direction, his brow furrowed. "I hope he's not bothering her."

"On the contrary, I think she's enjoying herself more than she has in quite some time." Cassie put down her cook spoon. "Lunch will be ready in about thirty minutes, but if you're hungry now I—"

He held up a hand. "I can wait. I don't expect you to go out of your way to accommodate me." Then he straightened. "I'll go say hello to Noah and Pru."

He returned a few minutes later. "Pru was sleeping when I looked in on her, so I didn't wake her."

"That's good. As long as she's sleeping, the itching can't bother her." Miss Vickers closed the cabinet door. "Did you see Noah?"

"Just for a moment. He and Mrs. Flanagan were in the middle of what appeared to be a tiebreaker game of checkers."

She grinned. "I told you Mrs. Flanagan would enjoy his company."

Riley inhaled appreciatively. "Whatever it is you're cooking smells mighty good."

"Thanks. It's lamb and vegetable stew."

"Sounds as good as it smells." Then he moved to the cupboard. "Why don't I get started on setting the table for you?"

"Thank you. I talked Mrs. Flanagan into having lunch here in the kitchen, so we won't need to carry the dishes very far. She's insisted that we will have our evening meal in the dining room, though, like civilized people."

He smiled at Miss Vickers's droll tone and began pulling out the dishes. "By the way, did our luggage arrive?"

She nodded, looking up at him. "It did. But I wasn't sure if you'd want it in the attic with you or in the room with the kids, so we set it in the parlor for now."

"I'll put it away before I head back to the livery this afternoon."

Miss Vickers waved her hand. "There's no rush. It's certainly not in anyone's way where it is."

She eyed him curiously. "Do you mind if I ask you a personal question?"

Riley paused, glad he had his back to her. What did she want to know? There was so much he couldn't say, so many secrets he had to keep. It was one reason he'd avoided making any kind of close friendships for the past year and a half.

But he could hardly refuse to let her ask her question, not with all she'd done for him in the past twenty-four hours. "What did you want to know?"

Please, God, don't let her ask me something I can't answer. I surely don't want to tell her a lie.

"I was just wondering, is that your only luggage?"

The relief that washed over him was almost a physical thing. That was a question he could answer freely. "It is. We travel light." He kept his tone carefully casual. There was no need to explain that they'd had to leave a large part of the kids' belongings behind three towns ago.

He began placing the dishes on the table.

After a few moments of silence, she asked another question. "Do you know if Pru likes to read?"

Her sudden change of subject surprised him, but he nodded. "She does. And she's trying to teach Noah to read, as well."

Miss Vickers straightened, a concerned frown on her face. "Did Noah have trouble with reading in school?"

Riley had said too much. How did she get under his guard that way? "Noah hasn't been able to spend much time in school this past year."

"Oh?"

He heard the question in her one-word response, but pretended not to. Her obvious concern over the children missing school chaffed at his conscience. But they'd moved around so much it just hadn't been practical.

After a moment, she seemed to get the message and gave him a bright, it's-none-of-my-business smile. "Well, school starts back up in about four weeks. If you all are still around at that time, perhaps you can enroll both Noah and Pru. Turnabout has some mighty fine teachers."

"I'm sure you do." Riley inserted a firmness in his tone. "But we won't be here that long. As I mentioned before, this was a temporary stop on our trip." Best to make sure she understood that was *not* going to change.

He needed to keep reminding himself of that, as well.

Cassie Lynn turned back to the stove. Wherever the three of them ended up, she hoped Noah would get the schooling he needed. Without the ability to read, a person missed out on so much.

Perhaps she'd mention something to Mrs. Flanagan about Noah needing reading lessons. The widow was a former schoolteacher and would probably relish having the opportunity to slip into that role again.

But Cassie Lynn still wondered why Noah hadn't spent much time in a classroom. Surely Mr. Walker hadn't pulled the kids out of school the way her father had done with her. Noah's uncle didn't seem the type to place such little value on education.

Mr. Walker had definitely looked uncomfortable with her question, though. There seemed to be something important he was leaving unsaid. Then again, she was a relative stranger to him—she shouldn't expect him to share confidences with her.

So why did she find herself wishing he would?

Chapter Nine

Once the kitchen was set back to rights after lunch, Riley turned to Miss Vickers. "I have a couple of hours before I go back to the livery. Why don't you show me to the attic, and I can tackle whatever needs doing to get it set up for tonight."

"Of course." She led him to the end of the hallway and opened a door to reveal a narrow set of stairs. Leading the way, she climbed with graceful movements.

When they reached the top, Riley paused to study the space. It was surprisingly roomy. The ceiling was tall in the center and sloped down near the eaves. There were two dormer windows on the front portion and large round ones on either end. The windows were a bit grimy, but provided enough light to make out the objects in the room.

There were a lot of odds and ends stored haphazardly about the place, but with some rearranging there should be more than enough open space to make a decent sleeping area.

"What do you think?" she asked.

He stepped farther into the attic. "This will work just fine."

She waved a hand toward the nearest window. "I thought we'd clear a space over there so you could take full advantage of the light. It'll mean moving quite a few things around, though." She pointed to the other dormer. "And if we move things away from that window and clean it up a bit, it will let in even more light."

He nodded. "I agree. I'll get started shifting items around. Does it matter where I place them?"

"As far as I can tell, there's no rhyme or reason to how objects are stored up here. Oh, and while you're working, if you see anything you can use as furniture or for storage, feel free to do so while you're here." She moved back toward the stairs. "I'll fetch the broom and some cleaning rags."

Riley went to work. Most of the pieces were light—someone had had to cart them up those stairs, after all. But there were a few heavier items that required muscle. He did find a few odd pieces of furniture he could make use of—a sturdy chair with a loose arm, a crate that would serve as a bedside table, a bench he could use as a shelf to set things on, and a trunk he could use for storage.

While he worked, Miss Vickers returned with her cleaning supplies and promptly started wiping down the window. Before long, the sun was shining through with unobstructed brightness.

Then she wended her way through the clutter to the other dormer and cleaned that window, as well.

Riley smiled as he caught the sound of her soft humming. Strange how comfortable this felt, as if they didn't need to fill the silences with words to feel connected.

She was still working on the windows when he finished moving things around, so he grabbed the broom and began sweeping.

A few minutes later she turned and met his gaze across the room. He saw surprise flicker across her expression before she bustled toward him.

"I'm sorry." She reached for the broom. "Here, let me do that."

What was the matter? Didn't she think he was capable of sweeping the floor? "No need. I'm just about finished."

She watched him uncertainly for a moment, then nodded. "In that case, I'll go fetch the quilts we can use to make your bed."

He watched her go, still wondering at her strange reaction. Did she really not expect him to do his own chores? What kind of people had she been raised around?

She made three trips, carrying two quilts the first two times. By the time she made it up with her third load, a pillow and sheets, he'd finished sweeping and had dragged his "furniture" pieces in place.

"I figured I would fold each quilt in half and stack them on top of each other to build your pallet."

"Easy enough." He grabbed two corners of the top quilt and waited for her to do the same.

When they were done, there was a pallet that was not only wide and long enough to accommodate him, but one that stood over a foot tall. She placed the pillow on top and covered the whole thing with one of the sheets.

Then, she stepped back. "I'll admit it's nothing fancy, but I hope you'll find it adequate."

He stroked his chin as he studied it. "Actually, considering the roominess of this place and the comfortable-looking furnishings, I could argue that I have the nicest room in the house."

She grinned. "I'll let Mrs. Flanagan know that you're pleased."

"All kidding aside, do you mind if I ask why you're doing all this for us—nursing the kids, inviting us to stay here? Don't get me wrong, I'm very grateful, but we're strangers to you. And this is no small service you've volunteered to perform." It was his experience that there were often ulterior motives behind offers of this sort. And even if that wasn't the case here, their current situation was precarious enough that a bit of good-intentioned interference could place them in a difficult situation.

"Not entirely strangers," she responded. "Even though I only met you two days ago, I think I know enough about you to know you're a good person."

He raised a brow. "Do you, now?"

She nodded, seeming absolutely confident. "I do. I can tell you really care about your niece and nephew, so you can't be all bad. And not only did you immediately find yourself a job your first day in town, but you've been helping out around here a good bit as well, so you're not a layabout. And you've taken all the right steps since you discovered your niece was sick, so you're a responsible person."

Then, Miss Vickers gave a curiously self-deprecating grin. "Besides, I've taken quite a liking to Noah and Pru. In fact, I sort of miss being around kids. I suppose it comes from growing up with four brothers."

It still didn't sound like reason enough to take in a sick child she barely knew, much less all three of them. But perhaps he should stop looking for reasons to question his good fortune and just accept it.

Then she spoke up again, her expression diffident. "Besides, I do have another reason to be happy you all are here."

"And that is?"

"Mrs. Flanagan, for all her bluster, is a lonely woman. Her husband and youngest son died in an accident about six years ago. Her oldest son, John, joined the army the year before that, so he's rarely around."

Riley sympathized with the woman—he, too, had lost people close to him. "But you're here with her, so it's not as if she's alone."

"True, but I work for her, so that's really not the same. Even though I've grown quite fond of Mrs. Flanagan in the time I've been here, from her perspective, I'm here because she pays me to be."

Riley wasn't sure he agreed with that. From what he'd seen so far, it appeared Mrs. Flanagan treated her a lot like family.

But he let Miss Vickers do the talking.

Her expression softened. "You should have seen her face when she was speaking to Noah after you left this morning. She came alive in a way I haven't seen her do before. I think she would truly be saddened if you should leave and take the children with you."

"But our stay here is only temporary—just until the children get better."

"I know, but by then she'll be that much closer to having the use of her leg again, and in the meantime you will have filled her days with something besides her own thoughts."

Riley lifted his hands in surrender. "Well, whatever your reasons, Miss Vickers, I hope you know how much I appreciate everything you're doing for me and the kids."

"I would consider it a favor if you would call me Cassie Lynn instead of Miss Vickers."

Her request startled him, but not unhappily so.

"After all," she continued, "it appears we'll be living under the same roof for a couple of weeks. It seems a bit silly to stand on ceremony."

"Of course, Cassie. And you should call me Riley."

He noticed a bit of pink staining her cheeks and that she wasn't quite meeting his gaze any longer.

"I think we've done all we can for now," she said, then finally turned to meet his gaze again. "If you don't have to return to the livery just yet, I do have a quick errand I'd like to run."

"Of course." Was she just trying to make her escape? He was fairly certain she'd made that request about names impulsively and that it had embarrassed her. But she wore the pink in her cheeks quite well.

Thinking back over all the reasons she'd given for helping him, a part of him wished there'd been something in there that indicated she'd wanted him close by, as well.

And the twinge of disappointment he'd just felt at that thought was yet another good reason to move on as soon as possible.

As Cassie Lynn headed down the sidewalk, she wondered if she'd been too bold in suggesting the use of first names. It wasn't something she'd planned, but it had seemed natural when she'd said it. It wasn't until she'd seen the surprise in his expression that she realized what she'd done.

Ah well, it was done now and she couldn't say she regretted it. Realizing she'd been moving slowly, Cassie

Lynn picked up the pace. She'd considered canceling her normal afternoon walk today. The additional responsibilities she'd taken on with the children didn't leave her with much free time. But there was one errand she really wanted to run.

Resisting the temptation to head out in the direction of the livery as usual, Cassie Lynn resolutely turned her steps toward the restaurant, which just so happened to also house the town's library.

As soon as she walked in the door, Daisy came bustling over to her. "Hello again. I have to say, my customers are loving those pies of yours. I'd like to order three for tomorrow if that's okay."

"Absolutely!" Then Cassie Lynn gestured toward the bookshelves to her left. "I was hoping to be able to find some reading material for a sick little girl who's staying with Mrs. Flanagan."

Daisy waved her on. "Abigail isn't here right now, but pick out what you want and leave the information in her ledger."

Conscious of the hour, Cassie Lynn resisted the urge to take her time browsing and quickly selected two works she thought a ten-year-old might enjoy.

On her way back to Mrs. Flanagan's house, she saw Mr. Drummond, the undertaker, step out of the mercantile. She tried to study him objectively without outright staring. This man could be her husband soon. Finicky was how Mrs. Flanagan had described him, and Cassie Lynn supposed he was.

As usual, he was fastidiously dressed, his clothing trim and neatly pressed, his hat perfectly situated on his no-hair-out-of-place head. He was a tall, spindly, bespectacled man who reminded her a bit of a farsighted grasshopper.

Chiding herself for the unkind comparison, she continued on her way. What would he think of her? Though she kept herself neat, she didn't consider herself fastidiously so. And would he expect his home to be kept completely spotless and perfectly organized? Would such a wifely requirement give Cassie Lynn much time to run her bakery business?

Those were things they would need to discuss if she made it to the point of proposing to him.

For some reason, thinking of that made her mood turn gloomy.

She arrived back at Mrs. Flanagan's house just in time to see Riley carrying the trunk on his shoulder down the hall. The effort had drawn his shirt taut across his back. She paused a moment to admire the play of muscles in his arm and back. Nothing spindly or grasshoppery about this man.

She quickly placed the books on the hall table and bustled forward. "Just a moment," she said as she slipped past him. "Let me get the door for you."

She tried hard not to stare as he set the trunk down in the children's room, but she couldn't seem to help herself. There was just something about this man...

He straightened, then turned back to her. "Now that you're here, I need to head out to the livery."

Hoping he hadn't caught her staring, she nodded quickly. "Of course. I'm sorry if waiting for me made you late."

He led her back into the hall and toward the kitchen. "Not at all. In fact, I have a favor to ask." His expression held a self-deprecating grimace. "If you don't mind my leaving the kids in your care for a little longer than planned, I'd like to take River for a run after I finish at the livery. He hasn't had a chance to really stretch his legs since we got here."

"Of course."

"Thank you. To be honest, I can use the exercise, as well. I always think better when I'm out riding."

"In that case, take as long as you wish." The man probably needed to do quite a bit of thinking, given the circumstances of the past twenty-four hours.

When he had gone, she remembered the books she'd left in the entryway. Fetching them, she headed to the kids' room, where she smiled at Pru. "I have a surprise for you."

The little girl sat up straighter, her expression uncertain.

"I stopped at the library today and picked up some new books for you to read."

A wide grin split her face. "For me?"

Cassie Lynn nodded, not certain if the girl understood what a library was. "You can take as long as you like reading them, and when you're done, I'll bring them back to the library and trade them for new ones."

Pru's expression changed to one of wonder. "You mean as many times as I want?"

Cassie Lynn nodded. "For as long as you are here in Turnabout, anyway."

Cassie Lynn could understand Pru's delight. As far as she was concerned, there was nothing better to help you forget how miserable you were feeling than to lose yourself in a good book.

Riley finished hitching Scarlett to the livery's buggy and led the conveyance to a waiting customer. It had been a busy afternoon, but he was glad of it. Working kept his mind from fretting over circumstances he couldn't change.

Horses were so much less complicated than people. Just one of the many reasons he preferred them to most folks.

As soon as Mr. Olson rode off in the rented buggy, the buckboard that had gone out earlier was returned. Riley unhitched the horse, checked her to make sure she was okay, and then brushed her down and gave her a bit of feed. Once that was done, he led the mare out to the corral and turned her loose.

And then he was free to leave.

Riley quickly saddled River and mounted up. Before long he was heading out of town, looking for a nice open stretch of road where he could let River have his head and stretch out in a full gallop.

He'd wired Claypool this morning to tell him the situation with the kids and to let him know he wouldn't be at the meeting on Wednesday. He'd received Claypool's response today and the detective had strongly encouraged Riley to find a way to attend. That he wasn't sure their informant would be forthcoming with him alone.

So now Riley was pondering options.

And there really was only one: ask the ladies to watch over the children while he went to Tyler. Which would mean he'd have to be away from Pru and Noah overnight.

Could he do that—go off and leave the kids in someone else's care while he was so many miles away?

If he *did* ask the ladies to do this, how much of the

children's story should he tell them? And if he did, would they still be as welcoming?

Growling in frustration, Riley saw the stretch of road he'd been looking for and nudged River into a full gallop.

Chapter Ten

After supper that evening, Cassie Lynn stood up from the table and fetched the pie that rested on the sideboard.

"So, what have you baked up for us tonight?" Mrs. Flanagan asked.

"A cinnamon-apple-pecan pie."

"Sounds delicious," Riley said.

"Baking is Cassie Lynn's specialty."

He nodded. "So I hear."

"She's always experimenting with new flavors."

"Experimenting, you say?" Riley raised a brow. "Should I be worried?"

"What, you're not adventurous?" Cassie Lynn teased as she set the pie tin on the table.

"Not when it comes to food."

Noah, however, leaned forward eagerly. "Well, I am, especially when it smells as good as this does."

"Why, thank you, Noah. Just for that, you get the first piece."

He sat up straighter, chest puffing out in self-importance. Cassie Lynn dished up a piece and handed the saucer to the little boy. Then she cut another serving and passed it to Pru, who had joined them at the table for supper tonight. The third slice went to Mrs. Flanagan.

Finally, Cassie Lynn turned to Riley. "What do you think? Have I given you enough time to gather your courage to try a piece?"

"Since no one else seems to have suffered any ill effects, I suppose I'm willing." His voice was solemn, but she saw the laughter in his eyes.

"It's good, Uncle Riley, real good," Noah assured him.

Riley accepted his serving of pie from her and tasted it with exaggerated caution. Then his eyes widened in exaggerated surprise. "Well, what do you know? This really *is* good."

Cassie Lynn rolled her eyes at his playacting, but her heart was warmed by the way he was willing to act foolish for the benefit of the kids. Not many a grown man would do that.

After the meal, Riley offered to help her clean up, and had the children help carry the dishes back to the kitchen.

"That's the last of it, Uncle Riley," Noah said as he and Pru each placed a bowl on the counter. "Mrs. Flanagan said she had something to show us in the parlor. Can we go now?"

Riley nodded. "Go ahead. I'll help Miss Vickers with the dishes."

Cassie Lynn was starting to get used to having him help her with the housework. "Just give me a minute to take my pies out of the oven."

"Are those for your customers?"

Cassie Lynn nodded. "Daisy over at the restaurant has ordered three for tomorrow. I set them to bake while we were eating." She placed the second one on the table next to the first. "I'll make the six fruit tarts for the tea shop later."

"Sounds like you're going to have a late night."

She shrugged. It was true, but that was just how things were going to be for a while.

He studied her a moment, then nodded, as if coming to a decision. "I tell you what. Why don't you let me handle the dishes while you go ahead and start work on your tarts now?"

He'd managed to surprise her yet again. "That's very kind of you, but it's not necessary. It won't take much time—"

"Exactly. It won't take much time for me to handle this while you work on that."

Deciding she was tired of arguing, she nodded. "All right. And thank you."

She floured the end of the table that was clear and began mixing her dough. "How was your ride?" she asked as she worked.

"Both River and I enjoyed it," he answered, looking back over his shoulder. "It was almost like old times."

"Old times?"

His expression closed off and he angled his face away from her. "Back before the kids and I began this trip."

But she got the distinct impression there was something he was leaving unsaid.

He asked her a question about the tarts she was baking and the conversation veered off into other inconsequential topics. Riley finished with the dishes before she had her tarts ready for the oven.

Drying his hands on a rag, he met her gaze. "If you'll

excuse me, Cassie, I think I'll go ahead and get the kids ready for bed."

She nodded and went back to work.

She'd give a pretty penny to know just what had put that unexpected strain into the conversation earlier.

Later, after she'd helped Mrs. Flanagan settle down for the night, Cassie Lynn returned to the kitchen to roll out the dough for her last two fruit tarts. She had just four tart pans, so she not only had to bake them in two batches, but had to wait until the first batch cooled enough to get them out of the pans before she could deal with the second batch. If this bakery business went well, she'd definitely need to purchase additional pans.

Once the tarts were in the oven, she stepped out on the back porch. Fireflies flickered across the lawn. A dog barked somewhere in the distance, but the sound was muffled and there was no sense of urgency in it.

She loved this time of day, when the world seemed to be pulling a blanket over itself in preparation for sleep. Most people waited until they were ready to slip into bed to say their prayers. But she preferred to be out here, where she was surrounded by the starry beauty of God's creation, to speak with the Heavenly Father. She bowed her head and closed her eyes.

Dear Lord God, thank You for this beautiful day and for the many blessings You've gifted to me. By Your grace I have a place to live, and work to occupy my hands. Watch over Mrs. Flanagan as she deals with the trials brought on by her injury, and help me to be a blessing to her. Thank You, too, for sending the Walker family our way—I know that was an answer to my prayer to

*find a way to help Mrs. Flanagan feel needed and en-
gaged again.*

*And please help me to figure out how to best plan
for my own future.*

Cassie Lynn opened her eyes again and sat on the
top step. She hugged her knees, inhaling deeply of the
warm summer air. A slight breeze stirred the leaves of
a woodbine vine growing near the far end of the porch,
wafting the floral scent around her like a fragrant ca-
ress. She found herself thinking of Riley and trying to
figure out yet again why she found him so interesting.

The door opened behind her and she glanced over
her shoulder. Riley stood on the threshold, hesitating.

"I hope I'm not intruding, Cassie," he said when she
met his gaze. "If you'd prefer to be alone, I can—"

Feeling her languor suddenly slough away, she smiled.
"Not at all. I'm just enjoying the evening breeze." She
waved him forward. "Feel free to do the same." She'd
noticed, since she'd invited him to use her given name,
that he called her Cassie rather than Cassie Lynn. The
first couple times she'd thought to correct him, but then
changed her mind, deciding she rather liked it. It seemed
more personal and grown-up than the other.

He stepped outside, then moved to lean a hip against
the porch rail beside her.

"Are Noah and Pru settled in?" she asked.

He nodded. "They are."

Cassie clutched the edge of the step. "I figured you'd
have turned in for the night after the day you had."

He gave her a direct look. "Actually, I wanted to talk
to you alone, if you don't mind."

Her heart did a funny little flutter at that. "About
what?"

"First, I want to thank you for all you did for Pru today. Not just watching over her, I mean. She showed me the books you got for her."

Cassie felt her cheeks warm. "I was glad to do it. Pru is a sweet child. And she's been a good patient. The itching is starting to bother her but she's doing her best not to complain and is apologetic every time she has to ask for something." In fact, Cassie was worried that the girl was a little *too* apologetic.

"Sweet is a good way to describe her. I've always thought she was a bit too fragile. Anyway, I appreciate you going out of your way for her."

"It was no trouble to stop at the library and pick out some books for her. In fact, I always enjoy perusing the new titles Abigail has brought in."

Then, uncomfortable with his gratitude, Cassie decided to redirect the conversation. "Was there something else you wanted to discuss?"

He folded his arms across his chest. "I know Mrs. Flanagan said she wouldn't take any payment for allowing us to stay here, but it doesn't sit well with me to not pay my way."

"If you want me to try to change her mind, I'm afraid—"

He held up a hand and Cassie stopped speaking.

"Not at all," he said. "I just figure, since she won't take my money, that maybe I can help out in other ways, at least while we're staying here. Are there any maintenance or other chores that need doing?"

That's why he wanted to talk to her? Ignoring the deflated feeling, she nodded. "I've noticed that the wire fence around the chicken coop is sagging in a few places.

I'd meant to tend to it myself but hadn't gotten around to it yet."

"Easy enough for me to take care of. What else?"

"One of the windows in the parlor is stuck tight. I haven't been able to open it since I moved in here."

He nodded. "I can take a look at that, as well. Anything else?"

Cassie searched her mind for other household needs. "I don't know if this is the sort of thing you would want to take on, but there's a limb from that old pecan tree around on the east side of the house that's touching the roof. I'm afraid it might do some damage to the shingles come the next big storm."

"I'll just need a ladder and a saw to handle that. And I'll take a look at the gutters while I'm up there." Then he waved a hand. "So far the items you've mentioned would take me two, maybe three afternoons. Surely there's more work that needs doing."

"You could always ask Mrs. Flanagan if there's anything she'd like taken care of."

He grimaced. "I'd rather not. Asking her would only give her the opportunity to tell me not to do any of it. Much better if I can just do the work and not say a thing."

Cassie did think of something else, but it was probably not the kind of task he had in mind.

Apparently, something in her expression gave her away, though. "What is it you're holding back?" he asked.

"Just a passing thought. I don't really think it qualifies as a household chore."

He raised a brow. "Why don't you let me be the judge of that?"

"All right." She took a deep breath, wondering what

he'd think of her unorthodox idea. "I think Mrs. Flanagan really chafes at not being able to come and go as she pleases. Right now, because of the steps, she can only go as far as the porch."

"Go on." His expression held a hint of puzzlement.

"I was thinking," Cassie said diffidently, "if you would offer to carry her down the porch steps while I roll her chair down, then I could push her wheelchair along the sidewalk and she could have a stroll of sorts. Of course, you'd also need to be available to carry her back up the steps at the end of her outing."

Riley rubbed his jaw. "You're right, it's not exactly what I had in mind." Then he grinned. "But I can sure sympathize with not wanting to be cooped up inside all day. If you can convince Mrs. Flanagan to let me carry her down the steps, then I'll be more than happy to perform the service."

"Excellent. However, as for convincing her, that might come better from you." Cassie gave him a knowing glance. "You are, after all, her guest, and as such your suggestions carry more weight than mine would. Just don't mention it was my idea."

"I'm not sure I agree with your thinking, but I'll see what I can do."

"Of course, once we convince her, it means you would need to keep an eye on the children while I am pushing her chair."

"I can do that." He lifted a hand. "In the meantime, if you can think of anything else, anything at all, that needs a handyman's attention around here, please let me know."

"I'll do that."

Now that they'd taken care of what he'd wanted to

speak to her about, she expected him to go back inside. But to her surprise, he merely looked out toward the fireflies as if he didn't have anywhere else to be. "I also want to thank you one more time for inviting us into your home. Pru and Noah really like it here."

What about him? Did he like it here, too? "You've already thanked us, multiple times. But to be fair, it's actually Mrs. Flanagan's home and it was her invitation."

He raised a brow at that. "No need to be coy, Cassie. We both know who I owe our current accommodations to, and you must allow me to thank you."

"In that case, you're quite welcome." She studied him a moment, realizing it wasn't his gratitude she wanted. "Do you mind if I ask you a question?"

His expression took on a hint of wariness, but he nodded. "Ask away."

"How long have the children been in your care?"

"About a year and a half."

"It can't have been easy for you, a bachelor trying to make a living and having to care for two young children."

He shrugged. "They're good kids and they are family, so I don't regret any of it. Except that I can't make a better home for them."

"Perhaps someday you'll find a place you like enough to settle down in, and then you can provide a nice home for them. A place where they can put down roots and make friends and go to school."

"That would be nice."

There was a resignation, a sort of regret in his voice that made her think he didn't believe that would happen.

"And if you found that place," she continued, "you

could find a kind, matronly housekeeper to help you give the children a feeling of home and permanency."

He didn't respond.

Cassie Lynn tilted her head to one side, studying him curiously. "That *is* what you want for them, isn't it?"

"Of course." He paused and she saw his jaw tighten. "We just don't always get what we want, when we want it."

"True. But that doesn't mean we shouldn't make the attempt."

He didn't say anything to that, just kept looking at the fireflies with an unreadable expression on his face.

Cassie realized she was trespassing on his privacy, just as Mrs. Flanagan had done earlier, and gave him an apologetic smile. "But they're your children, and I'm sure you're doing the best you can with them."

Then she stood and brushed at her skirt. "If you'll excuse me, I need to get my tarts out of the oven."

He nodded. "I think I'll stay out here a little longer, if you don't mind. I'll be sure to close the house up good and tight when I go in. And I'll check on the kids one last time before I turn in."

"Don't worry over much about the children. My room is right next to theirs, so I'll hear them if they should wake and need anything."

Cassie opened the oven a few moments later and was pleased to see the crust on the tarts was a nice golden brown. She pulled them out and set them on the table beside the pies.

She took care of the stove, then glanced out the back door before heading to her room. All she could see was the shadowy silhouette of Riley, who now sat on the porch step. There was something achingly lonely about that sight, something that made her want to go back out there and let him know he had a friend.

Instead, she turned and headed toward the bedrooms. She walked quietly past her door and paused outside the room where the children were sleeping. She opened the door and peered into the shadowy interior. Both were turned on their sides, and neither stirred at her intrusion. All she heard was their rhythmic breathing.

She smiled softly at the sweetness of that sound. Children were such precious gifts. She supposed she couldn't blame Riley for being so protective of them.

But how could she help him understand that he and his charges were safe here, that no one intended them harm?

Chapter Eleven

After Cassie went inside, Riley settled down on the spot she'd vacated. It was surprising how difficult it had been not to confide in her. He'd detected a faint note of censure in her voice and he'd found himself longing to replace it with admiration.

Which was altogether vain and totally irrelevant to the situation at hand. Because he had more than himself to worry about—he had those two kids sleeping inside counting on him.

Still, what if he could trust her with their story, tell her why things were the way they were? Being able to share that burden with someone, someone he could truly trust, would be such a gift.

But such thoughts were getting him nowhere and he'd had a long day. Riley placed his hands on his knees and levered himself up. Time to turn in.

As he stepped inside, he thought about what an unexpected turn this day had taken. From his restless night, to the unexpected invitation to move in here, to this feeling of almost being part of a family. Not that these cozy new accommodations didn't come with their own set of issues.

His first day at the livery had gone well, and Fred Humphries was an easy man to work for. And even though Riley had been worried about how Pru was doing, and whether he'd made the right choice in trusting the ladies to not get too close to their secrets, knowing that the children were being well looked after when he had to be away had brought him a measure of peace.

Trains stopped at the depot here in town twice a day, regular as clockwork, at ten in the morning and at three in the afternoon. He'd negotiated with Mr. Humphries to meet both trains each day to see if anyone needed to rent a wagon or have freight delivered. So Riley would be able to keep an eye on incoming visitors to town.

This was one of the benefits of stopping off in a small town—it was much easier to keep an eye out for his stepbrother, Guy. The disadvantage was that it was much more difficult to melt into the background and not stand out.

Riley paused at the door to the kids' room, and something in his chest tightened as he watched them sleep. Such precious little lives, and they'd been entrusted to his care. He simply could not fail them, doing so was unthinkable.

He stepped away and moved quietly to his attic room. Looking around, he smiled at the little touches that Cassie had gone to the trouble of adding at some point this afternoon. She'd placed a cloth on the crate he was using as a bedside table, and topped it with an oil lamp. There was also a braided rug next to his make-shift bed. A part of him wondered if she was just a little too good to be true. Perhaps it was cynical of him, but he'd been fooled too many times in his life to be completely trustful.

Still, it was hard to imagine there was any falseness or treachery behind the innocence he sensed in her. In fact, if it was only his own well-being at stake, he'd trust her with the whole story.

When Riley stepped into the kitchen the next morning, he was surprised to see Cassie sitting at the table hunched over a cup of coffee.

She glanced up with a smile, but he saw the circles under her eyes and the weary lines at her mouth.

He grabbed a cup, moved toward the stove and lifted the coffeepot. "Rough night?" he asked as he sat down across from her.

"I'll be fine as soon as I finish my coffee."

"It was the kids, wasn't it?"

"It wasn't her fault—she's sick."

"Tell me." When it appeared Cassie would try to put him off, he gave her a stern look. "I'm not wanting to cast blame, but I *am* Pru's uncle. I need to know how she's doing so I can better help."

Cassie nodded. "Of course. Pru's symptoms have moved deep into the itchy phase, and she was miserable." Cassie took a small sip from her cup. "I finally sent Noah to my room and spent the night on his bed, so I could read to her and try to take her mind off her misery."

"I'm sorry. That should have been me watching over her."

Cassie lifted a hand in a lazy wave. "Don't worry," she said with a lopsided smile. "I have a feeling there'll be enough of these episodes to go around over the next few days."

He smiled at her attempt at humor. But when she went to get up, he captured her hand with his. "Wait."

She stilled as if frozen. Her gaze went to their joined hands and then shot to his own. Something passed between them, something warm that he definitely needed to explore more deeply.

He released her hand and leaned back, clearing his throat. "I think it's my turn to apologize. You go do whatever it is you need to do to get Mrs. Flanagan ready to face the day, then send Noah back to his own bed, and get some rest yourself. I can handle cooking breakfast this morning. And I'll slip down to the livery to let Mr. Humphries know I need the morning off."

"That's very thoughtful of you, but I—"

"I insist. I only agreed to this arrangement on the condition you allow me to pull my weight in taking care of them, remember? Besides, as you said, there's going to be a lot of these episodes to go around the next few days. You won't do Pru or anyone else any good if you wear yourself out."

Cassie was silent for a moment and he could almost see her mind processing what he'd just said. Then she nodded. "Very well. But I'm only going to take a short nap, so there's no need for you to tell Mr. Humphries anything."

Riley made a noncommittal sound as he stood and moved around the table to help her stand.

She smiled with a raised brow. "Thank you, but I'm merely tired, not infirm."

He waved his hands in a shooing motion. "Then get

on with you—take care of whatever you need to with Mrs. Flanagan and then be off to bed."

She gave a little curtsy. "Yes, sir." And with a saucy smile, she headed out the door.

Smiling at her playful exit, Riley stoked the stove, then grabbed the egg basket and stepped outside. He'd have to make certain they shared the overnight duties tonight. He might not be as good at tending to sick kids as she was, but if it was just a matter of trying to soothe Pru, and read or otherwise distract her from her discomfort, he could manage that well enough.

Cassie opened her eyes and was confused by the bright sunlight streaming into the room. Then she remembered—she'd agreed to take a nap.

How long had she been asleep? She glanced at the small porcelain clock on her bedside table and saw that she had indeed slept for nearly two hours. Oh dear, she was going to be late making her deliveries.

She'd lain down fully dressed, so had only to pull her shoes back on and put her hair up again. She took care of that quickly, then hurried to the kitchen.

She entered the room to find it empty, but almost immediately the back door opened and Riley stepped inside.

"Oh, hello," he said, sounding inordinately pleased with himself. "Up already?"

"Already? I should have gotten up an hour ago." Then she looked around. "Where are my baked goods?"

"Delivered. I just got back."

"Oh." Realizing that had sounded less than grateful, she conjured up a smile. "Thank you."

"You're welcome. Care for some breakfast?"

She reached for one of the two biscuits on a plate in the middle of the table. "I'll just have these and a cup of coffee."

Before either of them could say anything else, Mrs. Flanagan appeared in the doorway, with Noah proudly pushing the wheelchair.

"Well, hello there," the woman said. "Thought I heard you in here."

"Where's Pru?" Riley asked with a frown.

The widow waved a hand. "Back in bed."

"Good." Cassie set her biscuit down as she reached for the cup of coffee Riley had poured for her. "She didn't sleep well and needs to get all the rest she can."

"Speaking of sleep," Riley said, turning to Mrs. Flanagan. "I have a favor to ask you."

The widow sat up straighter, as if happy to be asked. "And just what might that be?"

"There's a tree right outside my window with a limb hanging over the house. When the wind blows, it scratches and bumps against the roof, and that makes it hard to sleep. I was wondering if you'd mind if I trimmed it off."

Mrs. Flanagan nodded. "I suppose that would be all right. In fact, I was planning to take care of that myself before I had my accident."

"Then if you'll just tell me where to find a ladder and a saw, I'll get it all taken care of before I turn in tonight."

While her employer gave Riley the directions he needed, and some he didn't, Cassie smiled. She was impressed with how smoothly he'd handled that, getting the widow's permission to do one of the maintenance chores by making it sound as if she was doing him a favor.

And Cassie had noticed he'd been doing other chores, too, all without fanfare. The pantry door no longer squeaked, the cabinet door that had been sagging on its hinges was now tight, the broken slat on the porch rail had been fixed. He'd even replaced the rotten board on the old swing in the backyard with a new one.

Yep, Riley was one handy man to have around.

He glanced up and met her gaze for just a moment, and she let her smile tell him how much she appreciated his approach.

Chapter Twelve

Pru wasn't a very demanding patient. The biggest problem Cassie encountered that morning was trying to keep her from scratching at her blisters. She applied the calamine lotion Dr. Pratt had prescribed, which did seem to provide some relief, but not enough to sooth her completely. Cassie also trimmed the girl's fingernails short enough to minimize any damage she might do if she gave in to the urge to scratch.

When delivering a bowl of broth midmorning, Cassie nodded toward Pru's doll. "What a pretty little lady. Is that Bitsy?"

The girl nodded as she clutched the doll protectively against her chest.

Cassie could see the cloth doll had been lovely at one time. But one of the button eyes was hanging by a mere thread and the other seemed loose, as well. The yarn hair was frayed and tangled. The gingham dress was soiled and worn, but it was obvious the doll was well-loved.

"Bitsy is a perfectly lovely name for a lovely little lady."

Pru stroked the doll's hair. "My momma made it for me."

"Then that means she's an extra special doll, because she was made with lots of love."

The little girl moved the doll to her lap, where she studied her forlornly. "Her eye is messed up."

"I see that. Would you like me to fix it for you?"

Pru's expression was wary but hopeful. "Can you really?"

"I certainly can. It'll take just a few minutes with a needle and thread and it'll be good as new."

"I have something Ma made for me, too," Noah interjected.

Giving Pru time to decide if she would entrust her precious doll's well-being to her, Cassie turned to the boy. "And what might that be?"

He scrambled off the bed and moved to the trunk. After a moment of rummaging around, he pulled out a soft leather pouch and held it up proudly for Cassie to see. "Ma made it from a deer hide. And she stitched my name on it in blue thread. See?"

"I do. It looks like a very well-made pouch, and the stitching is exquisite."

"She said it was a special bag to hold all my treasures in."

"And what sorts of treasures do you keep in it?"

Noah opened the bag and poured the contents out on the bed. "This rock comes from the creek where I used to go fishing with Uncle Riley. And this is the brass hook that used to hang on the front porch to hold a lantern. And this is a blue jay feather I found once when Ma took us blackberry picking."

"What splendid treasures." Cassie noticed he hadn't mentioned his father. Was there a story there? She was tempted to ask, but decided not to. No point putting the boy on the spot if it was a sensitive topic.

She put a finger to her chin. "You know," she said slowly, "I imagine Mrs. Flanagan would enjoy getting a look at these fine treasures of yours."

Noah started tucking his things back into the pouch. "I'll go show her right now." And with that, he sprinted out of the room.

Cassie turned back to Pru. "So, shall I see about fixing Miss Bitsy's eyes for you?"

After another moment's hesitation, the little girl nodded. "Yes, please."

Cassie stood. "Then why don't I draw you a nice warm bath and add some baking soda to it? That ought to give you at least a small bit of relief from all that itching. Would you like that?"

Pru nodded, but her expression was uncertain.

Ignoring her reservations, Cassie smiled. "Very well. You stay here while I go draw your bath, and I'll fetch you once it's ready. Then, while you're soaking in the tub, I'll work on getting Bitsy fixed up."

Twenty minutes later, Cassie entered the parlor with the doll and her sewing box in hand.

Mrs. Flanagan sat near the sofa, an open book in her hands. Noah sat on the floor playing with a half-dozen tin soldiers, while Dapple watched him with lazily slitted eyes.

The widow glanced up and frowned. "What's that you've got there?"

Cassie explained the situation as she sat on the sofa. "Anyway, I could tell this doll means a lot to Pru and I thought it might cheer her up to have it fixed up."

She went to work immediately, reattaching Bitsy's left eye and securing the right one more firmly for good measure. Not satisfied leaving it at that, Cassie studied the doll critically. "Her dress could do with a good washing. I just wish I had something to fashion another garment from while this one dries."

Mrs. Flanagan straightened in her wheelchair. "I have just the thing." Turning adroitly, she exited the room and then returned a few moments later with a colorful scarf that she held out to Cassie. "Use this."

Cassie studied the bright yellow, flower-bedecked fabric and glanced up uncertainly. "Are you sure? I'll have to cut it."

The widow waved a hand dismissively. "Go right ahead. I never wear the thing—yellow is not a good color for me."

As Cassie washed the doll's original dress in the kitchen basin, she took note of the small, evenly spaced stitching. Pru's mother had taken a great deal of care when she'd stitched this for her daughter.

To fashion the new doll-sized garment, Cassie cut the scarf to a suitable length, then simply folded it in half and cut a hole at the fold large enough to fit the doll's head through. She quickly basted the sides together and then used one of her own ribbons to serve as a belt.

Then, for good measure, she worked on cleaning the doll's face and smoothing out her yarn hair.

She was quite pleased with the result and even Mrs. Flanagan called it a job well done.

Once Cassie was finished, she helped Pru dry off and dress, and then brought Bitsy to her. Pru was delighted with her changed appearance.

"Don't worry," Cassie assured her, "as soon as the dress your mother made for Bitsy is dry, you can change her right back into it. And then you can keep this one as a spare so she doesn't have to wear the same clothes all the time."

"Thank you." Pru held up the doll. "And Bitsy says thank you, too. She likes having two dresses."

Cassie was touched by the girl's simple gratitude. Perhaps, if she had some spare time, she would make the doll another proper dress.

When Riley retuned to Mrs. Flanagan's home that afternoon, he found the widow and Noah in the kitchen with Cassie. Cassie was at the table pouring a custard-like substance into a dough-lined pie dish.

He set a small sack of apples he'd picked up at the mercantile on the counter. "I had a hankering for an apple this afternoon and figured it would be rude to eat one in front of you all, so I bought enough for everyone." He picked one up and polished it on his shirt. Then he held it out. "Any takers?"

Mrs. Flanagan and Noah each accepted one, but Cassie shook her head.

"Maybe later," she said with a smile.

"Working on another pie, I see. Will this one be an experiment, as well?"

Mrs. Flanagan replied for Cassie. "Every dessert she makes these days is an experiment of one sort or another."

"She said I could help if I wanted to," Noah declared, his chest puffing out in self-importance.

"Helping is good," Riley said mildly. Then he remarked, to no one in particular, "You folks sure do have some fine weather in these parts."

"Better than where you came from?" Cassie asked curiously.

"It was raining there the day we left." Then he turned back to Mrs. Flanagan. "I imagine a lady as independent as you obviously are has a hard time being confined to the house."

The widow nodded. "I sure do miss being able to come and go as I please."

"Then how would you like to go for a bit of a stroll this afternoon?"

She glared at him. "That is not amusing."

"I didn't intend for it to be. In fact, I was quite serious."

"Then you must be addled. As you can see, I'm not in any condition to be doing any strolling."

"Perhaps I should have said how would you like to accompany Miss Vickers on a stroll."

Mrs. Flanagan's lips pinched even tighter. "Again, given the steps, I'm confined to the house and porch."

"Ah, but that's not strictly true. You need to use your imagination to see the possibilities."

Her frown took on a tinge of curiosity. "What do you mean?"

"Come on, I'll show you." Riley pushed the wheeled chair out onto the porch, inviting Cassie and Noah to follow.

Once they were all gathered there, Riley bent down and lifted the startled woman from her chair, cradling her carefully in his arms. Holding her as if she weighed nothing at all, he turned to the younger woman. "Miss Vickers, if you don't mind."

She quickly maneuvered the chair down the stairs and settled it on the walkway.

Riley followed with his surprised-speechless burden and settled her in the chair once again. "How's that?"

Mrs. Flanagan finally found her tongue. "That, young man, was highly impertinent. I will thank you not to ever take such liberties with my person again, at least not without my permission."

Riley schooled his expression in some semblance of contrition. "Yes, ma'am. I surely will not."

She shifted in her chair, her back straight as a fence post and her chin tilted up imperiously. "But now that I'm down here, I might as well take advantage of it. Cassie Lynn, I have a hankering to take a turn down Main Street."

"Yes, ma'am." Cassie's tone was bland, but Riley noticed the amused glint in her eye as she moved behind her employer and grasped the chair's handles.

Riley caught her gaze and gave her a quick wink. Cassie had a sudden coughing fit, no doubt to cover the laugh he saw threatening to spill out of her.

Then he stepped back. "Enjoy your stroll, ladies. And don't worry, Mrs. Flanagan, I'll be here to carry you back up the steps when you return."

With that, he nonchalantly stuck his hands in his pockets and went back inside. The fact that he'd made Cassie smile at him more favorably again had brightened his day more than it should have.

Cassie couldn't hide her smile as she began pushing the chair down the sidewalk. Who would have guessed Riley would be so good at charming her employer?

"Slow down," Mrs. Flanagan said. "We're not running a race here."

"Of course." She slowed her pace. "Just let me know if there's somewhere you want to stop, or when you're ready to turn around and head back for home."

"Of course I will," Mrs. Flanagan said acerbically. "You know I'm not one to be afraid to speak up."

It was nearly forty minutes later before they returned to the house. Noah was sitting on the porch, and as soon as he spotted them he sprinted inside. A few minutes later Riley stepped out, ready to carry Mrs. Flanagan up the stairs. This time, before he lifted her from her chair, he asked permission with exaggerated formality.

He was rewarded for his efforts with a glare. "Don't think you're fooling me, young man. I know impertinence when I see it." Then she gave a regal nod. "But yes, you may carry me back up the stairs."

Later that afternoon, after Riley had taken care of the wayward tree branch, he paused at the back door. Looking into the kitchen, he wasn't surprised to see Cassie at the stove.

He watched as she stirred a pot, and listened to her soft humming. The domesticity of the scene tugged at him, stirred a longing in him he hadn't realized was there.

A moment later she lifted her cook spoon and took a taste of whatever was in the pot. Her gaze met his just as she swallowed. Her eyes widened and her cheeks colored prettily, as if she were embarrassed to have been caught in the act.

Hiding a grin, he opened the door and stepped inside. "Hope I didn't startle you?"

She returned his smile self-consciously. "Just a little bit."

"Please let me make it up to you. What can I do to help?"

She shook her head. "You've been working all day. I'm sure you want to sit back and relax for a bit before supper."

But he was having none of that. "Surely there's something I can do."

Before she could answer, Mrs. Flanagan wheeled herself into the room, Noah at her side. "Good, you're both here. I wanted to speak to you."

Noting that Cassie once more looked like a schoolgirl who'd been caught at something, Riley turned with a smile to his hostess. "What can we do for you, ma'am?"

"I want to make certain you are both planning to go to church service tomorrow."

Cassie responded first. "Riley should go, by all means. But I'll stay. I can't leave you here to take care of Pru by yourself."

But the widow didn't agree. "I won't be by myself. Noah can help me keep Pru entertained."

Riley's nephew nodded. "Yes, ma'am. I'm real good at that."

Riley spoke up. "No, that's mighty generous of you to offer, but the kids are my responsibility. We'll be fine here while you ladies are at church."

Mrs. Flanagan drew herself up. "Young man, I'm not being generous, I'm being practical. As long as I'm stuck in this chair I won't be attending church service. My home's not the only building in town with porch steps that prevent me from entry on my own.

"And no," she continued before he could speak, "I

will *not* allow you to carry me up and down the church steps. You will please allow an old woman her dignity."

She settled back in her chair. "Now, you two will go on to church, Noah and I will watch over Pru and that's that." She eyed Riley sternly. "And don't tell me again that you aren't going. I won't be housing any heathens in my home."

"Yes, ma'am. I mean, no, ma'am. I mean, of course I'll go. If you're sure you can handle watching the children on your own."

"Oh, for goodness sake, I'm quite capable of watching over a sick child for a few hours. If you don't believe me, remember that I raised two boys of my own and nursed them through any number of illnesses and injuries. Besides, if there's something I can't reach or do because of this confounded chair, then, since Pru is not entirely bedridden, she'll be able to get up and help me."

Riley stepped out on the porch that evening to find Cassie in the exact spot he'd seen her in last night. Only this time she wasn't hugging her knees. She was leaning back, with her hands grasping the edge of the step on either side of her.

"Mind if I join you?"

"Not at all."

He leaned against the support post and folded his arms. "So how did your walk with Mrs. Flanagan this afternoon *really* go?"

Cassie looked up at him, her eyes sparkling in the moonlight. "Actually, I think she enjoyed it quite a bit. We stopped in at the mercantile and she told everyone there the story about how her roguish houseguest just picked her up without so much as a by-your-leave and carried her down the steps. But even though her words were tart, I could hear the smile in her voice. "

"Good. Then we'll try it again tomorrow afternoon. And I won't let her give me no for an answer." Then he grimaced. "Did she really call me roguish?"

Cassie grinned. "Her exact words."

Riley decided it was time to change the subject. "What did you do before you came to work for Mrs. Flanagan?"

"I worked at the restaurant."

That made sense. "Baking those tasty pies of yours, no doubt."

"Sometimes. But Daisy, the owner, is a terrific cook and she loves preparing the dishes for her customers, so I was mostly there to help with the cleanup and the serving."

"That's a waste of a good talent." He studied her curiously. "Will you stay here with Mrs. Flanagan when she's on her feet again, or go back to the restaurant?"

"I'm not sure." Cassie hugged her knees, as if in need of comfort. "I mean, I won't be going back to the restaurant—Daisy only hired me because she needed help when her youngest was born. Little Danielle is nearly nine months old now and, with her family's help, Daisy seems to have things well in hand."

Her tone had been matter-of-fact, but he detected some emotion under the surface.

"And staying with Mrs. Flanagan?"

Cassie kept her face turned away. "She's offered to help me with my bakery business, to let me live here and have the use of her kitchen, for a twenty percent share of the business."

"Sounds like a fair offer."

"Oh yes, more than fair."

When she didn't continue right away, Riley gave her a conversational nudge. "But?"

"But I'm not certain there will be a bakery business."

That surprised him. Cassie seemed so animated when she spoke of the orders she received and the new recipes she was concocting. "Have you decided it's too much work?"

"Not at all. I enjoy baking, and the idea of earning my own way doing something I truly enjoy is like a wonderful dream." Her enthusiasm faded as quickly as it had appeared. "But not all dreams are meant to come true."

He hadn't figured her as one to back down from a challenge. "Most good ideas start with a dream."

She lifted her hand in an uncharacteristically fatalistic gesture. "Perhaps."

Then she cut him a challenging look. "And if owning a horse ranch is your ultimate dream, why are you putting it off?"

He recognized that she was trying to move the attention away from herself, but he let it go. "It's definitely my long-term goal. But for the time being, I need to focus on caring for the kids and keeping them safe."

"An admirable goal. But you say that as if you can't you do both. I'm sure the children would enjoy living on a horse ranch. And not just enjoy it, but thrive there. Noah especially, since he seems quite fond of animals. And having a permanent place to call home would do them both good."

That again. "The timing's just not right at the moment. Maybe someday." How had she got him talking about himself? Time to change the subject.

But before he could do so, she spoke up again.

"You know, Mrs. Flanagan was right when she said there was plenty of land around here that would be perfect for a horse ranch. And Turnabout is a very nice place for a kid to grow up in."

Riley needed to snuff out this topic of conversation with the finality of a candle flame doused in a downpour. "I don't doubt it, but I'm afraid this is not the area of the country I aim to settle down in."

Her brows drew down. "You have something against Turnabout?"

Was she deliberately trying to misunderstand him? He raised his hands, palms out. "Turnabout seems like a fine town, but I think I'd like something a little farther West."

"And what can you find farther West that you can't find right here?"

"The land of opportunity."

She wrinkled her nose. "And California is where you find that?"

"That's right. Do you have something against California?"

"I don't know enough about the area to have an opinion one way or the other. I'm just curious as to what exactly you think you'll find there."

"Exploring a new place and learning new ways of doing things is part of the draw. And I imagine we'll see all sorts of other new and interesting sights along the way." He hoped his tone and expression didn't betray just how tired he was of traveling—no, running—from place to place.

Riley hated seeing the disapproval in Cassie's eyes,

hated not being able to explain to her why it was best for them to keep moving.

Part of him felt that she would understand, would even help him if he explained things to her. And if it was just his well-being at stake, he might have done so. But he knew he couldn't take that chance with Pru and Noah's future, no matter how tempted he was.

Cassie found Riley's words disturbing. That footloose way of life might appeal to someone with an adventurous nature and no real ties, but he had responsibilities, children who were depending on him. He appeared to care a great deal for Pru and Noah—did he really not understand how constantly moving around from town to town, without the opportunity to form any permanent connections, would affect them? For one thing, she suspected this was why Noah hadn't spent much time in a classroom.

Perhaps she'd been too hasty in forming an opinion of Riley's character. Was his concern for the children secondary to his own thirst for travel and adventure?

Land of opportunity indeed. Surely he wasn't trying to chase some pot of gold at the end of a rainbow. She hadn't figured him for the mercenary sort, but then again, how well did she really know him? But she felt a sharp stab of disappointment at the very idea that this might be true.

Later, as Cassie lay in bed, she tried to reconcile what she thought she knew about Riley with his seeming indifference to what his gallivanting about was doing to the children. A part of her refused to believe that indifference was real. Perhaps it was just her seeing what she wanted to see, but she sensed a struggle in him, a travel-weariness, whenever the subject came up.

Who was the real Riley Walker and what was his story? And why was it so important to her to find the answer?

Chapter Thirteen

Riley was surprised when he stepped into the kitchen
the next morning to find Cassie awake and up before him
once again. Not only was she up, but she'd stoked the
fire in the stove and gathered up the eggs. How much,
or little, sleep did the woman get in a night?

When she spotted him, she offered a polite smile.
"Good morning. How did it go with Pru last night?"

He shrugged. "She woke a few times whimpering
about how much she itched. I did what you suggested—
gave her the lotion to use, told her a few stories, tried to
keep her mind off her discomfort." He took a long swallow from his cup. "She's asleep right now, so I figured
I'd slip out to get some coffee."

Cassie nodded as she grabbed the flour. "Hopefully
there will just be another day or two of this severe itching before she starts feeling better."

Remembering her disappointment in him last evening, he studied her without further comment as she
prepared the dough to make biscuits, trying to gauge
her feelings this morning. But he couldn't really tell.

"I see you repaired the fence around the chicken

coop," she finally said as she placed the sheet of biscuits in the oven. "I suppose you took care of that while I was out with Mrs. Flanagan yesterday."

He nodded, encouraged by the friendliness of her tone.

She shoved a stray hair off her forehead with one flour-dusted wrist. "Thank you."

Was that thank-you prompted merely by gratitude for a good deed? Or had that small act been enough to sway her into letting him back into her good graces? "You're quite welcome. But there's no need to say anything to Mrs. Flanagan about it."

"Of course not. Informing her is entirely up to you."

Good. He really didn't want to deal with the woman's prickly pride. "Speaking of maintenance work, which of the windows is it that's stuck?"

"The one in the dining room that faces Dr. Pratt's home."

Riley made a mental note. That would be the next chore he tackled.

Cassie placed a large bowl on the table and started cracking eggs and dumping them into it.

"After sitting up with Pru last night, I'm wondering if I should leave Mrs. Flanagan alone with her, after all," Riley murmured.

Cassie paused and gave him a probing look, as if trying to gauge his motives. "There isn't anything in Pru's care that requires the person watching over her to stand up and walk. And Noah will be here to help."

The same arguments Mrs. Flanagan had used last night. "Still—"

"And it isn't as if we'll be gone all day." Cassie grabbed a whisk and began whipping the eggs. "However, if you want to tell Mrs. Flanagan that you don't think she's up to it, either because she's old, or she's in that chair, or both, then that's your right." Her expression took on an exaggeratedly pious look. "Perhaps you won't hurt her feelings too terribly."

He frowned at her. "You, Miss Vickers, do not play fair."

Her only response was a saucy grin.

Cassie strolled down the sidewalk toward church feeling slightly self-conscious. She'd never had a gentleman at her side like this, at least not one who wasn't her father or a brother.

And they were drawing quite a bit of notice. Most of the looks, she was sure, were due to the fact that Riley was new to town. And since most of his time had been spent either at the livery or Mrs. Flanagan's house, not many of the townsfolk had met him yet.

The two of them stopped along the way several times to exchange greetings and for Cassie to introduce Riley.

And was it her imagination or was he getting more than one interested second glance from some of the single ladies in town?

They arrived at church just as the bells rang to indicate the service would soon begin. Riley escorted her inside and then let her choose the pew.

Cassie slipped into one near the back, not wanting to walk the gauntlet of eyes that sitting farther up would have cost her.

As they settled in their seats, she remembered Mrs. Flanagan's instructions. The widow had pulled her aside just before they left. "I know you've had your hands full since our houseguests moved in, and haven't had much time to yourself. This will be a good opportunity to look around at the bachelors in this town and see if there are any other names you want to add to your husband list."

To be honest, Cassie was becoming more disenchanted with the whole idea of this husband-candidate list by the day. Not that her situation had changed any. Just her enthusiasm.

She spotted Mr. Edmondson seated two rows ahead of her. He was a broadly built, well-muscled man, as was fitting for a blacksmith. She could see why Mrs. Flanagan had suggested him. Though his beard sported more than a hint of gray, he seemed quite vital.

As unobtrusively as she could, Cassie glanced around the rest of the congregation while the last few stragglers took their seats. Ignoring the married men and those she considered too old or too young, she tried to identify any additional candidates she should consider for her list.

Her gaze paused when she spotted her older brother, Verne, and his wife, Dinah, across the aisle and three rows up. They had her youngest brother, Bart, with them. She was glad Dinah had taken a stand about going to church on Sunday and that Verne had supported her. After Ma died, Pa had decided going to church service was a waste of time, and allowed them to go only at Christmas and Easter.

Moving on, Cassie spotted a few men who seemed to be unattached, but who she didn't know by name. Perhaps—

"Looking for someone?"

Riley's question brought her back to her surroundings with a snap.

She shook her head as she tried unsuccessfully to

hold back the warmth climbing in her cheeks. "No one in particular."

Then, thankfully, the organist began to play and the two of them faced forward to participate in the service.

Reverend Harper's sermon was based on Colossians 3:17 this morning. As Cassie listened to him speak on doing everything in the name of the Lord, she wondered if she was truly doing that. Had she prayed for guidance on this matter of whether to return home to her father or not? Was this marriage-for-convenience's-sake that she was contemplating really what the Lord wanted for her?

Many people married for reasons other than love, but were her own strong enough to do so? Cassie couldn't shake the feeling that perhaps she had set her feet on the wrong path.

As they exited the church following the service, Reverend Harper was there to greet the members of his congregation.

"Well, hello, Cassie Lynn. It's so nice to see you here this morning. I trust Mrs. Flanagan is doing well."

"Thank you, Reverend, and yes, she is." She indicated Riley with a wave of her hand. "Allow me to introduce Mr. Riley Walker. He and his niece and nephew are visiting in Turnabout."

"Mr. Walker, welcome to Turnabout. I've heard about your niece's unfortunate situation. I hope she recovers soon."

Riley took the proffered hand and gave it a quick shake. "Thank you, Reverend. Fortunately, Miss Vickers and Mrs. Flanagan took pity on us and are helping with the nursing duties."

"You couldn't find two finer ladies to take you in."

After that, he turned to the next in line and Cassie and Riley moved on.

They hadn't taken more than a few steps into the churchyard when she was hailed from behind.

Turning, she saw her brothers and sister-in-law bearing down on them. Hoping they weren't going to mention anything about her father's plans for her, Cassie smiled and exchanged greetings, then introduced Riley.

Fifteen-year-old Bart seemed to be taken with a petite blond-haired girl across the way, and as soon as the introductions were complete, excused himself to join her.

Verne, however, didn't seem quite so eager to move on. He extended his hand toward Riley. "Mr. Walker, you're new to town, aren't you?"

Riley shook it firmly. "Just got here Wednesday."

Cassie was confused. It appeared to her that the men's hands were clasped a bit too tightly and that Verne was studying Riley with an assessing, none too friendly look. What had gotten into him?

"You planning to stay long?"

"Just until my niece gets over the chicken pox."

While Verne's tone continued to sound confrontational, Riley's had a slightly amused hint to it.

Ignoring the menfolk, Dinah linked her arm with Cassie's. "Did you hear that Verne and I are getting our own place?"

Trying to keep one ear on the other conversation, Cassie nodded and smiled. "Pa told me." She gave Dinah's arm a squeeze. "I'm so happy for you both."

"I'm so excited. Our own place at last." She spent several minutes talking about the new house Verne was working on, and then she paused and gave Cassie an abashed look. "Not that I don't enjoy living at your pa's place, but—"

Cassie squeezed her arm again. "No need to explain. I moved out as quickly as I could, remember?"

Dinah's lips curved up in a shared grin, but her smile quickly faded. "I'm sorry if our good fortune means you'll have to move back."

This time Cassie cut her off for an entirely different reason as she cast a quick glance Riley's way. "Let's not talk of that now. And no matter what, I'm still happy for you."

She caught sight of Verne's expression just then and was alarmed by how belligerent he looked. What had they just been discussing—something about Riley's living arrangements? Mercy, was Verne playing the role of her protector?

She quickly stepped forward. "Verne, Dinah has just been telling me about the new place you are building. It sounds wonderful."

Verne's expression immediately shifted to one of pride. "Nothing but the best for my wife."

Time to bring this exchange to a close before anything was said that shouldn't be. "Well, it was nice seeing you all, but I need to get back to the house. I don't want to leave Mrs. Flanagan alone with the sick little girl for too long. Tell Pa and Norris and Dwayne hi for me."

With that Cassie gave Riley a let's-go look and turned toward the sidewalk. To her relief he said his goodbyes and fell into step beside her.

"I apologize if my brother made you uncomfortable. I don't know what he was thinking."

"He was thinking 'who is this stranger with my little

sister?' And there's no need to apologize—I would probably have done the same thing if I'd been in his shoes."

She thought about that all the way back to Mrs. Flanagan's house.

The widow and the kids had indeed managed quite nicely on their own. When Cassie and Riley returned, they found the trio at the kitchen table, a child sitting on each side of the woman while they pored over a book with pictures of exotic animals. They seemed almost disappointed when Cassie and Riley walked in and Mrs. Flanagan said it was time to put the book away and get ready for lunch.

Riley struggled all through lunch with his decision over what to do about Wednesday's meeting. He'd held his own counsel, relied on his own resources, for so long that letting someone in at this point seemed both wrong and uncomfortable. But he couldn't let this opportunity to take care of Guy once and for all slip through his fingers out of misguided pride.

By the end of the meal he'd reached a decision. As soon as the table was cleared and the children had been sent off to take naps, he asked Cassie if they could talk out on the back porch.

She followed him out, took her customary seat on the steps, arranged her skirt and then looked up at him. "Now, what was it you wanted to speak to me about?"

Riley tugged one of his cuffs, gathering his resolve. This was it. He either trusted her enough to tell her the whole truth, or he didn't.

He looked into her concerned face and made his decision.

"I have a favor to ask of you."

Chapter Fourteen

Cassie could tell by the expression on Riley's face that there was something of great import on his mind. Was it just because he found it so difficult to ask for help, or was something else going on here?

"What can I do for you?"

"I need to be in Tyler early Wednesday morning for a very important business meeting. And of course, I can't take the kids with me in their current condition."

Was that all? "You want me to watch them while you're gone. I'll be glad—"

He lifted a hand to stop her. "Before you agree, there are some things I need to tell you that might change the way you feel about us."

She doubted that, but merely nodded. "Go on."

"It concerns the man who is the children's father and my stepbrother, Guy Simpson."

Now she was confused. "But, I mean, isn't the children's father deceased?"

"No, but their mother is." Riley tightened his lips for a moment, as if repressing some unpleasant thought. "Let me start at the beginning. My mother married Guy's father when I was eight years old and Guy was fifteen. They came to live on the horse ranch my father had built and operated before he passed. At first I not only liked but admired Guy. He was charming, athletic, handsome and very articulate—everything an eight-year-old boy would like to grow up to be. He could charm the rattle from a rattlesnake. And, as it turns out, he was just about as treacherous."

Cassie heard the disgust in Riley's voice and wasn't certain she really wanted to hear the rest of this story.

"After a while," he continued, "I began to sense he wasn't the person he appeared to be on the surface. But even then, it took some time for me to understand the depths of his corruption. He didn't seem to be bothered by any of the treachery he took part in, as if he didn't have a conscience."

Cassie's stomach tightened as she absorbed his words. How awful it must have been to know such a person was a part of his own household.

"Then he met Nancy Greene. She came from a fairly well-to-do family and spent most of her adolescence back east in boarding and finishing schools. It was when she returned home for good that her and Guy's paths crossed. Guy brought all his charm to bear in wooing her and quickly won her favor. Her father wasn't as easily won over, however. I'm not sure if it was because he suspected what kind of man Guy was or because he wanted better for his daughter than some horse rancher's son."

Already Cassie felt her heart go out to Nancy. It sounded as if neither her father nor her suitor were really honorable men.

"Mr. Greene promised to disown his daughter if she married Guy, but Guy vowed that it was Nancy he wanted, not her money. Of course, that was a lie. No one really believed Jerome Greene would disown his only child.

"But he did. On the day of their wedding, Greene made out a new will, leaving everything he owned to some distant cousin who lived hundreds of miles away." Riley's lips twisted in a crooked smile. "I think he would have eventually relented, but he never had the chance. Three days after the wedding he died of a heart attack."

Cassie could guess how the man Riley was describing would have reacted to that.

"My stepfather was more generous—he gave the newlyweds sixty acres of our ranch land, a piece that was suitable for farming, as a wedding gift. But Guy never thought he was cut out to be a rancher or farmer—he had much loftier ambitions. He blamed Nancy, and he was not above abusing her when he drank or his temper flared."

Cassie saw Riley's hands curl into fists and felt her own anger burn.

"Of course, not many people knew this darker side of Guy. He and Nancy put on a good front when they were in public. But I saw evidence of it with my own eyes."

There was a haunted look in his face and she refrained from asking exactly what it was he'd witnessed.

"Guy began hunting for other ways to make the kind of money he thought he deserved. He took long trips away from home, leaving Nancy to tend to the farm on her own, and would eventually return with large sums of money. At first I thought he'd taken to gambling, and that might have been part of it. But when Pru was barely four, he took her, against Nancy's will, on one of these trips, and when he returned I heard him brag about how easy it was to charm rich widows into just handing over their money, especially when there was a young child in the picture.

"Eventually, his crimes caught up with him. Four years ago Guy was arrested and put in prison for taking part in a bank robbery. He was given a three-year sentence."

Four years ago… Noah would have been little more than a toddler. But Pru would have been old enough to have a sense of what was happening.

"Nancy was left running the farm and raising the kids on her own, though that wasn't much different than it had been before Guy went to prison. She actually did well, until she got sick. That's when she contacted me for help.

"I stayed with her, keeping the farm running and doing what I could, until she passed two months later. Before she died, she made me promise not to let Guy get hold of the children again. She was afraid of how he would use them to further his own ends. And also what kind of treatment they'd receive at his hands."

There was a long pause and Cassie spoke up. "That's all so horrible. I can see why you're so protective of Noah and Pru. Where is their father now?" She'd done the math—the man had been out of prison for a year at this point.

"Unfortunately, I have reason to believe Guy's trying to track the kids down. That's why we move around so much. I'm trying to stay ahead of him."

"Do the children know that's the reason?"

"Yes. I thought it best to be honest with them so that if Guy does show up they won't be caught unawares."

"But I don't understand. If he's as bad as you say,

surely you can make a case for not letting him have control of the children."

Riley's jaw tightened. "There's no 'if' to it. And the stakes are too high for me to take a chance. He's their father, after all. I'm just their uncle. By law, he has more right to them than I do, and I'm afraid I'd ultimately be forced to hand them over." Riley shook his head. "You don't know Guy. I've seen him talk his way out of situations where he's been caught dead to rights, more times than you could imagine. When I said he's charming I wasn't exaggerating. You sit down and talk to him, and look into those sincere blue eyes of his, and before long you find yourself believing every word coming out of his mouth. I can't risk the kids' futures on my ability to convince the law that he's a liar and a crook. Especially a lawman or judge who has no reason to take my word over his."

Cassie turned the topic back to its original focus. "And this meeting on Wednesday... It has something to do with keeping him away from Noah and Pru?"

Riley nodded. "Before she died, Nancy told me about another crime Guy committed—the Ploverton bank robbery. That crime was much worse than the one he got arrested and went to prison for. In the Ploverton robbery a great deal more money was involved and two people were killed, including a young man whose wife was expecting their first child."

The black marks against the children's father just kept growing.

"Guy bragged to Nancy about his involvement, but there was no proof she could offer the law besides what they called hearsay."

"But now you've found some kind of proof?"

"One of the first things I did when Nancy died was hire a Pinkerton detective to try to find some evidence that would prove Guy was indeed involved in that robbery. If I can find that proof, then Guy will be sent back to prison, this time for much, much longer than three years. That detective, Mr. Claypool, thinks he's finally close to finding that proof."

Cassie placed a hand on Riley's arm. "Then of course you must go. And don't worry about the children, I'll keep a close eye on them."

He stared at her hand a minute and she started to pull it away. But then he covered it with his own and met her gaze. "I need to make certain you understand that Guy is actively looking for them. I think it's unlikely he'll show up here the one day I'm gone, but if he does, things could get ugly."

"I'll be ready. Besides, with the children having chicken pox, he won't be able to go anywhere with them." She drew herself up. "I can fetch Sheriff Gleason if Guy so much as thinks about doing so."

Riley grinned at that. "Feisty. Like a bear protecting her cubs."

Cassie's cheeks warmed, but so did her heart.

She reluctantly drew her hand away, missing the warmth of his touch almost immediately.

No wonder the children never spoke of their father. Noah, of course, would have been only two or three when the man went to prison, so he likely didn't remember much of him.

But Pru, poor Pru, who had been used in some of his schemes and who had likely witnessed how the man treated her mother... The memories she had were no doubt of the nightmare variety.

If there was anything she could do to help Riley keep those children safe, Cassie would do it.

Even if it meant watching them walk out of her life.

Chapter Fifteen

"Cassie, I need you to do me a favor when you go out to deliver your baked goods."

Cassie paused from packing the hamper and glanced up at her employer. Breakfast was over and she and Mrs. Flanagan had the kitchen to themselves for the moment. Riley was in the backyard with Noah, and Pru was settled in her room with a book.

"Of course," she replied. "Do you need me to pick something up from one of the merchants?"

Mrs. Flanagan held out a slip of paper. "I'd like you to deliver this to Betty Pratt on your way back. And wait for an answer."

Cassie took the missive and slipped it into her pocket. "Pru passed a much easier night last night. I know she has a way to go yet, but hopefully she's been through the worst of it now."

"That's good news," the widow said with a nod. "Especially since Noah's likely to show symptoms soon."

Cassie lifted her basket, feeling the weight of it. If she received many more orders she'd need to make her deliveries in two trips. All in all, not a terrible problem to have.

As she went about delivering her baked goods, she found her mind playing back the conversation with Riley yesterday evening. It was hard to believe that anyone could be as truly reprehensible as Riley had described his stepbrother. But she knew, even though she'd never experienced it herself, that there really was evil in the world.

It warmed her heart that he'd trusted her, not only with such a personal, painful story, but with the care of the children. She only hoped she could be strong enough to protect them should the need arise.

Cassie stopped at the Pratt home on her way back, as Mrs. Flanagan had asked, and gave Mrs. Pratt the note.

After reading it, the doctor's wife looked up and smiled at her. "Tell Irene that, yes, I'd be delighted." The twinkle in her eye made Cassie wonder just exactly what the two older women were cooking up.

When she reported back to Mrs. Flanagan, the widow gave a satisfied nod. "Excellent." Then she turned to Riley, stopping him as he headed out for the livery. "By the way, Mr. Walker, I would appreciate it if you could be back by ten thirty this morning. I have something I'd like you to do for me."

"That shouldn't be a problem." He raised an eyebrow. "Mind if I ask what it is you need me to do? Just in case I should pick up some tools or supplies."

She waved a hand. "No tools required. Now, there's no time to get into everything right now. I'll explain when you get back."

Riley exchanged a look with Cassie, and she shrugged to indicate she was as much in the dark as he was.

Not that she wasn't curious. But the widow was apparently enjoying this little touch of mystery, and Cassie wouldn't begrudge her that.

Riley had a smile on his face as he headed back to Mrs. Flanagan's home after his morning shift at the livery was complete. Had the widow put off the explanation because she was afraid he'd turn her down? Or was she planning some sort of surprise? Whatever it was she had for him to do, he'd do it. The woman had been too generous to him and the kids for him to refuse her anything.

He jammed his hands in his pockets, thinking about that. Mrs. Flanagan and Cassie had been more than generous. They'd treated him and the kids like family. And that was something he no longer took for granted.

He stepped into the kitchen to find Cassie, Mrs. Flanagan and a woman he'd never met already there.

Mrs. Flanagan was the first to greet him. "Oh, good, you're right on time."

"On time for what?"

"To meet Doc Pratt's wife. Riley Walker, this is Betty Pratt. Betty, this is Riley Walker."

"Pleased to meet you, ma'am." Was Mrs. Flanagan going to ask him to do something at the house next door?

"I've been watching you two young people work yourselves ragged trying to do everything—take care of the kids, the house, the upkeep, the cooking, your job." She waved a hand. "Like I said, everything."

Cassie's brow furrowed. "But that's what—"

Mrs. Flanagan didn't let her finish. "You two are not going to be any good to me or the children or anyone else if you wear yourself down to nubs."

Riley crossed his arms and waited, intrigued to see where she was going with this.

"Now, Betty has agreed to stay with the kids and me for the next several hours, and Riley here doesn't need to get back to the livery until later this afternoon, so that leaves about four hours for you two to get out of this house and do something relaxing. Take a walk, or better yet, go on a picnic. Cassie, you can show Riley here some of the nice spots in the area—Mercer's Pond, Gibson's meadow, the old lookout point on the bluff."

"Oh, and there's that pretty spot out near the Keeter farm," Mrs. Pratt added. "And see—" she pointed to a hamper on the kitchen table "—at Irene's request, I packed a cold meal for two, so there's no need to worry about your lunch."

"Of course, it's entirely up to you where you go and what you do," Mrs. Flanagan stated. "I just want you two away from this house for the next several hours. We'll all benefit if you come back refreshed."

Cassie crossed her arms over her chest, her raised brow and stiff posture making it obvious something had got her back up. "Are you saying you're not happy with the way I've been doing my job lately?" she asked.

"Goodness, girl, don't get prickly. All I'm saying is you deserve a bit of time off before you wear yourself out. And if you don't believe you do, then what about Riley here? Don't think I haven't noticed all the little things that are suddenly working again around here. Don't you think he deserves a bit of relaxation?"

Riley wasn't sure how he felt about Mrs. Flanagan using him as leverage to get Cassie to agree to her plan. Then again, he found he liked the idea of a guilt-free outing with Cassie, so he decided to hold his peace.

She glanced his way. "What do you think?"

He spread his hands in a gesture of surrender. "I'm thinking we don't have much choice."

A few minutes later Cassie found herself on the front porch, with Riley holding the food basket provided by Mrs. Pratt. She gave her companion a wry smile. "So what do we do now?"

He lifted the basket slightly. "I think we go on a picnic. I'll provide the transportation if you'll direct us to somewhere appropriate." He swept a hand out. "Shall we?"

Fifteen minutes later, when Riley handed her up into the wagon they'd procured at the livery, she noticed River was tied to the back. So he planned to get some riding done while they were out. She supposed she couldn't blame him—he'd had little chance to ride since he'd been here. Duchess was pulling the wagon so she could visit with her old friend while he was getting in his ride.

Riley took his seat and lifted the reins, then turned to her. "So, where shall we go?"

"Since you're bringing River along, I think we should head out to Mercer's Pond. It's a pretty spot and there's a meadow that's fairly open and level that'll be good for riding."

"Sounds perfect. Point the way."

"You know," Cassie said as they headed out of town, "if we'd already told Mrs. Flanagan about your plan to leave for Tyler tomorrow, she might not have thought this outing necessary."

"I don't know about that. It appeared to me that she was just as worried about you getting some time to yourself as she was me."

"For all her brusque ways, she really is a dear lady."

They rode in a comfortable silence for a while.

It was Cassie who broke that silence first. "Do you mind if I ask you a question about your stepbrother?"

He inwardly groaned. It wouldn't be much of an outing if they focused on Guy. But he could hardly tell her no. "Ask away."

"Why would he be so interested in the children? I mean, it sounds as if he didn't pay them much mind before he went to prison. And now that he's free once more, it doesn't seem as if a man like that would want to encumber himself with the care of young children."

That was a fair question. And an intelligent one. "You need to understand the kind of person Guy is. He viewed Nancy and the kids as possessions. They were his, and though he might not pay much attention to them, he never shares anything he considers his with anyone else."

Riley chose his next words carefully. "As I said last night, he's also used Pru to further some of his shady schemes in the past. I'm certain he has plans to do more of the same sort of thing."

Riley saw Cassie's jaw tense. "We can't let him get his hands on them," she declared.

He was warmed by her use of *we*. "We won't." Then he gave her a smile. "Let's not let Guy spoil our outing today. Tell me how your bakery business is going and what plans you have for it moving forward."

To his relief, she took her cue and the conversation moved on to more pleasant topics.

Cassie was almost sorry when they arrived at the pond. She'd enjoyed the ride, sitting close to Riley on the seat of the buckboard, having him listen so attentively to her dreams about the bakery, and not only listen but provide his own thoughts and opinions when she'd asked for them.

When he came around to help her down from the wagon, his hands seemed to stay at her waist a little longer than necessary, not that she found it at all unpleasant.

Once he released her, he let his gaze roam the open meadow and pond. "You were right—this is perfect for a nice ride."

Was he going to abandon her for River so soon?

He studied the pond for a moment. "That looks like a good fishing spot."

"From what I've heard, it is."

He glanced her way. "Don't you fish?"

"I tagged along with my brothers when I was younger, but haven't in a very long time."

"We should have brought some fishing poles today. It's been a while since I baited a hook."

Cassie started to say they could do that next time, but then he remembered there wouldn't be a next time. Instead she gave him an overly innocent look. "How are you at skipping stones?"

"Fair to middlin'." Then he raised a brow. "That wouldn't by any chance be your way of issuing me a challenge?"

"Maybe."

He rolled up his sleeves. "Then you're on."

She was inordinately pleased that he wasn't ready to abandon her for his ride just yet.

They spent the next fifteen minutes or so trying to best each other at the art of skipping stones, while haggling over whether the objective was to get the stone to skip the farthest or the most times.

In the end, they agreed to call it a draw.

Riley took her arm and began moving back to the wagon. "Now it's my turn to issue you a challenge."

"And what challenge would that be?"

He released her and moved toward Duchess. "I think it's high time a person as fond of horses as you are learns to ride."

She frowned, not sure what she thought about that. "Today?"

"No time like the present," he said cheerfully.

"But I'm not dressed for riding."

He studied her garment. "Your skirt is sufficiently full to protect your modesty and you can mount from the bed of the wagon to make it less awkward."

Once he had Duchess unhitched, he led the mare to the back of the wagon, where he lifted out a saddle that had been stowed under a sheet of canvas.

It didn't seem to take him much time at all to get the mare saddled. Then he turned to her. "Ready?"

With a nod she allowed him to assist her into the wagon bed, suddenly feeling quite daring.

Once Cassie was settled in the saddle, he smiled. "Don't worry. Duchess is a steady mount. And you two are already old friends. Now, I'm going to lead her around for a bit and let you get used to the feel of her, okay?"

Cassie nodded and he set Duchess in motion. Riley kept an eye on them, advising Cassie on how to adjust her position, and describing how to give instructions to the horse. He was a patient and articulate teacher and his love of horses really came through. Finally, he gave her an approving look. "I think you're ready to try this on your own."

Cassie wasn't certain she quite agreed with his assessment, but he was already turning to River.

Riley untied the horse from the back of the wagon and mounted him in one quick, graceful movement that earned her admiration. A moment later he had pulled his horse up alongside hers. "We'll ride side by side. Just relax and enjoy."

Easier said than done. By his own admission, he'd been riding since before he could walk. This was her first time riding a horse solo.

But Riley kept his word to stay beside her, mixing words of encouragement with casual conversation, and gradually Cassie felt her apprehension ease. And before long she was actually enjoying herself. So much so that when Riley asked her if she was up for increasing the pace she allowed Duchess to break into a trot without a moment's hesitation.

They ended their ride by letting the horses drink their fill at the pond, then rode them back to the wagon.

Riley dismounted first, then came around to assist Cassie. He had enjoyed watching her gain confidence as a rider. She'd taken to it as easily as he'd figured she would.

Cassie smiled down at him, her face flushed with triumph and exhilaration from her ride. In that moment, she was so achingly beautiful that she took his breath away.

As she slid down trustingly into his arms, his hands tightened around her. Their gazes met and locked, and he could not for the life of him release her. She felt nice in his arms like this—soft, warm, feminine. It was as if they were in a little bubble—isolated, protected, uplifted.

Her lips looked so sweet and kissable. What would she do if he put that thought into action?

Then Duchess nickered and the spell was broken.

Chapter Sixteen

Riley abruptly released her and stepped back.

Clearing his throat, he reached for Duchess's reins. "Why don't you get our picnic set up while I tend to the horses?"

"All right."

He heard the confusion in her voice. Was it because of what had almost happened? Or because he'd broken it off before anything could happen?

Best not to ponder that question. Instead he focused on tending to the animals while she retrieved the picnic basket and blanket.

By the time he had the horses taken care of she had the blanket spread under a tree and was unloading the food and dishes.

When he neared, she looked up and offered an easy smile of greeting, as if that little moment of awkwardness between them had never happened. Relieved, he sat down on the blanket across from her.

He wasn't going to push his luck by getting too close to her right now.

"So what did our friends pack us for lunch?" he asked.

"They did very well by us. There's some cold fried chicken, bread, cheese and a couple slices of pound cake."

"A feast, indeed."

Cassie filled their plates, and then Riley asked the blessing.

As they began eating, she gave him a smile. "I can see why you enjoy riding so much. It makes one feel on top of the world."

"So you don't think that'll be your last ride?"

"Not if I can help it."

If only he could stick around here to go on some of those rides with her.

Once they'd finished the main portion of the meal, Cassie placed a piece of cake on two plates and handed one to him. As he took his first bite, though, he realized she was just picking at hers with her fork. Was something worrying her?

"Not hungry?" he asked lightly. "Or do you just prefer pie?"

She glanced up guiltily and then smiled sheepishly. "Last night, you asked me for a favor and shared something very personal with me in order to explain exactly what it was you were asking."

He nodded. "And I truly appreciate your ready agreement to help."

"I was wondering if perhaps I could turn the tables on you now."

"How so?"

"I have a favor to ask, but it involves something a bit personal."

Now this sounded interesting. "Ask away." Whatever

this favor was, it must be something big. She seemed unduly nervous and slightly embarrassed.

"The thing is, I don't have much experience speaking to men besides my pa and brothers." She pushed a stray tendril behind her ear, not quite meeting Riley's gaze. "I mean, of course there are shopkeepers and such, but I'm talking about speaking to men on a more personal basis. In fact, there's only you and maybe Mr. Chandler."

Who was this Mr. Chandler? And why had she been speaking to him on a personal basis? But Riley supposed that was none of his business. "Go on."

She fidgeted a moment, then seemed to gather up her courage. "I need to propose marriage to someone, and I don't quite know how to go about it."

That completely unexpected confession set him back, hard. Propose marriage? Had he really heard her right?

She grimaced. "I suppose I should explain."

"That might be best."

"You heard me talking to my brother yesterday about how he and Dinah are going to be moving into their own place soon."

Riley nodded.

"Well, when they do, my pa wants me to move back home so I can take care of him and my other three brothers—cook their meals, do their laundry, keep the house clean, that sort of thing."

In other words, be an unpaid housekeeper. "And you don't want to go." Riley could certainly understand that.

She shook her head, looking miserable. "You must think me a wretchedly ungrateful daughter."

He reached over and clasped her hand. "Not at all. You're a grown woman, with a life of your own to live. And you deserve to have the opportunity to live it."

"I wish my pa felt that way." Then she sobered again. "The thing is, it's what I did for most of the last ten years. My ma died when I was thirteen, and my pa pulled me out of school so I could do all those chores she always managed." Cassie gave him a weak grin. "I'd never appreciated how much my ma really did until her chores became mine."

Pulled her out of school? Seeing as she set such a great score by schooling, that must have been hard on Cassie.

"The farm is several miles from town, and not on the main road, and after Ma passed, Pa didn't have much use for church. So without school or church services, I didn't get to see many folks besides the family."

"That must have been difficult." And lonely.

She shrugged off his sympathy and continued with her story. "All that changed eight months ago when Verne married Dinah. They moved into the house and I was able to turn it all over to her. I came to town and haven't been back since."

"I can't say I blame you for that. And now your father wants you to return home when your brother and his wife move out."

Cassie nodded. "But don't get me wrong, my pa has a good heart and is a very hard worker. He gets up when the sun rises and works until it sets. He just doesn't think he should be expected to do all the woman's work around the place, too."

Before Riley could respond to that, she hurried on. "That's why I need to find a husband. I've tried reasoning with my pa, and then I tried standing up to him, but he just waves aside everything I say. But I figure if I was married, he couldn't very well expect me to leave my husband to go take care of him."

That seemed a rather drastic solution. "Surely there are other options."

Her lips set in a stubborn line. "You don't know my father." Then she waved a hand impatiently. "Besides, I don't have much time. Pa expects me to return home as soon as Mrs. Flanagan is back on her feet."

"That's still no reason to get married."

"It may not be the *best* reason to get married, but it's better than some. At least I'll make certain we both know what we're getting into, unlike some lovesick pair who feel cheated later when the reality doesn't match their dream."

That was a mighty cynical outlook for a young woman. What sort of marriage had her parents had? "What about your bakery business?"

She nodded as if he'd just agreed with her. "That's yet another reason for me to go through with this. If I don't convince my father that I won't be returning home, then there won't *be* a bakery business."

Was Cassie so afraid of her father? Or was this some exaggerated form of daughterly obedience?

"Besides, it's my fault my ma is not around to do for him," she stated.

That brought Riley up short. "What do you mean?"

"I mean it's my fault she passed when she did."

Surely it hadn't been as dire as Cassie made it sound?

"Ma always made sure Pa didn't interfere with my schooling and that I had time to do my studies," she began. "She said she wanted me to have a chance to be a schoolteacher if I wanted." Cassie's expression turned bittersweet. "I think that had been her own dream before she gave it up to marry Pa."

"It sounds like she was a mighty fine woman."

"She was. Anyway, on this particular day, I was supposed to hoe the weeds in the garden. But I didn't want to. So I told Ma about a spelling bee we would be having in class the next day."

Wherever this was headed, Riley knew it wasn't going to end well. "You were a child. Sometimes children act childishly."

The look Cassie shot him said clearly just what she thought of *that* statement. "She insisted I stay in and study while she took care of the garden, just as I'd known she would." Cassie's gaze dropped to her hands. "I already knew most of the words, but I told myself I could use some more practice."

"I take it something happened."

She nodded. "While Ma was out in the garden, doing work I should have been doing, she got bit by a coral snake."

Riley saw the grief on Cassie's face, heard the self-blame in her tone. "That wasn't your fault," he said firmly.

She glared at him. "Wasn't it? I didn't really need to study. In fact, I was doing more daydreaming than studying. And while I was thinking about Asa Redding, who'd smiled at me in class that morning, my ma was dying in the garden. She never even made it back to the house."

"Your mother did what she did because she loved you and wanted you to have a better life. If she hadn't taken your place, and it had been you who died of a snakebite, how do you think she would have felt?"

Cassie waved her hand again, dismissing his argument. "I told you all of that so you would know why I need to take this step. Because unless I find a husband, something that allows me to turn down Pa's request with a reason he'll accept, then I will have no choice but to return home as he asks. And I need to do this before my work for Mrs. Flanagan is complete."

Riley raked a hand through his hair, not at all comfortable with where this conversation was headed.

"Well, will you help me or not?"

"Help you how?"

"Figure out how to go about this."

He couldn't believe he was in this situation. "Let me make sure I understand. What you're asking is if I can tell you the best way for you to propose to a man?"

She beamed at him. "Exactly."

"Any man in particular?" he asked, trying desperately to stall in giving her an answer.

"Actually, I have a list of men who meet the qualities I'm looking for."

She'd come up with a list of both requirements and men who fit them? That seemed to be a very…practical approach to finding a husband. "And what might those qualities be?"

She listed her three criteria, then leaned back. "So you see, I've given this quite a bit of thought."

"How well do you know these men?"

She picked at a piece of lint on her skirt. "Not well at all."

"Mind if I ask how many are on your list?"

"Three."

She said that proudly, as if it were a major accomplishment.

"And I've prioritized them. That way, if the first one turns me down, I have some backups."

"Very practical."

The look she shot him let him know she'd caught the hint of sarcasm in his tone. But she apparently decided to let it pass. "The first name on the list is Mr. Edmondson, the blacksmith, if that makes a difference."

Riley immediately pulled up a mental image of the man. Edmondson had to be more than twice her age. He was a big, burly fellow with hands the size of dinner plates, and who seemed to wear a perpetual scowl. The idea of him being married to young, sunny-tempered, idealistic Cassie was totally appalling.

But she hadn't asked for Riley's opinion on her choice. She'd asked for his help in executing her plan. And he owed it to her to give it his best shot. "However you approach Edmondson, he's going to be taken by surprise. Has he always been a bachelor or is he a widower?"

"Widower."

"How long ago did his wife pass?"

"About five years ago, I believe."

"Then his loss isn't so recent that your proposition would be unseemly."

"At least not on that account." Her wry tone told him she hadn't lost her sense of humor.

"Right. If this were me you were proposing to, I guess your best approach would be to explain, without any histrionics, what the situation is and what you are proposing. And if you could come up with any benefits to me in the arrangement, you should stress those, as well."

She hugged her knees with clasped hands. "That's the same thing I thought." Her lips curled in a crooked smile. "And don't worry, I never was one for histrionics." She cut him a sideways glance. "Mrs. Flanagan suggested I practice before I actually approach anyone."

"That makes sense."

"So, do you mind if I practice with you?"

He was afraid she'd ask that. But he saw the pink climbing up her neck and into her face. It hadn't been easy for her to ask this, so how could he refuse? "All right." Then he stood and reached down a hand to her. "But this will probably be a more effective practice if we stand face-to-face."

With a nod, Cassie took his hand and allowed him to help her up. She brushed her skirt for a few moments, not meeting his gaze.

Then she squared her shoulders and looked Riley in the eye. "Mr. Edmondson, may I have a moment of your time?"

Okay, so she was ready to move right into this. Riley crossed his arms over his chest and pasted on the kind of puzzled frown he expected the blacksmith to give her. "Is there something I can do for you—Miss Vickers, is it?"

"Yes, sir, Cassie Lynn Vickers, Alvin Vickers's daughter. I have a proposal for you, one I hope you will see as mutually beneficial."

He held on to his serious, slightly disapproving demeanor. "And what might that be?"

"I want to build a bakery business here in town, but my father wants me to move back home to be his housekeeper. The only thing that would please him more than that is for me to get married. So I'm looking for a husband."

Well, that was direct. "Now wait a minute, if you're suggesting—"

"Please hear me out, sir."

He was surprised by her tone. Somehow she managed to be both firm and polite.

"I'm not looking for romantic entanglements," she continued, managing to keep her voice mostly steady, "so you don't have to worry about that. And I'm a good cook and housekeeper. I would make sure you had hot, tasty meals every day and that your house was clean and neat and your laundry got done."

She moistened her lips as if they'd gone dry. "I would also provide as much or as little companionship as you wish. All I ask is that you give me your name and your word that I will be free to operate my bakery business."

Her gaze resolutely held Riley's as she stood there waiting for his answer. There was an earnestness about her, along with a touch of vulnerability in her eyes, that gave her an endearing, hard-to-say-no-to air. For a moment he was tempted to tell her yes, not as her stand-in practice partner, but as himself.

What would it be like to have a woman like Cassie at his side? A sweet, caring, giving companion to share his worries and burdens, joys and triumphs? The thought of that kind of life filled him with an aching yearning that was almost too strong to resist.

He almost reached out to her, but at the last minute regained control.

Still, the target of her proposal would have to be hardhearted indeed to tell her no.

Riley cleared his throat. "You did well. I think if you approach Mr. Edmondson in just that manner, then you will be giving yourself your best shot. It'll come down to how interested he is in acquiring a wife." The man would be a fool to turn her down.

Her relieved smile was Riley's payment.

"When do you plan to tender this proposal?" he asked, trying to come to terms with the idea that she would soon belong to another.

"I haven't quite decided, but soon."

"And what if Edmondson says no?" Not that Riley believed that would happen.

"There are those two other names on the list. And if all three turn me down—" she lifted her shoulders in a fatalistic shrug "—then perhaps that's my sign that I should just give in to my father's demand."

Riley had a feeling she didn't need to worry about that. There was no way three separate men would turn her down.

Determined to ignore the stab of jealousy that realization brought with it, he quickly changed the subject. "I think it's time to start packing up to head back. Much as I've enjoyed our outing, I do have to get back to the livery this afternoon, and then figure out when and what I'll tell Noah and Pru about being gone overnight tomorrow."

"Of course." Cassie immediately turned and began putting everything back in the basket.

Why wouldn't she look at him? Had he handled this wrong, not given her the kind of help she was looking for?

Or had she sensed something of his mood, his longing to be *that* man, the one who would stand by her side and care for her as she deserved?

Because, much as he hated to admit it, he really did.

Chapter Seventeen

Cassie wasn't sure what Riley was feeling right now. Strange how it had been both very easy and very difficult to practice that proposal with him.

He'd been so good about listening to her story without judging her, and then allowing her to practice with him. Much as she'd tried to picture herself speaking to the blacksmith while she talked, it was Riley's face she focused on, his answer she waited anxiously for.

Deep down—so deep that she hadn't acknowledged it even to herself before this very moment—she'd hoped he might step up when she explained her situation and told him she needed a husband. And for just a moment, when she'd spoken those potentially life-changing words, she'd seen his eyes darken and his jaw clench, as if he'd been taken by some strong emotion. Or had it only been her imagination, a fantasy conjured by a wishful heart?

A small part of her had hoped that he might...

Might what? Declare himself in love with her?

Which was totally ninny-witted of her. How many ways did he need to tell her he wasn't interested in settling down, before she accepted it as the absolute truth?

As she lifted the picnic basket, Riley took it from her and moved toward the wagon with it. She shook out the blanket and followed.

It was probably just as well he was leaving tomorrow for that meeting.

A day apart would allow her to get her bearings again, to figure out where she *really* wanted to go from here.

"Noah woke with a fever this morning. I'm afraid he's taking his turn with the illness." Cassie bustled around the kitchen, trying to get her biscuit dough ready to go in the oven.

Riley groaned. "I know Dr. Pratt said to expect this, but I was hoping Noah would somehow miss it this time."

She gave him a sympathetic smile. "I know it's worrisome, but try not to let it make you overly anxious. You see how Pru is getting better now, and Noah will, too. At least they didn't both go through the worst of it at the same time."

"It's not me I'm worried about. It doesn't feel right, me leaving you to bear the brunt of his care alone. Maybe I should—"

She quickly cut Riley off. "Don't even say it. It won't get really bad for a day or two, and by then you'll be back. If you look at it right, if it had to happen this is really the best time for it."

He leaned back. "How do you do that?"

"What?"

"No matter how much is thrown at you, you always seem to find a silver lining."

She smiled self-consciously. "I've found that looking only at the dark cloud serves no purpose but to make you feel sad, angry or helpless." She absently tucked a tendril behind her ear. "There is a Bible verse I took to heart many years ago. It states 'whatsoever things are true, whatsoever things are honest, whatsoever things are just, whatsoever things are pure, whatsoever things are lovely, whatsoever things are of good report; if there be any virtue, and if there be any praise, think on these things.'"

He smiled. "I can see the influence it's had on your life."

She returned his smile, then grew serious. "With your permission, I'd like to give Mrs. Flanagan at least part of the story you told me about your stepbrother."

Riley seemed to consider that for a moment, then nodded. "If you think that's best and that it won't rattle her too much."

"She's a lot stronger than you think. And you told me the story because you wanted me to be prepared if Guy came around and tried to get to the children. I think it only fair that we do the same for her. You can trust her to keep your secret, and to protect Noah and Pru with all that's in her."

Riley rubbed the back of his neck. "Speaking of secrets, it's probably time I tell the kids I'll be heading out of town today and won't be back until tomorrow."

"Do you want help?"

"Thank you, but I can do this on my own. They're good kids and they've gotten comfortable being here with you ladies. All things considered, I think they'll be fine."

Later that afternoon, as Cassie watched Riley head for the train station, she felt strangely bereft, as if it was a longtime friend walking away. Funny how quickly Riley had become familiar and comfortable.

How would it be when he and the children left for good?

She turned back to her work, not wanting to dwell on that very unhappy thought.

Instead she kept busy, experimenting with new pie recipes and doing her best to keep the children entertained and unconcerned about Riley's absence. And she sent up more than one prayer for the success of his quest.

When she finally heard the afternoon train whistle on Wednesday, it was all she could do not to hurry out to the depot to meet him.

Had he and the detective gotten the information they needed from the informant?

Would he stop at the livery before he came to the house, maybe take River out for a run? Or was he anxious about the children's safety, so would rush back to check on them first?

Ten minutes later her question was answered when Riley walked into the house. Funny how her first instinct was to run into his arms and give him a welcome-home hug.

"How did your meeting go?" she asked instead.

"It went quite well. Mr. Claypool now has some significant leads, and if things pan out the way we think they will, we may finally be able to put Guy away for quite some time."

"That *is* good news. Is it something that you think will happen soon?"

"Perhaps. Claypool is very hopeful." Riley moved toward the hall. "How are the kids?"

"Pru is getting stronger every day, but Noah is getting

worse, as was to be expected." Cassie smiled. "They'll be glad to have you back."

With a nod he disappeared in the direction of their room.

Cassie went back to work in the kitchen. While supper simmered on the stove, she planned her baked goods for the next day and checked that she had all the necessary ingredients on hand. But she found herself listening for the sound of Riley's footsteps.

He returned about ten minutes later, a smile on his face. "It appears they are doing well under your care. I hope they didn't cause you too much extra work."

"We managed quite well."

Riley watched her a moment, liking the efficiency of her movements and the gentle smile she seemed to always wear when busy. "And how is your husband hunting going? Did you approach Mr. Edmondson yet?" Almost as soon as the words were out of his mouth he wished them back. He'd promised himself he'd stay out of her business, would not torture himself asking about the progress of her scheme.

But it was too late to undo it now.

For her part, she didn't quite meet his gaze. "Not yet," she admitted. Then she changed the subject, asking him abut his trip and whether or not he'd stopped in to see River.

Riley got the message—she didn't want to discuss her husband hunt. Was it just that she didn't want to discuss it with him? Or was she having second thoughts?

He hated himself for wishing it was the latter, especially since he didn't have anything to offer her in its place.

* * *

That evening, as had become routine with them, Riley joined Cassie in the kitchen once the kids were put to bed. "Noah is finally asleep," he said, helping himself to one of her pecans.

She swatted at his hand. "Good. Let's hope he sleeps straight through the night."

Feeling not one whit remorseful for the theft, Riley crossed his arms. "So what delicacies are you preparing tonight?"

"Two pecan pies and a buttermilk pie for Daisy, four cherry tarts and two peach tarts for Eve, and two apple pies for Mrs. Ortolon over at the boardinghouse."

"Ah, so you have a new customer."

"I do." Cassie's smile had a satisfied edge. "And she sought me out rather than the other way around."

"Good for you." He glanced about. "What can I do to help?"

She cut him a skeptical look. "You know anything about pie making?"

"I know how to follow directions."

Cassie studied him a moment, then tilted her head toward the door. "There's an extra apron you can use, on that peg over there."

He hesitated, not at all interested in wearing one of those ruffled aprons. But she raised a brow as if to say *I thought as much* and he couldn't leave the challenge unmet. With a shrug, he grabbed the apron and tied it around his waist.

"Now what?"

"I've already taken care of the apple pies, and am going to work on the fruit tarts next. While I'm doing that, you can shell those pecans in that bowl on the table for me."

He reached for the bowl. "And for this you thought I needed to wear an apron?"

She grinned. "Kitchen work is kitchen work." Then she touched her chin. "You do know how to shell pecans, don't you?"

"I've shelled my share."

"Good. If you can clean 'em up and try to give me large pieces, that would be appreciated."

Nodding, he reached for a pecan. They worked in silence for a while until she had the tarts in the oven. When she'd shut the stove door, she returned to the table and peered into the bowl where he was putting the shelled nuts. "Nice job."

For some reason, those simple words gave him a feeling of pride.

A feeling she deflated with her next words. "How did you manage to get flour on your shirtsleeve?"

The amused light dancing in her eyes drew an answering grin from him. "You didn't come through this unscathed, either," he said with mock severity. "There's a large smudge of flour on your cheek."

She reached up guiltily to swipe at it, but missed.

"No, here, let me do it." He stood and reached over and brushed the hair from her face, then used his thumb to rub away the powdery substance. The sound of her soft, breathy inhalation made him pause as his gaze shot to hers. Had she felt it, too, that warm, tingly spark when his hand touched her face?

From the way her eyes darkened and her breathing quickened, he'd guess she had.

There was such a sweetness about her, such an enticing mix of courage and vulnerability, innocence and awareness.

Did she have any idea how she affected him?

He lowered his face, keeping his gaze locked with hers, looking for any sign that she didn't want this kiss he was aching to give her. But all he saw was invitation. When she tilted her face up in anticipation, he eagerly closed the distance and allowed himself to deliver the kiss he'd been longing to give her almost from the moment he'd met her.

And she seemed just as eager as he. It was sweet and tender and wonderfully electric. He'd never experienced anything quite like this before.

Then reality returned and he broke it off, pulling her into a hug, tucking her cheek against his chest, trying to get his breathing back under control.

What was he doing? He couldn't offer Cassie any kind of future that included him, and she was not a woman to be trifled with. She was a lady—sweet, generous, tenderhearted, and she deserved to be treated as such. Oh, but he couldn't find it in himself to be sorry for what he'd done. Holding her in his arms, tasting the sweetness of her lips, feeling her heart beat against his—the memory of this perfect moment would stay with him for some time to come.

But how could he undo what he'd just done?

Her first kiss. As she leaned her head against the warmth of Riley's chest, felt his hand rub small circles on her back, Cassie let all the wonderful, head-spinning sensations roll over her. She'd never imagined it could be this way. The emotions she felt from him—gentleness and possessiveness, tenderness and strength—made her feel cherished and needed. She'd never felt as if she mattered to someone in quite this way before.

Did he sense it, too, this connection, this feeling of meant-to-be?

Oh, he had to. He wouldn't still be holding her otherwise.

When they finally separated, Riley smiled down at her with such tenderness that it took her breath away. Could there be a future for them, after all?

Then his expression shifted and some distance crept in. Was he regretting having kissed her? If he apologized she would be absolutely mortified.

"Cassie, I—"

To stave off whatever was coming, she turned to the stove as if she hadn't heard him. "Time to check on my tarts—don't want them to burn."

But he didn't accept her not-so-subtle attempt to change the subject. He closed the distance between them and captured her hands with his. "The pies will be fine for another few minutes. We need to talk."

He gently drew her back to the table. Once she'd taken a seat, he pulled up a chair beside her and sat, as well.

She didn't meet his gaze, didn't want to see what might be reflected there.

After a few moments of silence, he grasped her hand again. "Cassie, look at me."

Reluctantly, she finally glanced up. His serious, what-do-I-say-to-her expression confirmed her worse fears.

"I want to apologize to you."

There they were, the words she'd dreaded hearing. He was sorry he'd kissed her.

He squeezed her fingers. "I can see what you're thinking and you're wrong. The apology is not because I regret that kiss. Kissing you was something I've wanted to do almost from the moment I saw you, and it was every bit as wonderful as I imagined it would be."

Still confused, she searched his eyes, looking for some insight.

"What I do need to apologize for is any expectations it might have given you. Nothing has changed as far as my situation. I still can't let Guy catch up with us and try to take the kids. So when Noah is able to travel, we will be leaving Turnabout and continuing our never-ending journey."

"I see." He wasn't asking her to go with him. Was he waiting for her to hint that she was willing to go? She gathered her courage in her hands. "Did you ever consider that you don't have to do this alone?"

Surprise flickered in his expression, along with some other emotion she couldn't quite identify.

He gave her hand another gentle squeeze. "No matter how much I might want that, I could never allow it. Not only because of how unfair it would be to that other person, but because of what a distraction it could be from my mission." He stood and paced across the room, as if unable to stay still. "Having someone else to be responsible for, to worry over, is not something I can add to my plate right now."

Was that how he saw her, as another burden to bear? Everything in Cassie screamed to tell him that she was perfectly able to care for herself, that she would be more than willing to help him keep the children safe.

But she knew that wasn't something he'd ever agree to. No, the best she could do right now, if she truly cared for him and wanted to help, was to relieve him of any guilt he might be feeling. "You should know I don't regret that kiss, either. You didn't force it on me, and I held no illusions as to your willingness to settle down here permanently."

She stood in turn, moving back to the oven. "At least now, when I do eventually marry, I will have an idea of what a kiss from a man should be like."

The silence stretched out, vibrating with an emotion she couldn't quite name, but which was anything but comfortable.

Finally, she heard him straighten the chairs at the table. "I'm glad I could be of service." His voice was strained, controlled.

She didn't respond—after all, what could she say to that? Instead, she kept her back to him as she removed the tarts from the oven. When she finally turned around, he had made his exit.

She set the kitchen to rights, trying not to think of anything but the task at hand. Then she padded down the hallway and checked on the children. Both were asleep.

Leaving just a sliver of space between the door and the frame, she moved to her own room.

She managed to keep her emotions under control until she slipped under the covers. How in the world had the evening gone from such a high note to that disaster? That kiss had been so wonderful—everything a first kiss should be. And she had wanted it with all her heart. Like Riley, she didn't regret that it had happened.

But would she be able to face him in the morning?

And how in the world had she managed to fall in love with the man in such a short space of time? Because she was in love with him. And now she knew why her mother had warned her about falling in love—because it hurt. It hurt a great deal.

But even so, it was so achingly sweet…

Cassie rolled on her side and peered into the darkness. Despite what she'd said, she couldn't go through with her marriage plan, not feeling as she did about Riley.

But she couldn't go back to her father's farm, either.

Which left her with what?

She closed her eyes and poured out her fears, questions, dreams and desires in a prayer.

And sometime around midnight, she finally fell asleep.

Riley lay in his attic room, calling himself all kinds of a fool. What had he been thinking, kissing her that way? Cassie deserved so much better than that. So much better than him.

Still, that kiss, and her innocent, trusting response to it, had been every bit as sweet as he'd imagined it would be. If only his life was his own…

He placed an arm behind his neck as he stared up at the night-shrouded rafters. Despite what he'd said about marriage, he knew they weren't all bad. His parents had seemed very happy together. He remembered lots of playful teasing and laughter in their home. And even when the barn had caught fire, something very scary to a six-year-old boy, his parents had pulled together and drawn strength from each other, and from prayer.

It was so tempting to ask Cassie to come with them, or at least wait for him, especially after the meeting in Tyler. Since his and Claypool's talk with Dixon, Riley was much more confident that this whole running nightmare would come to an end soon. But there was no guarantee, and he'd probably need to move on from Turnabout before that happened. Was it fair to Cassie for him to speak of all that now? Especially knowing she had to face her father with an answer soon.

But the thought of her proposing to the blacksmith set Riley's teeth on edge, made his stomach twist. To think of her bargaining her way into a loveless marriage turned him inside out. And it was so unnecessary. She had so much strength and courage when it came to other aspects of her life. Why couldn't she use those same qualities in standing up to her father?

Should he try to reason with her on that one more time? Perhaps he could enlist Mrs. Flanagan's help on that score. Or was the woman on Cassie's side? She had mentioned the widow was helping her with this husband-hunting scheme.

The way Cassie had turned from him so quickly after that kiss concerned him. Had she been upset or merely embarrassed? Or had it been something else altogether?

Which brought his thoughts full circle—what should he do now?

Chapter Eighteen

"About last night..."

Cassie didn't look up from her work at the stove. She had to keep an eye on the eggs in the skillet, after all. "Yes?"

"You have to know that I've grown to care about you a great deal," Riley went on.

"And I you." She really didn't want to rehash this again. "But you have responsibilities to the children and can't deal with any other distractions right now. You made that perfectly clear last night, and I understand your reasons. The children come first with you, and that's how it should be." She glanced over her shoulder at him. "In fact, I admire you for it. I just wish you would let me share that responsibility with you."

She heard the rattle of dishes as Riley retrieved a cup from the cupboard, and then forced herself not to tense as he reached past her to lift the coffeepot from the stove. Her effort met with mixed success. She was so attuned to him now, so affected by his nearness, that she couldn't completely tamp down her reaction.

He didn't say anything else, but she could feel his

stare on her as she worked. There was a tension between them now—did he feel it?

She put his plate of eggs and biscuits on the table in front of him. The butter and jam were already there.

"I hope you don't mind eating alone," she said as she wiped her hands on her apron. "I'm running a little behind this morning and I need to go tend to Mrs. Flanagan."

Something flickered in his expression, but he merely nodded.

She moved toward the hallway, then paused and turned back to him. "By the way, I have something I need to take care of today, and it'll probably take me most of the morning. Do you think you can stay around here to help out Mrs. Flanagan and the children until I return?"

"Of course. Just give me time to run by the livery and let Mr. Humphries know I won't be available this morning."

Riley pushed his chair back and made as if to stand, but she waved him back down.

"There's no need. I'll be going by the livery and I can let him know for you."

He studied her as he settled back in his seat, as if wanting to ask a question. But he just nodded once more and retrieved his fork.

Which was just as well, because she didn't want to discuss her errand with him.

Two hours later, Cassie stopped the buggy in front of her father's home. She sat there a moment, letting the familiar smells and sights wash over her. Life here hadn't been all bad. In fact, she had very fond memories of her childhood. Her father had always been more interested in the farm than in people, but her mother had had a way of softening him, of making him stop occasionally and take time to enjoy himself.

It was only after her mother's passing that he'd hardened, grown stricter, had retreated into the world of his farm with a focus that shut just about everything—and everyone—else out. Cassie would suffocate if she allowed herself to be sucked back into that world.

The door opened and Dinah stepped outside. A wide smile split her face. "Hi, Cassie Lynn." She wiped her hands on her apron. "It's so good to see you. We never get visitors out here."

Cassie climbed down from the buggy and returned Dinah's smile. She should have made more of an effort to come for an occasional visit. Dinah must have been lonely as the only female in this household of men.

"Hi. I come bearing pie."

"Well, bless your heart, your pa and the boys are going to love this. They're always telling me how much better your pies are than mine."

Cassie mentally winced as she approached the house. Yet another reason she should have befriended her sister-in-law sooner. Her father and brothers were anything but tactful. "Don't pay them any mind—they just don't take well to change. I'm sure your pies are wonderful."

Dinah held the door open and allowed her to enter the house first. Cassie looked around, noting the changes that had been made since she'd moved out. There were new curtains on the parlor windows and a pretty glass vase on the mantel that had replaced the canning jar she'd used to hold wildflowers in the past. And the cabinets had been painted a bright yellow. She was impressed that Dinah had been able to convince her pa to do even that much. Had Verne stepped in and backed her up? Or had Dinah up and done it herself without asking? Whatever had happened, Cassie's respect for her sister-in-law bumped up a notch.

"The place looks nice."

"Thanks." Dinah seemed inordinately pleased by the faint praise. "I have some ideas of the things I want to do with our own place once we move in."

"I'm sure it'll look lovely. You seem to have a real knack for decorating."

"Thank you." She touched her hair nervously. "It's nice to hear that. Menfolk don't really appreciate what little touches can do for a home." Then she waved a hand. "But here I go, nattering on. Was there a specific reason you came all this way?"

"I'm here to talk to Pa. Do you know where he is right now?"

Dinah studied her face a moment, then nodded, as if satisfied. "You're not moving back here, are you?"

Cassie shook her head. "No, I'm not."

"Good for you." Then she gave her a speculative look. "Is it because of that Mr. Walker?"

If only she could say yes. "No, he plans to move on after his niece and nephew get better."

"Too bad."

Cassie couldn't agree more.

"Your pa's over in the barn, I think. He said something earlier about the milking stall needing some work."

Cassie thanked Dinah, then headed for the barn. When she reached it, she stood in the doorway for a few moments, letting her eyes grow accustomed to the dim interior. She saw her father at his worktable, hunched over something he was applying a file to.

She loved him, she truly did—he was her father, after all. And she was very afraid he was going to be hurt by what she had to say to him. But it had to be said.

She stepped forward, leaving the bright sunshine behind her as she crossed into the half-light of the barn. "Hello, Pa," she said softly.

His head came up, a confused frown on his face. As soon as he recognized her, though, he smiled and pushed back his stool. "Well, hi there, Cassie Lynn. Is Irene Flanagan finally back on her feet?"

"No, sir."

He frowned, his confusion returning.

"I came to tell you I've reached a decision. I won't be moving back here once Mrs. Flanagan is able to get by on her own again."

The frown turned stern, authoritarian. "Now see here—"

She held up a hand. "Please, Pa, let me finish. I won't be abandoning you completely. Once Dinah and Verne move out, I'll come by here every Tuesday and Friday to cook and clean and do whatever else you need me to do." Those were the days the *Turnabout Gazette* came out. She figured she'd bring a copy when she came and deliver a little of the outside world to this isolated farmstead. If Pa didn't want to read it, perhaps her brothers would.

She pulled her thoughts back to the here and now. "But I won't be living here," she said firmly.

"Where will you stay?"

"Mrs. Flanagan is going to be my business partner in the bakery and she's offered me a room." Cassie swallowed, trying to hold on to her calm demeanor. "I'm sorry if this grieves you, Pa, but I'm a grown woman now and I need to make my own life."

"A woman needs a man to look out for her. If she doesn't have a husband, it falls to her family to fill that role."

"That may be true for some women, but not all. Not for me."

Her father's disapproving expression didn't relax.

On impulse she stepped forward and embraced him in a hug. After a moment she felt his arms go around her. "I worry about you, baby girl. The world isn't kind to women without a man's protection."

Her heart melted at those words, this proof that he was still her loving, albeit stern, pa.

She stepped back and smiled at him. "You can come to town and check on me whenever you like," she said, a gentle teasing tone in her voice. "And I just promised to return here twice a week."

"You've got your ma's stubborn streak, that's plain as day." Then he nodded, as if finally accepting her decision. "That will stand you in good stead, I suppose."

Cassie bit her lip, the old feelings of guilt ambushing her with unexpected force at his words. "I'm so sorry, Pa. About Ma, I mean." Her voice cracked on the last word, but she managed to hold the tears back.

Her father appeared startled by her sudden shift in mood. "What's the matter, Cassie girl? What about your ma?"

"It was my fault she was out in that garden, my fault she's gone. If I'd been doing my own chores—"

His arms went around her again. "Gracious, girl, you been carrying that around with you all this time?"

He set her back and stared solemnly into her eyes. "You got it wrong, Cassie Lynn. Your ma asked me to take her to town that day. She wanted to buy some fabric to make new curtains for the parlor. If I'd said yes instead of telling her what a wasteful notion that was, she might still be alive today."

"Oh, Pa, no." His confession touched Cassie, helped her relate to him in a way she hadn't in a very long time. "You can't go blaming yourself."

He brushed her hair with his gnarled, work-roughened hand. "I can and I did, for a long time. But I finally realized that thinking on such things does no one any good. You've got to trust in the Lord, forgive yourself and move on."

Easier said than done.

He must have seen something of her thoughts in her face because he squeezed her hands. "Now that you know the part I played, you can't take the blame on your shoulders without shifting some of that burden on mine, as well." He folded his arms across his chest. "We're tied together in this. You think about this anytime you go thinking the Lord ain't big enough to forgive us."

His words were a balm to the ache that had been gnawing inside Cassie for a very long time.

A few minutes later, as she turned the buggy back toward town, she felt as if a tremendous weight had been lifted from her shoulders.

She decided that, for the time being, she wouldn't mention this visit and its purpose to Riley. He might misunderstand her motives, might feel an added layer of guilt for something that had been no one's decision but her own.

She also didn't want him to feel that she'd read any-thing into last night's kiss that he hadn't intended.

If he inquired about her husband hunt, she would merely respond that it was progressing just as it should.

He'd be gone in a week and that would be that.

And if she was lucky, she'd wait until then to fall apart.

Riley had spent the morning wondering just what sort of business it was that had taken Cassie away from the house. She'd said she was going by the livery, and the blacksmith's place was just down from there. Was she proposing to Edmondson? It was all Riley could do not to march out there and stop her.

But he knew he had no rights where she was con-cerned.

Still, as one hour turned into two and then three, he found himself growing concerned on her behalf. Had she had to go down to the second or even the third choice on her list? Or was she merely spending time with her new fiancé?"

It was nearly eleven o'clock when Cassie returned to the house.

"How are the kids?" she asked promptly.

There was a new look about her, as if she'd accom-plished some major feat, as if a burden had been lifted from her. So had she gone through with her proposal, after all? If so, why didn't she just announce that she had a fiancé?

Pulling his thoughts back to her question, Riley an-swered as coherently as possible. "Noah is complaining about the itching. Mrs. Flanagan's been trying to entertain him with stories and games, but she's been meeting with mixed results. "

"Oh dear, I don't know whether to feel more sympathy for Noah or Mrs. Flanagan. I'll go check on them in just a moment."

Riley decided to do a bit of subtle probing to see if she'd reveal anything. "Did you get your business taken care of?"

"I did."

That still didn't give him the answers he wanted, so he tried again. "It all went well, I hope."

Cassie nodded, a satisfied expression on her face. "It wasn't an easy step to take, but yes, it ended even better than expected."

She didn't elaborate, and other than out and out asking her what she'd been up to, he had to be satisfied with that.

Later, as Riley brushed Duchess with long even strokes, his mind was still on that cryptic conversation. He'd just unhitched the animal from the freight wagon and the horse was now contentedly munching some oats while Riley groomed her.

Cassie had remained closemouthed as to the nature of her errand all through lunch and the cleanup after. Perhaps he'd misread her intent.

If she had proposed marriage this morning and one of her three candidates had accepted, surely she would have announced it? And if the man had refused her, she wouldn't appear nearly so serene. There was a third option, of course—the man may have asked for time to think it over.

No, that couldn't be it. She had the look of a woman

who had settled matters. Perhaps she had been dealing with another matter altogether.

This was ridiculous. The only way he was going to get peace of mind was to come right out and ask her. Maybe tonight, when they were doing the supper dishes—

"Hello, Riley."

Riley froze. He knew that voice, would know it anywhere, anytime.

Guy had found them.

Chapter Nineteen

Riley turned and faced his stepbrother, trying to keep hold of his emotions.

"You're quite predictable," Guy said with a self-satisfied sneer. "When I arrive in a new town, I always check at the livery first."

"What do you want?"

"What do you think I want? I want my kids."

"Nancy entrusted them to me."

"But Nancy's not here anymore. I'm their father and by rights they belong to me, not you."

"You talk about them like they're animals or furniture. They're not possessions, they're children."

"And they're *my* children. And I aim to have them come with me."

"That's not going to happen."

"Shall we let the law decide?"

"Your record with the law is far from stellar."

"But I've done my time, and now I'm a changed man, ready to walk the straight and narrow."

Riley very much doubted that. "I've heard that all before."

"But this time, it's true. And you can't prove otherwise. So, take me to my kids."

"You might want to wait on that. They have chicken pox." The surprise on Guy's face was quite satisfying to see.

"You're lying."

"Not at all."

"Do you mean to tell me that you went off and left them on their own with them being sick?"

"Who said they were by themselves?"

"I want to see for myself." Guy straightened. "I can just ask around town if I want to know where they're staying. A little backwater like this, everyone here likely knows everyone else's business."

It appeared there was no putting this off. "Let me finish up here and then I'll take you to them."

Guy tugged his sleeve in that irritatingly superior way he had. "I'll wait."

"Riley, why'd you knock? You know you can bring a visitor right on in," Cassie said as she opened the door.

Before Riley could respond, his stepbrother doffed his hat and stepped forward. "Good day to you, ma'am. I'm Guy Simpson, Pru and Noah's father."

"Oh." Cassie's gaze flew to Riley's and he saw the surprise and uncertainty there. She recovered quickly and gave his stepbrother a nod of greeting. "Good afternoon." But she stepped out on the porch, casually pulling the door shut behind her.

If Guy noticed anything awkward in her greeting, he gave no sign of it. "Riley tells me the kids are a bit under the weather right now, but didn't mention the cause. I hope it's not anything serious?"

So Guy was trying to confirm his story.

"It's chicken pox." She tilted her head slightly, her nose wrinkled in apparent concern. "May I ask if you've had this illness yourself?"

An uncertain look crossed Guy's otherwise smooth expression. "I'm not really sure."

She lifted a hand in a gesture of dismay. "Oh, dear. Chicken pox is highly contagious, so we have the children under quarantine. And according to Dr. Pratt, it's much worse for an adult to catch it than a child."

Guy rubbed his jaw. "I don't care so much for myself, but I don't suppose it would do the kids any good for me to finally show up just to become too sick to care for them." Then he met her gaze, his expression troubled. "Are they suffering much from it?"

Riley wanted to roll his eyes. Guy was a consummate actor.

But Cassie was continuing to speak to him as she would to any genuinely concerned parent. "They're definitely uncomfortable and a bit cranky when they go through the worst of it. But thankfully, they're not suffering any real pain."

"Well, thank the Good Lord for that." Guy gave her one of those charming, self-deprecating smiles of his that could make women swoon. "It's very kind of you to be caring for them. I hope you'll allow me to repay you for all your trouble. I'm afraid I don't have much in the way of funds, but I'm willing to help out in other ways."

"Thank you, but there's no need. Mr. Walker here has been doing some fix-up work around here and he's really been doing a lot of the looking after Noah and Pru."

"I'm glad my little brother here has been doing his part, but I'm their father and I like to pay my own debts."

"There's no debt here." Her tone was firmer this time. "I've grown quite fond of the children and I am happy to do what I can to help."

"Miss Vickers is very forthright," Riley said.

Guy ignored his comment and kept his smile focused on her. "I can see why Riley was so comfortable leaving them in your care. Tell me, how much longer do you reckon they'll be contagious? I certainly don't want to impose on your kindness any longer than necessary."

"Another week, at least. And as I said, it's no imposition."

"Well then, since I can't see the children just yet, I guess I'd best find myself a place to stay for the next week." He turned to Riley. "Where are you staying—the hotel? A boardinghouse?"

"Actually, I'm staying right here, where I can help take care of the kids when I'm not working at the livery." He rather enjoyed the flash of irritation he saw in his stepbrother's face.

Guy frowned. "I'm surprised that you would impose on the kindness of this lady, not to mention put her in such a socially precarious position."

Before Riley could respond, Cassie spoke up. If anything, her spine got straighter and her chin higher. "I believe you are under some misapprehensions, sir. Mr. Walker was invited to stay here by Mrs. Flanagan, my employer and the owner of this house. She issued the invitation so he could be close to Pru and Noah. He's a welcome guest, there is nothing socially precarious about his presence here and he has been nothing but a gentleman his entire stay."

Riley felt a little prickling of guilt at that statement.

That kiss last night didn't exactly qualify as a gentlemanly act.

But Guy was already bowing to her in his courtliest fashion. "My apologies, ma'am. I meant no offense." Then he turned to Riley. "Perhaps you will be so good as to show me the way to the hotel and we can catch up on the latest news while we walk."

Riley was tempted to refuse, but decided it was best to hear what Guy had to say.

As Cassie watched the men walk away, her hands began to tremble. The only thing that had kept her from panicking earlier was Riley's reassuring presence. It had been obvious, to her at least, that he wasn't happy with the circumstances—undoubtedly a major understatement—but he had remained calm and businesslike.

She hugged herself with arms crossed tightly over her chest. Riley's fears had come to pass. The children's father had caught up with them.

What would happen now? Surely there was something they could do to prevent Guy from gaining control of the children. She understood now why Riley was so protective of them. The thought of those precious little ones falling into the hands of a man who would use them in the manner Riley had described was absolutely unthinkable.

Would Sheriff Gleason help them? Or would his hands be tied by the law?

Cassie stepped back inside and closed the door, leaning against it while she tried to pull her thoughts together. She should tell Mrs. Flanagan as soon as possible, but she would leave it to Riley to tell Noah and Pru, when he thought the time was right.

How would the kids feel if they knew their father was here? Would they want to see him? Would they fear him?

It was hard to believe the man she'd just met had done all those things Riley had described. Even though he'd told her his stepbrother was charming, she'd pictured a brute of a man with a boorish demeanor, not this very pleasant-looking, well-mannered gentleman. Not that she doubted Riley's story.

Which made his stepbrother all the more dangerous.

She looked into the dining room, to find Mrs. Flanagan reading a book, flanked by the children. Cassie took a moment to savor that sweet picture, then reluctantly cleared her throat.

The trio glanced her way and she flashed them all a calm smile. "What story are you reading?"

Noah gave a wide grin. "Mrs. Flanagan is reading us a story about a prince who was turned into a frog."

"Oh my, that poor prince."

Noah puffed out his chest. "I think it would be fun to be a frog. You could hop around and get as dirty and wet as you want and never have to do chores."

Pru wrinkled her nose. "But you would be green and squishy and have to eat flies."

Noah merely shrugged, as if he didn't consider that a hardship.

Cassie smiled and then turned to Mrs. Flanagan. "Can I speak to you for just a minute?" She tried to communicate the importance with her eyes.

"Of course." Her employer handed the book to Pru as Cassie moved to the back of the wheelchair. "Why don't you continue reading while I see what Cassie Lynn needs?"

"Yes, ma'am."

Cassie pushed the chair into the kitchen and then quickly updated Mrs. Flanagan on the situation.

"That man is going to have to climb over me to get to those little darlings." The widow's grim expression made it clear she meant every word.

After she returned Mrs. Flanagan to the children, Cassie went back to the kitchen and finished chopping the carrots that would be a side dish for this evening's supper.

What was Riley doing right now? Was he still with his stepbrother? Had he taken River out for a gallop so he could think?

Waiting for him to come back was excruciating. She needed to know what he was thinking, what he might be planning to keep the children safe.

Because there had to be a way.

As she'd hoped, Riley soon reappeared, entering through the back door. She immediately turned to him and her heart nearly broke at the drawn, worried look on his face.

"Where are Noah and Pru?" he asked.

"Mrs. Flanagan is reading to them in the dining room."

He nodded and crossed the room.

"Oh, Riley, what are we going to do?"

He dropped down on one of the chairs. "Whatever I have to do to keep Guy away from those kids."

She grabbed the coffeepot and poured a cup, figuring he needed something to grab on to. While she was still at the counter, he shot her a suspicious look. "You didn't say anything to them, did you?"

"Of course not." How could he think she would

scare them that way? She set the cup in front of him and crossed her arms.

"I'm sorry, I should have known better. It's just…"

"It's just that your stepbrother's arrival has rattled you."

He grimaced. "That's an understatement."

She sat at the table across from him. "I did tell Mrs. Flanagan, though. I thought she needed to know."

Riley nodded, but didn't respond.

"Are you going to tell the children that their father is here?"

He absently turned the cup of coffee in his hands. "I don't want to put that burden, and that fear, on them."

"But he may find a way to make his presence known."

Riley nodded. "I know." He stared at the cup as if just now realizing it was there, then took a sip. "I'll tell them. But I think I'll wait until morning. Let them have one more night of peace."

"Perhaps, in the next day or two, this detective of yours will find what he needs to put your stepbrother away."

"Doubtful. He only left Tyler today."

"What did the two of you discuss just now, when you left here? Did Guy tell you what his plans are?"

"He did all the talking. He tried to convince me that he was truly reformed, that he had learned his lesson and paid for his transgressions, and that he was ready to be a proper father to the children."

"But you don't believe him."

Riley grimaced. "I've been fooled by that kind of talk from him too many times. He comes to you with eyes filled with sorrow, and confides how deeply he regrets the wrong he's done. You hear the emotion in his voice, see it in his expression and bearing, and you just know that this time it's genuine." Riley waved a hand in disgust. "But as time passes, you watch as he slips back into his old ways, begin to doubt that he ever truly abandoned them, and you come to realize that the only thing he truly regrets is having been found out."

Cassie reached across the table and touched his arm. "Oh Riley, I am so sorry."

He took her hand and gave it a gentle squeeze—a silent thank-you—then released it. "This is my fault. I let down my guard."

"It is *not* your fault. Pru and Noah catching chicken pox was not your doing, and that's the only reason he was able to catch up with you."

"Still, I should have found a way."

"You just stop that right now. Wallowing in self-recrimination will not do you or the children any good."

Cassie suddenly realized this was what her father had said to her, what he'd wanted her to understand.

But this discussion was about Riley, not her. "Those two kids need you to be sharp and alert right now."

His tense expression relaxed into a crooked grin. "Yes, ma'am."

"That's better."

"It appears I only have one choice. I need to find a way to slip away with the kids before Guy realizes they are able to travel."

"You don't think he'll be keeping an eye on the train station?"

"The train isn't the only way to leave. I'll camp out in the woods with them if I have to, until Guy gives up searching for us."

"Surely it won't come to that."

Riley gave her a meaningful look, but didn't say anything.

He didn't have to.

She knew that Riley was prepared to do whatever it took to keep Noah and Pru safe. And while she admired him for that inherent love and courage, a part of her was frightened of what that could lead to.

Especially if there was an actual face off between the two men.

And regardless of what else happened, he'd just told her that he and the children were leaving. Without her.

Chapter Twenty

The next morning Riley took Cassie up on her offer to help him break the news to Noah and Pru. He figured she might be better able to soothe their fears than he was.

And he was correct.

She knew all the right things to say to calm Pru's worst fears, to explain matters to Noah in a way that made sense to him.

Later, when he and Cassie were alone in the kitchen, Riley took a deep breath, feeling as if a major chasm had been crossed. "Thank you for that. I appreciate how you were able to find the right words to ease the majority of their fears."

"You're welcome, but I'm sure you would have done just as well without me. Those children look up to you, trust you."

If only he felt he deserved that trust. Time to change the subject. "I think it'll be best if I stay close to home now that Guy is here. I'm going to head for the livery and tell Mr. Humphries I can't work there anymore."

"You must do what you feel best, but what about River's stabling fees, if I may be so bold as to ask? Because I'd be glad to give you some of my pie money if you need it. For the children's sake, of course."

"That's mighty generous of you, but it won't be necessary. I have some funds put by."

Cassie continued to amaze him with her unselfish generosity. And it hurt more than he cared to admit that he had nothing to give her in return except his gratitude. He couldn't even promise her he would return anytime soon.

But oh, how he wished he could.

Cassie stepped out of the restaurant, her mind troubled. She'd delivered three pies, and Daisy had requested that she begin delivering four. At this rate she would soon have enough saved up to order the extra baking tins she wanted. And then she could begin saving her way to true independence.

That thought should have brought her joy, but her mind was too troubled about the uncertain future of the children to let that be so.

Please, Lord Jesus, keep those little lambs safe, give Riley the strength and discernment to know what to do, and show me how best to help them all.

"Miss Vickers."

Hearing her name called brought Cassie back to her surroundings. She was passing the Rose Palace Hotel, and Guy Simpson was standing in the doorway.

She offered a smile that carried a politeness she didn't feel. "Mr. Simpson, good morning. I trust you slept well."

He stepped forward to join her. "Unfortunately, no. But it wasn't the fault of the hotel. I was just too worried about my children to relax."

"Quite understandable." If it were true. "But please try not to worry overmuch. It's quite common for children to get chicken pox and the vast majority come out unscathed."

"Thank you for those reassurances to a concerned father. And I must say, I do feel better knowing they are in such good hands."

She nodded her acknowledgment of the implied compliment, then straightened. "If you'll excuse me, I have some errands to run and I don't want to be away from the house for too long."

"Of course. But if you don't mind, I'd like to walk along with you for a while so we can chat."

What could she say to that? "By all means."

Cassie started forward again and he fell into step beside her. "I suppose Riley has warned you about me."

Startled by his directness, she faltered slightly, then resumed her pace.

"That's all right," Guy said with a rueful shake of his head. "You don't need to answer. And I really can't say as I blame him. Riley was always the responsible one, so serious, so loyal."

"You say that as if those were bad things."

"No, of course not. It's just that, well, there is such a thing as self-righteous as opposed to righteous. Riley doesn't seem to have it in him to forgive those of us who are weaker than he is, who stumble and fall at times."

Guy waved a hand. "I'll be the first to admit that I did some terrible things, things that hurt my family, things that broke the law. But I served my time for those crimes and I've deeply repented of the hurt I caused my family."

"I understand you've repented before."

"So Riley *has* been talking. He's right, of course.

But there's one big difference this time. While I was in prison there was a preacher who came by to visit us. At first I didn't want anything to do with him. But that man of God was nothing if not persistent. And he eventually got through to me, and after that, the Good Lord got through to me, too."

Could he be telling the truth? Cassie wanted to give him the benefit of the doubt, but Riley had warned her how convincing he could be.

His smile took on a self-mocking edge. "Of course you don't believe me—that's to be expected. Perhaps this forced layover here in your town is a good thing. It will give you and Riley a chance to see the truth of what I'm saying."

"Mr. Simpson, it's not my place to judge you or what you are saying. My only concern in this matter is making sure the best interests of the children are focused on."

"For which I'm grateful, because that is what I want, as well."

He looked and sounded so sincere, but Cassie refused to be taken in. As Riley had said, the stakes were too high. "Then I suggest you go very slowly with this so that you don't upset them. Give the children a chance to get used to the idea of having you back in their lives. And, as you yourself said, give everyone else a chance to see that you have indeed changed your ways." *And give Riley time to figure out what to do.*

Guy executed a short bow. "Those are very wise words."

She didn't believe for a minute she'd changed his mind about anything at all.

"It saddens me to think what my brother might have told my children about me these past months."

"Mr. Walker would never lie to them."

"No, of course not. My brother is too sanctimonious for that. But his own feelings about me, no matter how well deserved they might be, no doubt colored everything he said."

"Knowing your stepbrother as I do, I'm certain he did his best to be fair."

"But is he really looking out for their best interests? To know that he's been dragging them across the country, from town to town, never staying in one place very long—well, as their father, it just breaks my heart. That way of life may suit Riley—even as a kid he was restless. In fact, he left home as soon as he was able. I doubt he'll ever be happy settling down anywhere."

That seemed a deliberate jab aimed her way.

"But subjecting my children to that sort of life," he continued, "not allowing them to set down roots anywhere, make friends or even go to school, saddens and angers me. My kids deserve so much more. They deserve stability and a real home and a chance to just be children. And that is what I aim to give them."

"Mr. Simpson, your stepbrother is a good man. Regardless of any inclinations he may have about how he wants to live his life, he is now entirely focused on doing what he thinks is best for Noah and Pru, what he believes he must do to keep them safe." No matter who he has to leave behind.

"Safe from me, you mean."

The only bitterness Cassie detected seemed self-directed. If the man was acting, he was doing a very good job of it. "Safe from anything, or anyone, that could do them harm."

She stopped in front of the Blue Bottle. "Now, if you will excuse me, I have some business to conduct inside."

"Then I shall leave you to it. But I am certain we will be seeing each other again very soon."

Had Guy Simpson been deliberately trying to drive a wedge between her and Riley, with all his talk of how his stepbrother would never settle down and what a disservice he'd done to the kids by keeping them on the move?

Well, it hadn't worked.

She'd take Riley's side over Guy's no matter what the issue.

True to his word, Guy showed up at the front door around eleven o'clock, holding a bunch of flowers.

"These are for the other lady of the house—I believe you said her name was Mrs. Flanagan. I would like to meet her, and thank her as well for the kindness she's extended to my children."

"But do you think that wise? I mean, with the quarantine—"

"It was my hope, if it isn't too much of an imposition, that she would join me here on the porch for a few moments." He smiled apologetically. "I heard about her injury, which makes it even more remarkable that she would go out of her way on my children's behalf."

Cassie noticed that he never called Noah and Pru by their given names. It was always "my children" in that possessive way that set her teeth on edge. She also realized that he must have been checking up on them if he now knew about Mrs. Flanagan's condition.

Cassie hesitated a heartbeat, then nodded. This wasn't her decision to make. "I'll check to see if Mrs. Flanagan is available to come out here." She waved to a pair of wooden chairs located by the swing. "Please, have a seat while you wait."

She found her employer where she'd left her, in the dining room with Riley. "That was Mr. Simpson at the door. He'd like to meet you."

Riley immediately stood, his expression darkening. "You don't have to see him if you don't want to. I'll deal with—"

"Sit down, Mr. Walker." Mrs. Flanagan had drawn herself up to her full sitting height. "It's me he asked to see, not you." She set down her book and folded her hands in her lap. "I believe I would like to meet him, as well. Take me to him, Cassie."

"Perhaps I should be the one to push your chair—"

"No, I want to see him without interference from you, Mr. Walker. The children are in their room, but I think it would be best if you joined them just in case they get a notion to get up and go wandering around."

Without waiting for his response, she looked up at Cassie. "What are you waiting for? Let's go."

Cassie, seeing the frustrated expression on Riley's face, almost felt sorry for him. She'd been on that side of Mrs. Flanagan's high-handedness before and it had left her feeling the same.

As soon as she rolled the wheelchair out onto the porch, Mr. Simpson was on his feet, holding out the flowers and smiling down at the older woman.

"What beautiful flowers," Mrs. Flanagan exclaimed. "It's been such a long time since anyone has brought me such a lovely gift."

"Why, I find that hard to believe—a lady as charming and generous as yourself."

"Oh, pish-posh, go on with you."

"It's just a small token to thank you for all you've done for my children."

"Your children are easy to do for. I can see where Noah gets his charm and Pru gets her lovely looks from."

"You flatter me, ma'am."

Cassie could scarcely believe it. Was Mrs. Flanagan actually *flirting* with the man?

"Cassie Lynn, dear, would you take these flowers inside and put them in some water?"

Leave that man alone with her? "But—"

Mrs. Flanagan waved her hand to halt the protest. "Run along now, we don't want these lovely flowers to wilt. Mr. Simpson and I will be just fine out here, getting to know each other better."

"Please, call me Guy."

"Then you must call me Irene."

Cassie couldn't figure out what had brought on the change in Mrs. Flanagan. Surely the woman was just putting on an act. She couldn't be that taken with the man.

Uncomfortable leaving them alone for any length of time, Cassie quickly poured two glasses of lemonade and carried them out to the porch. "I thought you and your guest might enjoy a little refreshment," she said by way of explanation as she stepped outside once more.

"Thank you, dear." Mrs. Flanagan accepted the glass, then turned to Guy, continuing their conversation. "It does my heart good to know that you have turned to God and away from wickedness. The Good Book says that there is more joy in heaven over a sinner that repents than over ninety and nine just persons. You must attend service at our local church on Sunday. Reverend

Harper is a fine preacher and I know you will find joy in being part of the congregation."

Cassie thought she spied just a hint of smugness in Mr. Simpson's expression, but he covered quickly.

He took Mrs. Flanagan's hand in both of his. "Dear lady, you are most kind—your words both humble me and bring me joy. And of course I will attend the church service here—it was already my intent to do so. May I have the honor of escorting you?"

"Oh no. I'm afraid our church isn't set up in such a way as to make it easy for a person in a wheelchair to attend. Besides, someone needs to stay here with the children, since they aren't able to leave the house yet."

Then she frowned. "But you shouldn't have to walk in alone—not that a charming man such as yourself wouldn't be immediately welcomed. But it is always nice to have someone at your side." Mrs. Flanagan's expression suddenly cleared. "I know, you can accompany Cassie Lynn and your stepbrother. I'm sure they'd be happy for you to join them." She turned to Cassie expectantly.

Cassie took her cue. "Of course. We'll be passing right by the hotel on our way."

Guy smiled in acknowledgment, then turned back to the widow. "But it's a shame you're trapped here in this house."

"Your brother is kind enough to help me down these stairs occasionally so that Cassie Lynn can push me about town and give me a bit of air. Though I do hate to add to her already heavy burdens here."

"I don't mind at all," Cassie said.

Guy jumped on Mrs. Flanagan's statement as if Cassie hadn't spoken up. "Oh, but please, you must allow me to take over this most delightful task. I am sadly without employment while I'm here, and since the quarantine makes it impossible for me to go inside and help with the children, at least I can do this."

"Oh, but surely you have something better to do than to be pushing an old widow woman about town." Her tone was almost embarrassingly coy.

"There is nothing I would enjoy more. I'll hear no further arguments. This is but a small way to repay your kindness."

"Then I accept. Cassie usually takes me for my stroll around four o'clock, but I would much prefer two o'clock, if that is all right with you?" Mrs. Flanagan smiled sweetly. "That way, at the end of my outing, I could stop in at the Blue Bottle and have some tea and visit with that nice Eve Dawson. If you don't mind such frivolous indulgences, that is."

"I have always thought afternoon tea to be a very civilized practice. Two o'clock it is." He stood. "Now, I will bid you goodbye until then."

Mrs. Flanagan waited until Guy had turned from her front walk onto the sidewalk before she allowed Cassie to push her back into the house.

"I take it from your disapproving frown that my performance was convincing."

"Performance?" So it had been an act.

"Of course. I've met men like him before. Trying to win you over with gifts, pretty words and grand gestures. Smooth and pleasant as rose petals on the outside, but dark and nasty as rotted fruit on the inside."

"But why did you fawn over him?"

"Cassie Lynn, I know you don't have a deceptive bone in your body, and that's a good thing. However,

I've learned that if you allow people like Guy to think they have you under their spell, there are all kinds of things you can find out about them."

"And is that why you're allowing him to push your chair through town?"

"That, and the fact that if he's with me, he can't be causing mischief here or elsewhere. It also leaves you and Riley time to take a breather from keeping such close guard over the children."

"I just realized, you actually manipulated him into offering to take over that task, didn't you?"

The woman shrugged. "It's always best if they think the idea was theirs."

"But why two o'clock?"

"Because the three o'clock train is never late and I intend to keep him out until we hear the whistle. That way you'll have a bit of warning before we return home."

Cassie shook her head. "I never imagined you could be so outright devious."

"I'll take that as a compliment."

Riley joined them, seeming a bit agitated. "Noah's awake and complaining about the itching. And we're all out of calamine lotion."

Cassie grimaced. "I meant to get more while I was out earlier. I'll run down to the pharmacy right now. In the meantime, if you would fill the kettles with water and put them on the stove to heat, we'll let him take a nice warm soak with some baking soda."

Riley nodded, then looked from one to the other of them. "How did it go with my stepbrother?"

Cassie gave a quick recap of Mrs. Flanagan's performance and Guy's reaction to it.

When she was done, Riley had a worried frown on

his face. "I appreciate what you're trying to do," he told the widow, "but please be careful. Guy is very good at reading people."

"Well, he's never encountered me before. I think that stepbrother of yours wouldn't ever dream that an old woman like myself, especially one who's stuck in a wheelchair, wouldn't be taken in by his charm and flattery."

"Still, please promise me that you will be careful."

"You have my word."

Seeing the smugly confident look on the widow's face, however, Cassie found herself as worried as Riley.

Chapter Twenty-One

Later that afternoon, Cassie watched Guy carry Mrs. Flanagan down the steps and settle her in her chair before wheeling her down the sidewalk. There was nothing improper about his manner, but she still had an uneasy feeling about the whole business.

Stepping inside, she sought out Riley. "Now that we know your stepbrother will be occupied elsewhere, I was thinking perhaps we could let the children go outside in the backyard for a little while."

"Do you think that wise?"

"As long as we don't let them overdo it, and keep a close eye on them, then I think the fresh air and sunshine would actually be good for them."

The children were excited by the idea and eagerly followed the grown-ups out the back door.

Riley turned to Pru. "I think what you need, young lady, is a ride on a swing. What do you say? Would you like me to push you?

"I want to swing, too." Noah's expression threatened to turn to a pout.

"Maybe in another day or two," Cassie responded.

Would they still be here then? "But don't worry," she continued, "we're not going to let them have all the fun. I've got something for the two of us."

"What's that?"

She reached into her skirt pocket and pulled out the two long pieces of chalk she'd purchased at the mercantile. "I thought we could draw some pictures right here on the porch floor."

"Pictures of what?" Most of the enthusiasm had gone out of his voice.

"Remember those fairy tales Mrs. Flanagan has been reading to you and Pru?"

He nodded.

"Well, I was thinking we could draw some of our favorite things from the stories. Like a castle, or a dragon, or a knight with a sword."

"Or the frog prince?"

"Absolutely. You could even draw him as a giant frog, bigger than Dapple here."

"Yeah, with a crown on his head and everything." Noah's enthusiasm had definitely increased. "And I could draw a castle next to him?"

"Whatever you like."

The boy reached for the piece of chalk, then met her gaze. "What are you going to draw?"

"I think I'll draw a princess to go with your frog."

Noah shrugged. "I guess that'll be okay."

Cassie supposed princesses were not particularly exciting to little boys. "Would you rather I drew something else?"

Noah started work on his frog. "I didn't like that princess very much. She tried to go back on her word to the poor Frog Prince after he dived down really deep and got her golden ball back for her."

"I see. But she did finally keep her word, didn't she?"

He grimaced, obviously unimpressed. "Only because her pa made her. I just think the Frog Prince should've had a nicer princess, like Cinderella, maybe."

"So you liked Cinderella."

"Uh-huh. She worked really hard and even when her stepmother and stepsisters were mean to her she was always really nice. Kinda like you." Noah looked up and met Cassie's gaze. "Not that you have a mean stepmother and stepsister, but you always seem to be working and you're really nice to everyone."

"Why, thank you, Noah. I believe that is the nicest thing anyone has ever said to me." Oh, how she was going to miss them when they were gone. "Why don't I draw Cinderella and we can pretend that she and the Frog Prince are really good friends?"

The boy nodded enthusiastically.

As they drew their pictures, Cassie made up a story of how Cinderella and the Frog Prince met and became friends. Noah contributed bits and pieces about some of the adventures they had together.

Occasionally little-girl giggles drifted their way and Cassie would glance over to Riley and Pru at the swing. They made such a poignantly beautiful father-and-daughter picture, even if Riley wasn't truly the girl's parent.

How dear these three people had become to her. A lump formed in her throat and she had to fight to swallow it. The thought of them leaving in a few days and disappearing from her life entirely was nearly more than she could bear.

"Are you okay, Miss Vickers?"

Cassie glanced up to find Noah watching her with a concerned look. "I'm fine." She waved to her drawing, which so far consisted of a head and face. "I'm just trying to decide if I should draw Cinderella dressed in her ball gown or in her rags."

Noah seemed to give that some thought. "Not in her rags, because that was the unhappy time for her. But ball gowns aren't very good for adventures." He looked up again. "Do you reckon, after she became a princess, that she had any regular clothes?"

Cassie hid her grin. "I imagine she did."

He gave a satisfied nod. "Then that's what you should draw. And she could still wear her crown, just so everyone knows she's a princess."

"Perfect!" Cassie went back to work with a smile at the child's unique but very valid insights.

Yes, she was definitely going to miss these precious children.

And their uncle.

Riley was waiting on the porch when Guy escorted Mrs. Flanagan back to her house. "And how did you enjoy your outing?"

Guy lifted her from the chair before Riley could perform that service, so instead he carried the chair up the steps.

Mrs. Flanagan smiled up at him. "I had a grand time. You never told me you had such a charming stepbrother. Why, I declare, he was turning heads everywhere we went."

Guy laughed good-naturedly. "I don't know about that, Irene. I only had eyes for you."

Mrs. Flanagan actually tittered. "Go on with you. I only hope all my silly errands didn't overtax your patience."

"Not at all. It gave me a chance to get better acquainted with the town."

She sighed as he lowered her into the chair. "Like I said, simply charming."

Guy gave her a short bow. "I will leave you now, gracious lady, but will return tomorrow so that we can do this again."

"I shall be looking forward to it." She turned to Riley. "Will you be so good as to roll me inside?"

"Of course."

As soon as they were safely in, Mrs. Flanagan laughed. "I haven't had so much fun in quite a while. I had Guy taking me to the dress shop to check out the new fabrics, the restaurant to look through the new romance books in Abigail's library and the Blue Bottle for afternoon tea." She gave them a waggish smile. "We happened on Eunice Ortolon on the way to the Blue Bottle and I invited her to join us and catch me up on all the news about town."

Riley raised a brow. "Should I know who this Eunice Ortolon is?"

"Eunice runs the boardinghouse," Cassie said. "She is also quite fond of talking."

"I see."

Mrs. Flanagan gave a very unladylike snort. "Cassie is just being polite. Eunice is actually the town's most notorious busybody. And I do believe she was quite taken with your brother."

"Of course she was."

"An interesting thing, though. We left the Blue Bottle about the same time as the train whistle sounded. Your stepbrother then asked me if I'd mind making a stop at the depot. He professed to enjoy watching people come and go on the train and imagining where they were coming from or going to."

"He's watching the trains to make certain I don't try to slip away."

The widow nodded. "That was my guess, as well." She straightened, and tapped her cheek with her forefinger. "I think tomorrow I shall need to visit the apothecary to pick up some more of my liniment. And now that Constance Harper is back from her schooling and is working there again, I'll have all kinds of questions for her. I also may have to stop at several merchants to pay my bills." She nodded confidently. "Between that and having tea at the Blue Bottle, I should be able to keep Guy busy until the train comes in."

Riley bent down and planted a kiss on her cheek. "You, my dear, are a true treasure."

Mrs. Flanagan turned to Cassie. "In case you were wondering, this is what genuine charm looks like."

Cassie couldn't agree more.

Chapter Twenty-Two

The first part of Saturday passed pretty much the same way Friday had. Riley stayed close to the house, Cassie delivered her baked goods to her three customers and took orders for Monday, and Mrs. Flanagan had her outing with Guy.

The only difference was, when Mrs. Flanagan and Guy had their outing, Cassie insisted Riley take River for a ride.

"As good as that sounds," he answered, "I wouldn't feel right going off and leaving you alone with the kids."

"Nonsense. Pru's almost completely recovered and Noah is getting better—we'll be fine. And Mrs. Flanagan is keeping Guy occupied, so there's no worries on that front."

When Riley still hesitated, Cassie pressed harder. "It's been a few days since you've taken River out for a run and the poor animal is probably pining for it. And you said yourself that a good ride clears your head and helps you think through your problems better." She put a hand on her hip. "And goodness knows we need some good problem-fixin' thinking right now."

"You're right." He grabbed her hand and gave it a squeeze. "Thank you."

She waved off his gratitude. "Get on with you. If you're going to be back before the train whistle sounds, you'd best not tarry."

Cassie watched him go, a worried frown on her face. Riley seemed outwardly calm, but she could feel the tension thrumming from him. This had to be difficult for a man who was used to taking action. She wanted to help, but didn't know how. She didn't think Riley had figured out a solution yet, either.

What were they going to do?

She thought about trying to hide them all at her father's farm—it was certainly remote enough. But Guy would find out about it sooner or later and then they'd be right back where they started, and maybe worse. Then again, it could buy them a little time, and if Riley's detective was really close to proving the case against Guy, it might be enough.

She would mention her idea to Riley as soon as he returned. Of course, if they decided to actually follow through with it, she'd have to convince her father to let them stay. And that could be a difficult task.

Riley found a long stretch of open road and gave River his head. The horse immediately surged into a gallop. For a few moments Riley just savored the movement, the sensation of almost flying, of the powerful animal beneath him and the open sky above.

But his mind wouldn't empty of his worries for long.

Sheriff Gleason had come to him after having that same welcome-to-town meeting with Guy that he'd had with him.

"I understand Guy Simpson is your brother," he'd said.

"Stepbrother."

"Anything you care to tell me about him?"

The sheriff's expression had been impassive, but Riley got the distinct impression the lawman was troubled by something he'd seen in or heard from Guy. His respect for the man went up several notches.

He'd given Sheriff Gleason the information about Guy's crimes and time in prison, but he'd left off anything to do with Nancy or the kids. He didn't see any point in airing that particular dirty laundry.

The sheriff had accepted the information with a nod and moved on. He was prepared now, if Guy should attempt to break the law. Not that that was particularly comforting, because Riley knew Guy well enough to know he wouldn't make any attempts to break the law until he had everything he'd come here for, namely Noah and Pru.

Riley felt the walls closing in on him. Noah would be better soon and then there'd be no excuse to keep Guy from seeing the boy and his sister. Pru was already terrified her father would snatch her away again, as he had when she was younger. Riley didn't like to think what his stepbrother had put her through back then.

He had to protect those two innocent children from Guy, no matter what.

But how?

Cassie and Riley didn't have a chance to speak when he returned. Noah was having a hard time with his illness and that kept everyone hopping most of the afternoon.

After Noah and Pru had been settled in bed for the

night, Mrs. Flanagan called Riley and Cassie into the parlor. "We should discuss who goes to church tomorrow," she announced without preamble.

Riley spoke up first. "I should stay here." He held up a hand to forestall any protest his hostess might make. "Not because I think you can't handle the children, but because there's no telling what Guy might do if he knows I won't be around the entire duration of the church service. It gives him too large a window of opportunity to act. And forgive me, but you are not equipped to stop him if he sets his mind to take the kids."

Mrs. Flanagan made an inelegant noise. "If worse came to worse, I have my husband's shotgun. But that won't be necessary. I've already considered all that, which is why I made sure you and Cassie Lynn would be escorting him to church. If you get to the hotel and he's not there, or makes an excuse not to accompany you, then you can come right back here and guard us to your heart's content."

Riley raised a brow. "You arranged for us to escort him?"

Cassie nodded. "Yes, as a matter of fact, she did. I was there. And it was masterfully done, I might add."

"And I reminded him of it on our outing today, so he will have no excuse to forget." The woman sounded understandably smug.

Then she waved a hand. "I know Pru is no longer contagious, but she does have a few lingering spots. I think it best we keep her here, since contact with her father in such a public venue could upset her and cause a scene. Besides, she can help me tend to Noah if I should need a hand."

"It seems you've given this quite a bit of consideration," Riley said, eyeing her thoughtfully.

She nodded. "The children and I will have our own prayer and Bible study service here while you two are gone."

"Is Guy planning to take you on your afternoon outing tomorrow?" Cassie asked.

Mrs. Flanagan nodded. "Oh yes. I specifically told him I wished to visit the graves of my dear Ernest and Willy. That I hadn't been able to do so since I'd been confined to this chair." She grinned impishly. "He should have fun pushing it over that rough ground."

Cassie spoke up in dismay. "Do you really want him to take you on such a personal visitation?"

"Land sakes, girl, Ernest wouldn't mind. In fact, he'd probably enjoy the joke as much as I do. As for my boy Willy, ah well, a grave is just a grave. Both those menfolk of mine are up in heaven with the Lord."

Riley shook his head. "As I said, a true treasure."

Mrs. Flanagan's eyes twinkled. "And don't you forget it."

Later, after the widow retired for the night, Riley and Cassie headed for the kitchen.

"I'll just be making pies tonight," she told him. "The Blue Bottle will be closed tomorrow, since it's Sunday."

He professed himself ready to lend a hand regardless.

He'd gotten quite good with handling the dough these past few nights. He would have made a good partner if her business expanded.

As they worked, Cassie gathered her courage and cleared her throat. "I hope you won't think me too forward, but I've been trying to think of some way to get you and the kids out of your stepbrother's reach, and I have an idea."

Riley smiled, obviously intrigued. "I don't think that's too forward at all. In fact I'd love to hear what you came up with."

Cassie explained her idea. "What do you think?" she asked when she had finished. "I mean, I know it's not ideal, and we would have to convince my father, who can be quite stubborn, I'm afraid. But I thought it worth a try."

Riley nodded and she could see him mulling over what she'd just said. "The idea does have merit. It would be a quick, easy move from here, and we'd be helped by someone familiar with the place. The problem is that it *is* close. If Guy should discover our location, and then bring the sheriff in on it, he'd have the law on his side. I'd be forced to turn the children over to him."

"I just thought—"

Riley touched Cassie's hand, his smile tender. "It's a good plan. I'll keep it in mind as a backup, in case I can't come up with something else."

So he hadn't decided on a course of action yet.

And time was running out.

Chapter Twenty-Three

Sunday morning, Cassie and Riley left a little early for church so that Cassie could drop off her baked goods at the boardinghouse and the restaurant. Then they headed for the Rose Palace Hotel, where Guy was already waiting for them in the lobby.

As they headed for the churchyard, Guy turned to Cassie. "Once the children are better and your duties are not so onerous, I would like to take you out for a meal at your fine restaurant. As a thank-you for all you've done for my children."

"That is most kind," she said noncommittally. "Does this mean you plan to stick around for a while once the children are well?"

"I do. As we discussed, it'll take a bit of time for this skeptical brother of mine to see that I'm truly a changed man. And I'm also coming to appreciate Turnabout and all it has to offer." He smiled at her meaningfully. "It might be the perfect place to raise my children."

"We do take pride in being an open, welcoming town." Could they take him at his word? If he planned to stay here, at least for the time being, that would give

Riley some breathing room, might get them through until the detective was able to close his case.

They made small talk for the rest of the walk, though Cassie found the effort to continue to be pleasant trying.

She sat in the pew between Riley and Guy. When it came time to sing the opening hymn, she was surprised by the richness of Guy's voice. It was deep, full and absolutely on key. She noticed that he had quite a number of heads turning his way with smiles of appreciation.

How could a man be gifted with so many blessings and still turn to wrongdoing?

Once the church service was over Cassie and Riley were put in the position of introducing Guy to Reverend Harper and others of the community.

Guy, with his gallant smile and boyish looks, seemed to be making a good impression. Which made Cassie feel like a bit of a fraud.

As they walked away from the churchyard, Guy invited them to have lunch with him at the hotel, but they refused, referring to the need to check in on the children. It was a relief when they left him at the hotel and continued on to Mrs. Flanagan's place.

When they stepped inside the house, it was to discover that Pru, with Mrs. Flanagan's help, had prepared their lunch. It was a simple meal consisting of sliced ham, boiled potatoes, some pickled squash and green beans that had been put up from last year's garden, and the second batch of biscuits Cassie had baked before heading out this morning.

Cassie clasped her hands together. "What a pleasant surprise! I can't believe you did all this."

"Pru has the makings of a fine cook," Mrs. Flanagan

said proudly. "All she needs is a good teacher and a little bit of experience."

Both of which Cassie would love to provide for her.

When Guy arrived at Mrs. Flanagan's that afternoon, he was carrying a large brown paper bag with something inside.

"What have you got there?" Mrs. Flanagan asked archly.

"It's a surprise, but it will have to wait until after our outing."

"Oh, I do like surprises."

"As do I."

Riley didn't care much for the smug look on Guy's face as he made that last statement. The man was up to something.

Guy set the bag on the porch near the swing, then glanced at Riley. "Can I have your word that you won't look inside? That would spoil the surprise."

Yep, he was definitely up to something. But Guy had him—he knew if Riley gave his word he wouldn't break it. He nodded assent.

After Guy had taken Mrs. Flanagan away, Riley turned to Cassie. "I need to go down to the livery for a little while. I want to check on River." He'd finally come up with plan.

Riley was once more waiting on the porch when Guy returned with Mrs. Flanagan. Once they had the widow settled in her chair at the top of the steps, Guy straightened and gave him a direct look. "I would like to see my daughter now."

Riley was taken aback by the unexpected request. Though in hindsight he should have seen it coming.

Mrs. Flanagan spoke up before he could marshal his thoughts. "I know the doctors say patients aren't contagious anymore after new blisters stop forming, but she still has a few spots left and we thought it best to be safe."

"I'll take my chances. I haven't seen my children in over four years now, and I think it's high time I remedy that."

"She's napping right now," Riley protested.

"Then I'll wait." Guy moved to the porch swing and sat.

After a long moment during which the stepbrothers stared at each other without blinking, Mrs. Flanagan spoke up again. "Bless your heart, of course you want to see your baby girl—what father wouldn't? It does my heart good to know that you care about her so much that you'd risk exposure to the chicken pox at your age. If Riley will be so kind as to roll me inside, I'll go check on the little lamb myself."

Riley gritted his teeth. Mrs. Flanagan was taking this act of hers a bit too far. But he obediently pushed her chair inside the house and straight to the kitchen, where he knew Guy couldn't overhear their conversation.

"I am not letting Guy anywhere near Pru."

"You don't have any choice."

"What's this all about?" Cassie asked, looking from one to the other.

"Guy is sitting out on the porch, demanding to see Pru now that she's no longer contagious."

"Oh no."

"Listen, you two, I know this is not ideal, but she's going to have to face her father sooner or later—"

"Not if I can help it."

"You can't. Do you want to test the legalities of your guardianship right here and now? Because all Guy has to do is go talk to Sheriff Gleason, and then you'd have to face that showdown you've been dreading."

Riley raked his hand through his hair. "But Pru doesn't want to see him."

"I'm well aware of that. But she'll have us close by."

"Absolutely. I'm going to be right by her side, and if Guy so much as—"

"You will do no such thing. You'll be in the children's room, making sure Noah is not upset by what's going on around him. Cassie Lynn, pull out your sewing box. You're going to sit on the other end of the porch, doing your mending, while Pru and her daddy get reacquainted."

Riley didn't move. "I don't like this."

"Neither do I. But the sooner we get to it, the sooner it will be over. Now, who should tell Pru?" The widow held up a hand. "I don't mean who wants to do it. I mean who can best explain this without frightening the girl or unduly upsetting her."

Riley looked to Cassie and saw her staring back at him. Finally he turned to Mrs. Flanagan. "I think perhaps Cassie and I should do it together."

The woman nodded. "Now you're thinking and not just reacting."

Five minutes later, when Cassie led a pale and frightened-looking Pru from her room, Mrs. Flanagan stopped them. "I just wanted you to know that I told Pru's daddy that she shouldn't stay out very long because she's still weak from her illness. I also told him you would be on the bench nearby in case Pru shows signs of needing to retreat."

The widow patted Pru's arm. "Don't be frightened. We're all right here and we won't let anything happen to you."

Pru nodded, then looked up at Cassie.

Cassie had one hand on Pru's shoulder and her sewing basket handle in the other. "It'll be all right." She tried to infuse as much assurance in her tone as she could. "I'll be sitting a few feet away the whole time. I promise I won't leave you alone."

As soon as they stepped out on the porch, Guy stood. "Prudence, what a beautiful young lady you've become. You look so much like your mother."

"Thank you." The little girl's words were barely above a whisper and she moved closer to Cassie's side, practically gluing herself to her leg.

Guy retook his seat on the swing and patted the spot next to him. "Come here and sit beside me. I have something I want to show you."

Pru glanced up at Cassie as if asking what she should do. The girl's terrified eyes tore into Cassie's heart and fueled her anger against the man. What had the child's father done to her all those years ago that she should still fear him so much?

She gave Pru's shoulder a little squeeze. "Go on, sweetie, sit with your pa. And just remember, I'm right here."

Pru nodded resignedly, then turned and slowly plodded across the porch. The poor girl had the air of a prisoner going to meet her executioner. It would be a blessing if this little family reunion didn't last too long.

Cassie moved to the bench on the other end of the porch, though she turned it to face the swing before sitting down. As she opened her sewing basket, she saw Guy reach for the brown paper bag that had been placed nearby. Did he refrain from hugging his daughter out of deference for her feelings or because he himself had no real interest?

He drew a large box out of the bag, one tied with a wide pink satin ribbon that formed a bow on top.

"This is for you," he said, laying it in Pru's lap. "A present to make up for all those birthdays and Christmases I missed."

For a moment Pru just sat staring at the package, as if uncertain what to do with it.

"Aren't you going to open it?" her father finally asked.

With a nod, she began delicately tackling the ribbon. After several minutes, when she'd made very little progress, Guy reached down. "Here, let me help you with that."

He quickly removed the ribbon, then sat back, allowing her to open the lid on her own.

Curious, Cassie ignored her mending to see just what it was he'd brought Pru.

Setting the lid aside, the little girl reached in and drew out a doll. From what Cassie could see, it was breathtaking. The doll had a porcelain face and hands. The head was covered in springy golden curls and the dress was a frothy cascade of ivory lace and pink fabric.

For a long time Pru just stared at the doll, not saying anything, and then she gently laid it back in its box. "Thank you," she said politely. Then she reached for the lid.

This restrained politeness was obviously not the reaction Guy had been hoping for. "Don't you like the doll? The shopkeeper assured me this was the best one on the market."

"She's very pretty." Pru's toned remained unenthusiastically polite.

"It's okay to play with it, you know. That's why I bought it for you."

"I already have a doll to play with—Bitsy. Momma made her for me."

This drew a frown from him. "A rag doll? You'd prefer a rag doll to this beautiful little lady?"

Pru's chin went up stubbornly. "Bitsy's my friend, even if she doesn't have fancy hair or fancy clothes. And *Momma* made her for me." She repeated that last as if he hadn't heard it the first time and it should explain everything.

And to Cassie, it did.

But apparently not to Guy. It was obvious he didn't like the way his grand gesture had been received. But then he cut a quick glance her way, as if just remembering her presence, and his whole demeanor changed.

He smiled down at his daughter, and when he spoke, his tone had softened once more. "I can see as how you are very loyal to your old friend Bitsy, and loyalty is a very fine quality." He tapped the box, which still sat in her lap. "But this little lady needs a home and someone to love her, as well. Do you think you and Bitsy can find it in your hearts to take care of her?"

It was exactly the right thing to say to get Pru to accept the doll. She glanced down at the box, her expression changing from rejection to uncertainty to tentative acceptance. Then she nodded. "We can do that."

"That's my girl."

A look of panic crossed Pru's face and she cast a quick glance toward Cassie.

The look wasn't lost on Guy. But instead of showing irritation, he smiled fondly at the little girl. "I imagine you want to show your new friend to Bitsy and your brother, so I won't keep you sitting here much longer. But I do have one more thing." He drew another, much smaller box from the bag. "This one is for your brother. Since I can't visit him just yet, would you give it to him for me?"

Pru nodded and accepted the second box.

"Before you go," he added, touching a finger to his cheek, "it would please me to no end if you would give me a goodbye kiss right here." And he leaned closer to her.

Pru hesitated a heartbeat, then gave him a quick peck and scrambled off the swing and moved toward the door, as if afraid he would try to pull her back.

Cassie hastily put her mending away and stood.

Guy stood, as well, and gave her a chagrined smile. "It appears my first attempt to make friends met with mixed success."

"She'll need some time to adjust to the idea."

He nodded. "I know. I guess it was unrealistic of me to expect her to love me right away, the way I do her."

He was the picture of a forlorn but hopeful parent. "But as you say, time will mend those broken fences. And I aim to give her and Noah all the time they need." He twisted his hat in his hands. "I just hope Riley doesn't try to keep poisoning them against me."

"He wouldn't do that."

Gut's look said he believed differently. But he set his bowler hat back on his head and then moved to open the door for her. "I will bid you good day and hope to see you when I return again tomorrow."

Cassie nodded and then walked past him to enter the house. He stood in such a way that it forced her into closer proximity than she liked. It gave her an unpleasant, queasy kind of feeling that lasted for a moment even after she closed the door. How could it be that so many women apparently found him charming?

Then Riley appeared in front of her. "I take it he's gone?"

Cassie nodded and pulled herself together. "Your stepbrother behaved with decorum." Mostly. "How is Pru?"

"A little quieter than usual, but otherwise okay. She and Noah are playing with their gifts—Guy's way of trying to win their affection."

"What did he give Noah?"

"A whole bag of marbles, including a few aggies and a shooter." Riley grimaced. "Noah's thrilled with his present."

"Any boy would be." She remembered how much her brothers prized their marbles, all the more because they didn't have many.

"And Pru is busy introducing her new doll to Bitsy. Seeing how delighted they are made me realize I haven't been much for gift giving since they've been in my care. I'm not even sure when their birthdays are." Riley gave Cassie a troubled look. "Little kids should get to celebrate their birthdays—especially kids who don't have much else to celebrate."

She placed her hand on his arm. "You've given them so much more than mere things. You've given them your love, and have put them first over your own needs, and have done everything in your power to keep them safe. Believe me, those things are much more important than a doll and a bag of marbles."

He placed his hand over hers and gave it a squeeze. "Thanks."

With a nod, she turned and headed down the hall to check on the children, wanting to reassure herself that Pru was okay.

She smiled when she saw them playing with their gifts, just as Riley had said. Cassie sat on the edge of Pru's bed. "Have you given your new doll a name yet?"

Pru nodded. "Cindy."

"That's a pretty name."

"I named her after Cinderella, because she was mostly alone and looking for someone to love her. And now she's a princess."

"I see. That is quite fitting." Apparently both children had been taken with the Cinderella story. Mrs. Flanagan must have done an extraordinary job reading it to them.

Pru looked at her other doll. "I'm worried about Bitsy. She doesn't have beautiful clothes like Cindy and she's not a princess. Do you think that will make her sad?"

"Not if you continue to love her. That's the greatest thing for any doll, to be loved by the little girl who owns her."

Pru hugged the rag doll tightly against her chest. "I do love her a whole bunch."

Cassie had an idea. "Wait here just a minute. I'll be right back."

She went to her room, opened the top drawer of the dresser and lifted out a small, somewhat battered cardboard box nestled there. Opening it, she stared at the contents. Inside was a bracelet, a delicate gold chain barely long enough to fit around her wrist, with a single red stone. Her mother had given it to her on her thirteenth birthday and it was the only piece of jewelry she owned.

Cassie stared at it a moment, then closed her fist around it and headed out of the room.

She sat down next to Pru. "I believe that even though Cindy is a princess, Bitsy is secretly a queen. She just doesn't make a lot of fuss about it because she's a very practical queen who likes to wear sensible clothes that she can play in and not have to worry about getting dirty."

Pru cocked her head, studying her doll thoughtfully. "She is?"

"Yes indeed. One can always tell a queen by her good character and her generous spirit." Cassie opened her hand to show the bracelet. "But occasionally she still wants to feel like a queen, so when she does, she puts on her crown, like so." Cassie placed the bracelet on Bitsy's head, carefully displaying the stone in the center of the doll's forehead. Just as she'd hoped, it fit nicely.

Pru's eyes widened. "She *does* look like a queen now." Then the girl turned to Cassie. "And being a queen is better than being a princess, isn't it?"

"Well, a queen is usually older and wiser than a princess."

Pru nodded, obviously satisfied with that answer.

"Of course, we both know Bitsy won't want to wear her crown all the time. She's much too practical for that. So you must keep it safe for her when she's not wearing it." Cassie lifted the bracelet and undid the clasp. "And perhaps Bitsy will allow you to wear it on your arm sometimes, as a bracelet." She placed it on the girl's wrist and fastened it there. "And when you wear it you must promise to think of me and how very much I love you." She pulled Noah over and embraced them both in a tight hug. "How much I love both of you."

How would she bear watching these precious children walk out of her life when the time came for them to go?

Chapter Twenty-Four

Riley stood quietly in the doorway to the children's room. He'd arrived in time to observe that entire exchange with the bracelet. He didn't know anything about the gold chain, but would be willing to put River on the line to bet it had a very special meaning to Cassie.

And she'd just handed it over to his niece and her doll as if it wasn't difficult at all to part with.

He'd never met another woman—another person— who was as selfless and courageous as Cassie Lynn Vickers, someone who could touch his heart with a word or gesture, someone he could love for the rest of his days.

Riley abruptly turned and walked away. He headed for the backyard, feeling the need to get out in the fresh air, to do something physical. He retrieved an ax from the tool shed and proceeded to make kindling from one of the chunks of firewood stacked near the house.

Love her—how could he? He cared for her, of course. Who wouldn't—she was sweet, generous, practical, and she'd been exceptionally kind to him and his charges.

But true love, the man-and-wife kind, that wasn't for him. Besides, he'd known her for only a little over a week and most of that time had been under extraordinary circumstances.

He wasn't the settling down kind of man, and that's what she needed, what she deserved. Riley reached for another piece of wood and began attacking it with the same fervor.

And even if he *was* in love, he'd made his plans with Mr. Humphries earlier. The wheels were in motion and soon he and the kids would be leaving here. And there was a chance they wouldn't be back. Then again, even if they did come back, Cassie would likely be married to one of the names on that confounded list of hers. In fact, she could be engaged to one of them already.

He swung the ax with a force that jarred his arm all the way to the shoulder when it hit.

"What are you doing?"

He looked up to see Cassie standing on the porch, staring at him with a frown on her face.

He wiped his brow with his sleeve. "Just chopping a bit of wood. Sorry if the noise bothered you."

"It's not the noise. Members of this household don't do that sort of unnecessary labor on the Sabbath."

Riley winced. "I'm sorry. I guess I forgot it was Sunday. I just felt the need for some fresh air and physical activity."

Her expression turned sympathetic. "I know having your stepbrother around is trying, but don't let it get to you this way."

Riley was guiltily relieved that she had misread the situation. "Hard not to."

"I know. But you'll figure out something, I have confidence in you."

Riley slammed the ax into the chopping block, then

joined her on the porch. "Have a seat," he said, waving to the steps. "I want to talk to you."

Her expression grew apprehensive, but she nodded and did as he asked. Once she'd seated herself and arranged her skirts, Riley joined her, careful to leave what space he could between them on the narrow stairs.

"What did you want to talk to me about?"

"That something you were confident I'd figure out, I think I have." At least he sincerely hoped so.

"You're planning to leave, aren't you?"

He hated to see the sadness in her expression, the brave resignation. But she deserved to hear this, to know what was coming. "I am. Noah is not completely well, I know, but he's no longer contagious and he's getting better every day. Before long Guy will demand to see him, too, and then there will be nothing to stop him from laying claim to them."

"He said he would take it slow, would give them time to get used to him. If your detective is close to—"

"I've learned to never trust Guy's promises. And even so, there is no guarantee Claypool will get the answers this week or next week or the week after. And I can't afford to take the chance that things will just magically all work out. The stakes are much too high."

"I understand." Cassie's tone said she wished she didn't. "But how are you going to get out of town? We already know he's keeping an eye on the depot when trains pull in and out. It'll be hard to slip by him."

"We're not leaving by train. I took Mr. Humphries into my confidence and he's agreed to help."

"So you're leaving by wagon."

"Yes. Mr. Humphries is going to meet me at the edge

of town with a horse and buggy just before dawn on Tuesday morning."

"So soon!" She grimaced. "Sorry, of course you must get away as quickly as you can."

"I'd actually hoped to leave tomorrow, but he'd already promised the buggy to someone else and he didn't have another wagon to spare." Riley just hoped the delay didn't cost him. There was an itch in him, an instinct, that said they should leave as soon as possible.

"What do you need me to do?"

She uttered no more protests, just looked for ways to help. Always practical, even if it hurt her to the quick.

"I need you to go about your day as usual, as if nothing has changed," he answered. "The longer we can keep Guy thinking me and the kids are still here, the better." He raked his fingers through his hair. "I'm not asking you to lie to anyone, mind you, just don't make it obvious we're gone."

"Of course. The three of you haven't been out in public much, so your absence shouldn't be noted by anyone. But won't you need help getting the children to where the carriage will be parked?"

He shook his head. "We don't have far to go—he's meeting me on the western edge of town. I can carry Noah if need be and Pru's got most of her strength back, so she can walk." He rubbed the back of his neck. "But that means we won't be able to take many of our things with us."

Cassie waved a hand dismissively. "We'll keep your luggage for you, of course. When you think it safe, you can let us know where you are and we'll send it to you."

"There's more than luggage." Riley clenched his jaw. "I won't be able to take River with me, either."

She placed a hand on his arm. "Oh, Riley, no."

Her dismay, and the touch of her hand, were oddly soothing. "It can't be helped. The town Mr. Humphries is directing us to, Burnt Pine, is off the railroad line, which is what I wanted. It'll make it that much harder for Guy to track us."

"But doesn't that mean you'll be more or less trapped there without a quick exit?"

"No, because we won't be staying. About two miles outside of Burnt Pine is a stagecoach relay station. Mr. Humphries knows the man who runs it. It's where I'll leave the buggy for someone to pick up and return to him, and it's where the kids and I will begin the next leg of our journey. We'll head out on the first stage that passes through and then look for a crossroads and take a roundabout path to just about anywhere. That should make it harder for Guy to locate us. Until we're ready to be found."

"Which is why you can't take River."

She was quick. "There's no way to take him with me if we're traveling by stage. I have no guarantee I'd be allowed to tie him behind the vehicle, and even if I could, such travel would be very difficult for him."

"I give you my word I'll take real good care of him. I'll treat him as if he were my very own. And he'll be waiting right here for you when you return."

But would *she* be waiting, as well?

Cassie felt a stab of pride. Riley was putting his beloved horse into her keeping—not just for a day or a week, but for however long it took him to work this all out and return. He must really trust her.

But his next words took some of the starch out of her sheets.

"I already spoke to Mr. Humphries about this and gave him some money I'd put aside. It's enough to pay for River's stabling and feed for about two months. "

So she'd misunderstood—he wasn't putting River into her keeping. "Oh, I see. You don't need—"

"I told him that in my absence he is to consider you River's owner. If any issues at all come up concerning River, he is to come to you about them." Riley took her hand. "Mr. Humphries will have the responsibility of the day to day boarding and feeding of my horse, but I am entrusting you with his ultimate care. But only if you are willing to accept such a burden."

She nodded. "Gladly." This meant he would have to come back. He would never abandon River altogether.

"Any word from your Pinkerton detective yet?"

"No."

Cassie heard the world of frustration Riley managed to infuse into that one word. It was easy to recognize, because it mirrored exactly what she herself was feeling.

She decided to change the subject. "When will you tell the children?"

"Not until the last minute. I don't want them fretting about this any sooner than need be."

She nodded, hoping she didn't give it all away with her longing looks.

"As for Mrs. Flanagan," he continued, "I thought we'd wait until after her outing with Guy tomorrow afternoon. There's no need to burden her with keeping this secret if we don't need to."

Cassie nodded, pleased by the way he'd said *we*, as if they were in this together.

Which they absolutely were.

Until they left her behind.

Chapter Twenty-Five

Monday morning Cassie woke with a sick feeling in her heart. It was her last day with Riley and the children—at least the last day for some time to come.

Mrs. Flanagan received a note from Guy midmorning apologizing for the fact that he would have to cancel their afternoon outing—he was feeling under the weather.

The widow cackled as she read it. "Under the weather—hah! More likely I plum wore him out with our trek through the graveyard yesterday. I'll have to think of something extra special for tomorrow, if he dares show up."

With that distraction out of the way, Riley and Cassie sat down with Mrs. Flanagan and told her of the getaway plans.

She nodded when he mentioned Mr. Humphries would be helping them. "Fred Humphries is a good man."

She turned to Cassie. "You need to bake a pie to deliver to Fred Humphries this afternoon. You'll carry it to him in that extra large hamper we have. Along with it I want you to pull together whatever food you can find that Riley and the kids can eat on the road. Bread, fruit, cheese, pickles—you know what to look for. Riley, you can also gather up any of the smaller items you want to take with you that will fit in the hamper, too."

Before Cassie could ask, the widow explained. "Fred can put all of this in the buggy tonight, so it'll be there for you tomorrow. That'll be less you have to carry when you leave here on foot."

Cassie stood and gave the woman a hug. "You are amazing. I don't know why I didn't think of all that myself."

Later that afternoon, Cassie had the kitchen all to herself.

Mrs. Flanagan was in the parlor reading her Bible. She'd mumbled something about needing some extra fortifying this afternoon.

Pru was on the back porch with Dapple and her dolls, drawing chalk pictures of castles and rainbows. She was also wearing the bracelet. She said it made her feel like a princess, too.

Riley was with Noah in the kids' room. Last time she'd checked on them, Noah was asking him questions about how kites were able to fly.

Oh, but she was going to miss this so much. The people and the feeling of family and having these children who looked up to her. But Cassie couldn't let herself think about that. Not today, when they were all still here. Tomorrow would be soon enough for the mourning.

She'd decided to go all out for supper tonight, to make it really memorable. She would prepare sweet corn pudding, which seemed to be Pru's favorite, and thick slices of ham, which Noah had told her he liked best. And to add to that, she had smothered turnip greens with bacon and cornbread. For dessert she'd decided to bake an apple, cinnamon and raisin cobbler.

The pie Mrs. Flanagan had instructed her to bake for Mr. Humphries was on the counter, waiting for her to deliver it. Beside it was an extra one she'd made, and on impulse she decided to slice it and offer everyone an afternoon treat.

She served the first piece to Pru, carrying it out to the porch to let her eat it picnic style. After taking a moment to praise the child's drawings, she stepped back and sliced two more pieces. Loading them on a tray to deliver to Riley and Noah, she smiled as she heard Pru explain to Dapple and the two dolls just why she had drawn four towers on her castle.

As Cassie headed down the hall, she reflected on how Pru was really starting to come out of her shell, becoming more an active ten-year-old girl than a subdued shadow.

When she got to the kids' room, she eased the door open with her hip. "Hello, you two. Anyone interested in a slice of cherry pie?"

Noah's head shot up and he gave her a wide, gap-toothed grin. "I sure am."

Riley's smile was warmer, more intimate. "Me, too." He stood to take the tray from her.

"What are you two up to in here?"

"Uncle Riley is teaching me how to tie different kinds of knots. Want to see?"

"Well, of course I do." She sat on Pru's bed across from them. "Show me."

For the next ten minutes or so, Noah tried, and mostly succeeded, in showing her his newly acquired skill, carefully explaining the various uses for each type of knot.

Finally, Cassie stood. "That's quite impressive, but I need to get back to the kitchen and check on supper." She turned to Riley. "I thought I'd deliver that pie to Mr. Humphries in about an hour, if you'd like to accompany me."

He nodded and she made her exit to the sound of Noah begging his uncle to please show him just one more.

She hadn't quite made it to the kitchen when she heard a knock at the front door.

Who could that be? The only visitors they ever received were Reverend Harper and Doc Pratt, and both of those gentlemen normally made their visits in the mornings.

Had Guy decided to take Mrs. Flanagan on an outing, after all? She glanced at the hall clock. It was nearly three o'clock—a bit late for that.

She bustled forward and to her surprise saw Betty Pratt from next door.

Cassie opened the door wider and smiled as she waved her in. "Mrs. Pratt, what a pleasant surprise. If you'll come on in you'll find Mrs. Flanagan in the parlor."

But the woman didn't move and Cassie realized she looked a bit agitated and uncomfortable. "I'm sorry, is something the matter?"

"I'm not sure. At least I hope not. Oh dear, I hope you won't think I'm poking my nose in where it doesn't belong."

"I would never think that. Now tell me, what's the matter?" What was bothering the woman? Cassie had never seen her so agitated before.

"It's just that I was coming home from the mercantile

a little while ago and I saw him with her, and the little girl looked so uncomfortable." Mrs. Pratt was wringing her hands now. "I mean, I know Mr. Simpson is her father and he seems like a nice man, and all children can be a bit fractious with their parents at times, but something just seemed a bit odd about the way they were acting that I just thought I'd stop by and make sure everything was all right."

Cassie had felt the blood drain from her face about halfway through the woman's convoluted explanation. "Are you telling me Guy Simpson has Pru?"

The woman had barely gotten the word *yes* out of her mouth before Cassie was flying through the house, yelling for Riley. She found herself on the back porch without remembering how she got there, and leaned heavily against the doorjamb as she took in the scene—a half-eaten piece of pie being examined by the cat, two abandoned dolls and a smudged drawing of a once pristine castle.

A great shuddering sob tore from her throat and then she felt strong arms go around her, pulling her to him.

"What is it?" he asked gently. "What's happened to upset you?"

"It's Pru," Cassie choked out. "Guy has her."

At that moment, as she watched the horror spread across Riley's features, they heard the sound of a whistle, signaling the train's departure from the Turnabout depot.

Chapter Twenty-Six

"You've got to do something, Sheriff! We can't leave
that child in that horrible man's clutches!" Cassie was
wringing her hands, mostly to keep them from trembling.

As soon as Riley verified that Guy and Pru had indeed been on the train when it departed, he'd raced to
the livery to saddle up River. Mr. Humphries had told
him about a shortcut to the next stop on the train line, but
even so it was going to be close. If Riley didn't catch up
with that train before it departed its next stop, he might
never find Pru.

Once he'd galloped off, right after answering Cassie's
"what will you do if you catch up to them" question with
a grim-faced "whatever it takes," she had headed directly
to the sheriff's office. It hadn't escaped her notice that
Riley had had a gun with him when he rode off.

"Miss Vickers, I want to help—you can't imagine just
how *much* I want to help—but there's nothing I can do.
The man served his time and he is her father, so he is
well within his rights to take her wherever he cares to."

Cassie fisted her hands in frustration. She was equally

as concerned over what would happen if Riley did find them as she was over what would happen if he didn't.

"Unless…" the sheriff murmured.

She glance up hopefully. "Unless what?"

"Unless he was guilty of some kind of crime that we could arrest him for, or at least hold him on." The lawman gave her a speculative look. "For instance, has anything gone missing at your place, anything at all that one could reasonably suspect him of having taken?"

Cassie was sorely tempted to lie. Then she had a sudden thought. "My bracelet!"

Sheriff Gleason straightened. "Tell me."

"There is this gold chain bracelet my mother gave me when I was younger. Pru was playing with it this afternoon and I assume she still had it when Guy took her. Will that work?" Cassie had left out the part about her having given the bracelet to Pru, but maybe she could be forgiven for that.

"Absolutely. The charges may not stick, but it is definitely enough to get him hauled off that train and held in custody until you can get there and clear the matter up." He moved to the door. "I'll send a telegram to Sheriff Calhoun over in Needle Creek to be on the lookout for him."

"And Pru?"

"Sheriff Calhoun is a good man. He'll make sure she's looked after until Riley gets there."

A great wave of relief washed over Cassie as her knees threatened to buckle. She felt for the chair behind her and plopped down.

The sheriff moved toward her. "Are you all right? Do you need me to get you some water? Or the doctor?"

She waved him away. "I'm fine, just a little overexcited. Go, take care of that telegram. I'll be right here when you get back."

Cassie twisted the fabric of her skirt in her hands, feeling the guilt trying to beat down her defenses. Why had she left Pru outside unattended? She should have know better, should have been more alert.

But why hadn't the girl struggled, made more noise? What had Guy threatened her with?

Cassie was worried about what Pru was going through, worried about what Riley was thinking and feeling, and what he was prepared to do to get Pru back. And Cassie was scared, more scared than she'd ever been in her life, of how this all might turn out.

She bowed her head and prayed, pouring out her fear and desires, her heart and soul into those prayers, focusing on every Bible verse she could remember that promised solace, mercy and love.

She wasn't certain how much time passed, but the door suddenly opened, bringing her back to the present. A curious little man, one Cassie had never seen before, walked in. He was short, not much taller than her in fact, and rather rotund, with a bespectacled face and mutton chop whiskers, and carried a derby hat and a sheaf of papers in his hands.

He glanced around, obviously looking for the sheriff, and then his gaze rested on her. He gave a short bow. "Forgive me, miss, but might I inquire as to whether the sheriff is about?"

Cassie was immediately taken with his formal, slightly accented speech and his gentlemanly manner. "He's stepped away to send a telegram, but he should be back shortly." She waved to the chair a short distance from hers. "You can wait if you like."

"Thank you." He moved to the chair, but before he sat, executed another short bow. "Allow me to introduce myself. I am Alexander Claypool."

Cassie immediately straightened. This was Riley's Pinkerton detective? He wasn't at all as she'd pictured him. "Mr. Claypool, I am so very glad to meet you. I'm Cassie Lynn Vickers, a friend of Riley Walker's, and I sincerely hope you have good news for him."

His face split in a smile of genuine pleasure. "Ah, Miss Vickers, of course. Mr. Walker has spoken of you in the most glowing of terms." Then he sobered. "But I'm sorry, I can only divulge the information I've brought to Mr. Walker himself."

"I understand, but that may be difficult to do right now."

The man must have heard the tightness in her voice because he frowned. "What is it? Has something happened to Mr. Walker?"

"Not Mr. Walker, at least not yet. His stepbrother, Mr. Simpson, grabbed Pru this afternoon and left with her on the train before we had time to react. Riley's ridden off after them on his horse, but he may be too late."

"How could this have happened?"

"It's my fault." Cassie's voice threatened to crack. "I should have been watching her more closely, should have—" She couldn't go on.

Mr. Claypool reached out and touched her arm briefly. "Dear lady, please do not do this to yourself. The only person at fault here is that criminal Guy Simpson."

"Thank you. But that doesn't make me feel any better."

"But I don't understand. I told Mr. Walker in my telegram that I would be here today with the proof we've been searching for. He only had to hold out for one more day."

"What telegram?"

"Why, the telegram he should have received yesterday."

"I assure you he didn't receive a telegram from you yesterday." She was absolutely certain Riley would have told her had something this significant occurred.

She stood. "Come on, we're going down to the telegraph office at the train depot to find out just what happened."

With a nod, Mr. Claypool crossed the room and opened the door, allowing her to sweep past him before joining her in her rapid march down the sidewalk.

Cassie's mind was churning. Had Guy somehow gotten hold of that telegram? It would explain so much—why he'd canceled the outing with Mrs. Flanagan, why he'd picked today of all days to leave town.

About two blocks from the train station they met Sheriff Gleason heading back to his office. Cassie made quick introductions and then told the sheriff he needed to follow them to the depot. "I think I know why Pru's dad took her and left town." And without another word, she headed off again, leaving the two men no choice but to follow her.

Not waiting for either man to open the door for her, Cassie pushed into the depot and made a beeline for the counter. "Zeke Tarn, I need to have a word with you."

The young man looked up guiltily, his Adam's apple bobbing convulsively. "Miss Vickers. What can I do for you?"

"This gentleman here is Mr. Alexander Claypool, a Pinkerton detective. He tells me he sent Mr. Walker an official telegram yesterday, a telegram I know for a fact Mr. Walker never received. Would you care to explain that?"

Zeke glanced from one to the other of them, looking like a mouse caught in a trap. "I'm so sorry," he finally blurted. "I thought it would be okay."

"Slow down, Zeke," Sheriff Gleason said. "You thought what would be okay?"

"Lionel's been sick for two days now and I've been running this place all by myself. We were sure enough busy yesterday when the morning train came in, what with that big order for the mercantile and Mr. Johnston's crate getting busted and all. And Mr. Johnston was sure 'nuff angry."

"Yes, you were busy," Cassie said impatiently. "Get to the part about the telegram."

Sheriff Gleason shot her a quelling look, then turned back to Zeke. "Then what happened?"

"That telegram came right in the middle of all that ruckus and I had to set it aside while I tried to calm Mr. Johnston down. But then Mr. Simpson, he heard me say who it was for, and offered to deliver it for me. I thought it would be okay, him being Mr. Walker's brother and all."

The sheriff stared the man down. "Zeke, I'm afraid you've caused quite a bit of trouble. We're going to need to talk about the proper handling of telegrams, but not right now. You go on about your business and we'll discuss this after Lionel gets back on his feet."

"Yes, sir, Sheriff. And I promise it won't ever happen again."

The sheriff turned to Mr. Claypool. "What exactly did that telegram say?"

"It advised Mr. Walker that I had finally found the evidence he'd been looking for in regards to the Ploverton robbery, and that I would be here today with the information in hand."

The sheriff nodded to the sheaf of papers in the detective's grasp. "And is that the evidence?"

"Yes, sir. And this is your copy."

Sheriff Gleason perused the papers while Cassie fidgeted impatiently. Why were they all just standing here? They should be doing something, anything, to help Pru and keep Riley from doing something he'd have to live with the rest of his life.

Finally the sheriff looked up, his expression grim. "This changes everything." He turned back to the depot worker. "Zeke, I need to send another telegram to Sheriff Calhoun over in Needle Creek."

Gleason turned to Cassie. "Rest assured, the sheriff is going to yank him off that train as soon as it arrives, and Guy Simpson is going to be put away for quite a long time."

That relieved Cassie a bit, but there was still a worry nagging at her, a feeling that the nightmare wasn't completely over yet. "I'm going to Needle Creek myself," she blurted out.

"Now, Miss Vickers—"

But Cassie wasn't going to let herself be deterred. "I'm going and that's the end of it. No matter what comes of this, I need to be there for Pru." And for Riley.

"The next train to Needle Creek won't come through until tomorrow afternoon. By then, God willing, Mr. Walker and his niece will likely be headed back this way."

"That's not quick enough. I'll rent a buggy and horse from the livery."

"Now, you know I can't let you go gallivanting around the countryside on your own, especially somewhere you've never been before."

She lifted her chin and headed for the door. "I don't believe you have the right to stop me." Then she changed her tone as she stepped outside. "I'm sorry, Sheriff, I know you mean well, but this is just something I have to do."

"I'll go with her."

Startled by this sudden support from the Pinkerton detective, Cassie gave him an uncertain smile, but didn't pause. Her sense of urgency was growing. "That's very kind of you, Mr. Claypool, but you don't have to—"

"Oh, but I think I do. Mr. Walker hired me to take care of his interests in this matter, and something tells me you have become one of his interests. In fact, I do believe he would be very angry with me if I didn't do my utmost to assure that you reached your destination safely."

Riley hated to drive River this hard, but he had to get to Needle Creek before the train pulled out. The alternative was too nightmarish to contemplate.

How had Guy anticipated his plans this way? Or was it mere coincidence that his viper of a stepbrother had made his move on this particular day?

Whatever the reason, it was all Riley's fault. He'd let down his guard, relaxed his vigilance just when he should have been shoring it up. He'd been so intent on making sure they enjoyed this last day with Cassie and

Mrs. Flanagan that he'd let the weasel traipse right into the henhouse.

He wanted to howl in anger at the thought of what Pru must be going through right now. Would she ever forgive him, ever trust him again?

Riley leaned forward and rubbed River's neck, trying to coax a little more speed out of the already over-exerted horse. No time to think about forgiveness right now. He had to focus all his efforts on getting her back.

He would deal with the aftermath later.

Ten minutes had passed when the first outbuildings of what had to be Needle Creek came into view. He was close now, just a little bit farther.

In the distance, he heard the sound of a train whistle.

Chapter Twenty-Seven

Cassie and Mr. Claypool accomplished most of the one-hour trip from Turnabout to Needle Creek in silence, for which Cassie was grateful. Her tangled thoughts weren't conducive to conversation and small talk.

When they'd left the train depot, Mr. Claypool had gone to the livery to make arrangements for the buggy, while Cassie returned to Mrs. Flanagan's to update her on the situation. Noah was understandably upset and Cassie wished she could stay longer to help soothe his fears, but she couldn't shake the feeling that every minute counted and that she needed to get on the road. She quickly made arrangements for Mrs. Pratt to spend the night at Mrs. Flanagan's home, to tend to those things a wheelchair-bound woman could not. Dr. Pratt insisted on accompanying his wife, so Cassie felt relieved to know she was leaving the widow and Noah in such good hands.

When the first homes on the outskirts of Needle Creek came into sight, Cassie leaned forward, as if she could see through them into town and search out Riley and Pru.

"I know it's futile to tell you to relax, Miss Vickers,

so instead I will say take heart. We will soon be able to appraise the situation for ourselves."

She cast a glance at the detective, whose kind eyes mirrored some of her own worry. She liked this man, and understood now why Riley had put such trust in him. It wasn't just the prestige and reputation of the agency he worked for, it was the man himself.

Five minutes later, they had made it into the town proper. Mr. Claypool stopped the first person he saw and asked for directions to the sheriff's office.

"You turn left there on Pine Street and go three blocks and you'll see it on the right." The helpful stranger frowned. "But you won't find Sheriff Calhoun there right now, if that's who you're looking for."

"Why not?" Mr. Claypool asked.

"'Cause he's got a big ole ruckus to take care of. Some stranger got off the train dragging a little girl with him and tried to steal a horse. He's holed up in the livery stable right now, threatening to shoot anyone who steps inside."

Pru! She must be frightened beyond bearing. And where was Riley?

Cassie looked down from her seat on the wagon. "There was a man headed this way who was trying to get back the little girl. He was riding a silver-gray horse. Have you seen him?"

The helpful stranger nodded. "He's down at the livery, too, and the sheriff is having a hard time keeping him out of things." Their informant narrowed his eyes. "You folks mixed up in this, too?"

Mr. Claypool stepped in again, ignoring the man's question to ask one of his own. "Where is this livery?"

"One block over on Second Street, down toward the

train tracks. You'll see the crowd of gawkers before you get there. Fools all of 'em. Likely to get themselves hit by a stray bullet."

Cassie's heart lurched. "There's been shooting?"

"Not yet. But it's coming, you just wait and see. I don't plan to be there when it does."

Cassie turned to her companion. "Let's go."

To her surprise, he didn't argue, merely flicked the reins to set the horse in motion again.

When they were within a block of the livery, Mr. Claypool pulled the buggy to a halt, unable to continue due to the crowd.

Not waiting for him to so much as set the brake, Cassie jumped down and began searching the crowd for Riley. She spotted him almost immediately, arguing with someone, who from the looks of the badge on his shirt, was the sheriff.

Hands tried to hold her back, but she kept elbowing her way through, until she was close enough for him to hear her call.

Riley halted midargument and turned. He had to be hearing things. He'd know that voice anywhere, but Cassie couldn't be...

Then he saw her, struggling with a deputy who was trying to hold her back. Riley abandoned his argument with the sheriff without a backward glance and crossed the distance to her in quick, ground-eating strides. Without a word he pulled her into his arms, buried his head in her hair and hugged her for all he was worth. She felt so good, so right. He could draw strength from her, wanted to hold on to her as if she were a lifeline.

Then sanity returned and he pulled back. "What in the world are you doing here?"

"I came to help." She said the words matter-of-factly, as if they provided the most reasonable answer in the world.

"Help? The best thing you can do right now is get yourself out of harm's way."

"I intend to stand with you."

He had no answer for that, so tried a different approach. "How did you get here?"

"Mr. Claypool and I came by buggy."

"Clayp—" He looked around and spotted the detective standing a few feet away, his signature sardonic smile on his lips.

"Hello, Riley," the detective said in greeting. "I assure you I had no choice in the matter. If I hadn't come with her, I have no doubt Miss Vickers would have attempted to make the journey on her own."

Riley had no doubt of that, either. "So you've noticed how stubborn she is, have you?"

Cassie gave an inelegant sniff. "I believe the word you're looking for is *determined*." Then she waved her hand. "But we can discuss all of this later. Tell us what's happening."

Riley relayed basically the same story they'd heard from the man on the street earlier. He rubbed the back of his neck as he finished. "He's demanding we give him a horse and let him ride away, or he's going to come out shooting, using Pru as a shield."

Cassie's hand flew to her mouth. "Oh, how awful." Then her brow crinkled. "But I don't understand. All he wants is a horse, and he's in a livery…"

Riley shook his head. "It just so happened that at

the time Guy ran in, the owner had all the horses that weren't leased penned in the corral behind the stable. As soon as he realized what was happening, he opened the gate and ran 'em out."

She shook her head over that, then moved on. "Have you been able to see or talk to Pru?"

Riley shook his head in turn. "He was already holed up inside when I arrived and he hasn't allowed Pru to say anything." Which could mean any number of things, some of them worse than others.

"What does the sheriff want to do?"

"That's what we were just discussing when you arrived." Arguing about, actually. "Sheriff Calhoun thinks the best way to keep Pru safe is to let Guy have what he wants for now, in the hopes that he can be recaptured and dealt with later under better circumstances."

"And what do you think?"

Without answering her question, he turned to the detective. "I take it your presence means you have the evidence we've been searching for?"

"I do, and it's about as ironclad as it can be."

Cassie spoke up again. "And Guy knows all about it."

Again, Riley felt the urge to howl in frustration. But he had to keep his wits about him. "That's it, then. If we let Guy drive out of town with Pru, we will likely never see her again. She's become a liability to him. He knows he needs to travel light, travel fast and change his entire identity if he's going to escape capture. Pru just won't fit into those plans once she helps him get out of town."

"You can't mean—"

"He will either abandon her somewhere, or worse. We have to end this here." Riley gave Cassie's hands a squeeze, trying to draw strength from her. Then he reluctantly let them go. "Stay here, out of the line of fire, in case he makes good with his threats. I need to speak to the sheriff again."

Riley headed toward the lawman, rock-solid determination in his steps. His argument was no longer based on a hunch. Sheriff Calhoun had to listen to him now. Pru's life depended on it.

But he'd hardly launched into his argument when Cassie stepped up beside them.

"Let me talk to him." Her voice was steady, as if she'd just commented on the fine weather they were having.

"Absolutely not!" Riley felt his voice thunder from him, but Cassie didn't look the least bit fazed.

"I wasn't speaking to you," she answered calmly. "I was speaking to the sheriff."

"And just who might you be?" Sheriff Calhoun asked.

"I'm Cassie Lynn Vickers from over in Turnabout. And I'm also someone who cares very much about that terrified little girl in there."

"Cassie…" Riley's voice was a growl now. This was ridiculous. It was bad enough he had Pru's safety to worry about. He would not allow Cassie to put herself in Guy's hands, as well.

But the sheriff raised his hands to halt Riley's protest. "I want to hear what the lady has to say."

"Thank you, Sheriff. I think we're all agreed that the primary concern is getting Pru to safety. What happens to or with Guy Simpson is secondary."

"I'm with you so far."

"Mr. Walker tells me that no one has seen or heard Pru since Guy dragged her in there. I want to try to make certain she's all right, to see if she needs any medical help."

Cassie was voicing thoughts Riley had been trying to avoid since his arrival.

"I want to try to talk to him, to get him to let me in."

Riley opened his mouth to issue another strong protest, but the sheriff's glower held him off. He clamped his teeth tight enough to tense his jaw. He'd let the sheriff hear her out, but he'd be hanged if he'd let her go through with any of it.

The lawman crossed his arms. "And what makes you think he'll listen to you?"

"Because I'm a woman, he won't see me as a threat. In fact, he'll likely see me as another potential hostage, doubling his chances of negotiating his way out."

"And you don't think that's what you'll be handing him?"

She shook her head. "I'm pretty nimble and more clever than I look. If he lets me get close to Pru, and if she's not seriously injured, I'm pretty sure I can get her out. I have to try, at least."

"I heard a lot of ifs and pretty sures in that statement."

At least the sheriff wasn't letting himself be bowled over by Cassie's harebrained logic.

"But none of them were very long shots. Besides, I don't believe either you or Mr. Walker here has come up with a better plan, have you?"

Riley fumed as the silence drew out. Finally, he bit out the only response he had. "Any plan would be better than that one." He could not bear to have her fall into Guy's clutches, too.

She raised a brow. "I'm listening."

This time it was the sheriff who spoke up. "I know you want to save that little girl, but I don't see how giving this Simpson fellow another helpless hostage—no offense, Miss Vickers—is going to do that."

"And what makes you think I plan to be a helpless hostage?" Cassie reached into her pocket and drew out a derringer. "Mrs. Flanagan gave me this before I left Turnabout. And don't worry, I know exactly how to use it."

Riley had had enough. "So now you're planning to shoot your way out, with Pru in tow, no less? This is utterly ridiculous. I won't have it."

Claypool cleared his throat, making his presence known. "Actually, I think the lady's plan makes a great deal of sense, given the dire circumstances. And I think that for her to even suggest it, much less do so in the calm, logical manner she has, makes her one of the bravest women I have ever known."

Didn't Claypool think he knew that? "Miss Vickers's courage is not in doubt here, it's the soundness of her plan." Riley just couldn't risk losing both her and Pru. It would kill him.

Cassie patted his hand as if he were a child, and then turned to the sheriff. "What do you think of my plan?"

"It could work. Or it could get you killed."

Cassie offered him a crooked smile. "Let's focus on the *could work* part."

A great deal more discussion ensued, but in the end, the sheriff was convinced to let her do it.

Riley, however, was *not* happy.

She looked at him, her eyes liquid wells of emotion. "Before I do this, there's one thing I need from you."

There was nothing on this earth he could refuse her when she gazed at him that way. "Name it."

"Kiss me. Kiss me like you want me to come back out

of there. Like you wish you could go in with me. Like I truly matter to you."

He stepped forward and took her gently into his arms. "Yes, to all of the above," he whispered. Then he bent down and gave her the kiss she'd asked for, a kiss that came pouring from him with all the force of his pent-up emotions, a kiss that didn't care who was watching or what they might think.

When he finally pulled away, he gently pushed a few tendrils of hair from her forehead, not surprised to see his hand trembling slightly. How could he let her do this? "Now I need you to do something for me."

"Anything," she whispered.

"Promise me you won't do anything stupid in there, that you will do all in your power to come back to me."

"I promise." Then she stepped away from him and faced the livery. She didn't see him reach for her again and then drop his hands in defeat.

Cassie took a deep breath. Now that the moment was upon her, doubts were creeping in.

But she had the memory of that amazing, soul-searing kiss to give her courage.

"Guy!" She was surprised that her voice came out steady and strong. "It's me, Cassie Lynn Vickers."

It took a moment for him to respond, and when he did, she could tell he was close to the door. "Well, well, so it is. It appears my do-gooder brother has got his woman to do the talking for him."

She heard a snarl from somewhere behind her, but ignored it. "No one has gotten me to do anything. It's Pru I'm worried about and it's her I'm here for."

"I've already told the sheriff what needs to happen if he wants to keep Pru safe."

"I just want to see her, to talk to her and make sure she's all right."

"You think I would hurt my own flesh and blood?"

That's exactly what she thought. "You've both been through a lot these past several hours. Lots of bad things could have happened to a little girl in that time."

"I told you all, she's fine. But she won't be if I don't get my horse."

"Come on, Guy, I just want to see her, assure myself she's okay, maybe cosset her a little bit and let her know it's all going to turn out okay." Cassie infused a touch of incredulousness in her voice. "Surely you're not afraid of what I'll do if I get inside?"

He made an inelegant noise. "That's a laugh."

"Then let me see her. I'll just come in, check her over and come right back out. Then I can reassure all these gents that you're a man of your word and maybe they'll give you that horse." Not that she really thought he'd willingly let her back outside once he had her in there.

There were a few moments of tense silence, and then Guy finally answered. "All right, have it your way. Come on in, but only you, and you'd better not try any tricks."

Resisting the urge to look back and draw support from Riley, Cassie squared her shoulders and started forward. If she turned around and saw that passion in his eyes, she might not be able to go through with this.

She finally reached the livery door. It was a large, two-panel affair, with the panels sliding in opposite directions. She grasped one with both hands and began opening it.

"Only far enough for you to step inside," Guy called out. She realized he'd move farther back into the interior.

She followed his instructions and slipped through the narrow opening.

"Now close it."

She did so and the space was immediately shrouded in shadows. It took a moment for her eyes to adjust, but she moved forward, toward the sound of his voice. Then she spotted them, man and child standing in the middle of the spacious building. Guy held a gun in one hand and the collar of Pru's dress in his other.

"Pru, sweetheart, are you okay?"

The little girl nodded. Her sniffles, though, told a different story.

Cassie was within a few feet of them now. And as expected, Guy put a halt to her progress.

"That's far enough. You wanted to see her? Well, here she is, fit as a fiddle, just like I said."

Cassie smiled, trying to disguise the bile rising in her throat. "I told them you wouldn't hurt your own little girl. You're not that kind of man. Why, anyone can tell how truly deep your love for her is by looking at how you risked getting caught by taking her with you, rather than leaving her behind and running off on your own." It was the one thing she couldn't figure out. If he'd slipped away as soon as he intercepted that telegram, he'd probably have been able to disappear cleanly.

"You think I'd leave my daughter, *my* daughter, in the hands of my do-gooder, self-righteous stepbrother? No, and if I could have, I would have grabbed the boy, too. And I will someday, mark my words. Riley will *never* have anything that's rightfully mine, no matter how jealous he is of me."

The man was truly mad. Cassie knew now that he would never willingly let Pru go.

But right now she had a part to play. She frowned petulantly. "Must you wave that gun around?" She gave a delicate shiver. "I have a strong distaste for such instruments of violence. Surely a grown man such as yourself can control one little girl without it."

"The gun's not for little girls or women." His sneer made it clear he was speaking of her. "It's to protect myself against those men out there."

She nodded, as if in agreement. "Before I go and tell the others that Pru is okay, can I at least give her a hug?"

He rolled his eyes and then nodded. "Make it quick."

Was he really planning to let her leave, after all? Cassie knelt before Pru, heartbroken by the fear and despair she saw in the little girl's eyes. "You are so, so brave," she said, as she brushed hair back from the child's face. "Your uncle Riley and Noah and Mrs. Flanagan all send their love to you."

"I want to be back with them," Pru said in a voice that trembled.

"I know, sweetheart. And you will be. You need to just hold on a little longer."

Guy laughed at that—an ugly, hateful sound.

Cassie embraced the girl in a gentle hug, and pitched her voice so that only the child could hear. "When I say the word," she whispered, "run to the door, just as fast as you can. Your uncle Riley is waiting on the other side."

"That's enough," Guy growled. "And I've changed my mind. I don't think you'll be heading back outside, after all. I like the idea of having two things Riley wants. He might even trade the boy for you, if he's properly motivated."

Cassie gave Pru a tight squeeze, then released her. She yanked Guy's hand, surprising him enough to have him release the child's collar.

"Now!" Cassie yelled, and still in a stooped position, rolled into Guy, catching him at the knees and causing him to fall backward.

She scrambled to her feet, pleased to note Pru was already halfway to the door. This was going to work! And she hadn't had to use the gun. But before Cassie could get way, Guy grabbed a fistful of her hem and yanked hard, pulling himself up into a sitting position. Calling her a vile name, he raised his gun and, to her horror, pointed it toward Pru rather than her.

Desperate to stop him, Cassie reached in her pocket for the derringer.

A moment later, a shot rang out through the stable.

Chapter Twenty-Eight

Riley shoved the door to the livery open with an almost superhuman force. Where were Pru and Cassie? Who had fired that shot? More importantly, who had it hit?

The first thing he saw was Pru, just inside the door, lying facedown. His knees nearly buckled. *No. Please, God, no.*

Then she moved and looked up. When she saw Riley, her face split into the most beautiful smile he'd ever seen, and she scrambled to her feet and ran to him. "Uncle Riley, Uncle Riley." He stooped down to catch her and she latched on to his neck. "I ran and ran, just like Miss Cassie told me to, but then I heard the gun and I tripped."

"It's okay, kitten, you did just fine."

He stood, his eyes scanning the interior over Pru's shoulder. Where was Cassie? Now that he knew his niece was safe, he frantically searched for some sign that she was okay, too. But other men had swarmed the stable— the sheriff, his deputy and a half dozen other deputized men. Riley couldn't see past them.

Then he felt a touch on his shoulder and looked

around to see Claypool standing there, hands out to take Pru.

Riley gently disengaged his niece's arms from around his neck. "Pru, honey, this nice man here is Mr. Claypool, a friend of mine. Would you go with him for a moment while I look for Cassie and make sure she's okay?"

Pru nodded and allowed herself to be transferred to the other man's hold. Then she pointed behind Riley. "She's okay, Uncle Riley. Look!"

He spun around and there Cassie was, apparently unharmed, making a beeline for him. He saved her some steps and met her halfway.

He caught her up in an embrace and without preamble kissed her soundly. This time the emotions that poured from him were relief and victory and exultation. Somehow, against all odds, both his girls were safe.

When they finally parted, he took Cassie's face in his hands. "You did it. You saved Pru and came out of it whole."

"Which is more than I can say for Guy." There was more than a hint of amusement in the sheriff's voice.

"What do you mean?" Riley glanced from the sheriff back to Cassie and saw her face turning beet red in embarrassment.

The lawman laughed. "That shot we heard that got you charging inside like a bull after an interloper? That wasn't Guy's gun we heard, it was Miss Vickers's derringer."

Riley stared at her incredulously. "You shot Guy?"

"He'd pointed his gun at Pru. I had to do something to stop him."

"She stopped him, all right. Shot his big toe right off."

"I just aimed for his foot. It seemed the least gruesome of my possible targets." She lifted her chin. "And it worked."

Riley grinned, deciding she was quite beautiful when she was embarrassed.

She frowned at him and the sheriff both. "This is not funny, gentlemen. I don't take what I did lightly."

"No, ma'am," the sheriff said meekly.

But Riley heard the man chuckle again as he walked off.

He linked his arm with Cassie's, not wanting to let her go so soon after he'd discovered her again, and turned to Claypool. "What do you say we take these two lovely ladies out of this stable and find them somewhere more comfortable to relax?"

The sheriff told them that they would have a couple hotel rooms free of charge for the night, compliments of the town council. Cassie asked Riley to order some food to be sent upstairs for Pru, and took the girl upstairs to settle her in. She carried with her the small carpetbag Mr. Claypool had retrieved from the buggy, and set it on the bed. She opened it and pulled out two things—a hairbrush so that she could brush the tangles from Pru's locks, and a surprise she'd packed as an act of faith that they would get Pru safely home.

"Look who came along to keep you company to-night."

"Bitsy!" The girl's delighted smile warmed Cassie's heart.

"Cindy will be waiting for you when you get back to Mrs. Flanagan's," Cassie said. "I'm sorry I couldn't fit both of them in my bag."

Pru's gaze shifted and her gaze didn't meet Cassie's. "That's okay."

Guessing what the little girl was feeling, Cassie took one of her hands. "It's okay if you don't want to play with Cindy anymore. But I want you to think about this. It's not Cindy's fault she came from your father, any more than it's your fault that he's your pa."

Cassie stood up. "Now, let's get you cleaned up and get your hair brushed. What do you say?"

With a nod, Pru followed her to the vanity.

An hour later the child was freshened up, fed and tucked into bed, sound asleep.

Cassie headed downstairs, knowing she would find Riley waiting for her there.

And she did.

Her heart gave a little pitter-patter as she saw the way he looked at her. Could he possibly return her feelings? Those kisses today had certainly said yes. Or was she fooling herself, and was this all merely gratitude for what she'd done for Pru?

He stepped forward to greet her as she reached the bottom step, and tucked her arm in his.

"How's Pru doing?"

"She's still a bit clingy, but that's to be expected after all she's been through. But right now she's sound asleep. One of the hotel maids is sitting with her, in case she wakes up before I return, but I honestly think she'll sleep through the night."

Riley nodded as he led her to a secluded corner of the lobby. "I sent a telegram earlier to Sheriff Gleason to inform him that it all ended well and we would be back in Turnabout tomorrow. I asked him to share the information with Mrs. Flanagan and Mr. Humphries.

"Thank you. I know Mrs. Flanagan and Noah will sleep better tonight."

Riley seated her on a padded bench, then settled beside her. Taking her hands, he held her gaze with a steady one of his own. "We need to talk."

Her heart fluttered again, but she ignored it. This could be about anything. "I'm listening."

He shifted, as if uncertain what he was about to say. "I know you're probably already spoken for, but—"

"What?"

"Perhaps 'spoken for' is not the right term here. Should I have said you've already made your marriage bargain?"

"Whatever are you talking about?"

"That day you were gone all morning, weren't you visiting the men on your husband list?"

"Absolutely not." She held his gaze. "I was actually visiting with my father that day. To tell him I would not be returning home on a permanent basis, that I had my own life to live and would be opening a bakery business."

Riley's whole demeanor brightened, as if a weight had been lifted. "Good for you."

"I did agree to a compromise, however." She explained to him the bargain she'd struck with her father, then frowned. "How could you think I would kiss you like I did today if I'd promised to marry another man?"

He had the grace to look sheepish. "To be honest, I didn't know what to think. Why didn't you tell me about the visit to your father?"

Now it was her turn to squirm. "I didn't want you to think… I mean, it was…"

He grinned. "You didn't want me to think it had been on my account."

"And it wasn't." At least not entirely. "It was something I had to do for myself."

"I'm proud of you."

That should have sounded condescending, but somehow it didn't. She sat up straighter. "Was that all you wanted to speak to me about, or was there something else?"

He grinned. "Oh yes, there's definitely something else. And now that I know you've given up that husband hunt of yours, it is even more pressing. Cassie, you have to know, especially after all that happened today, that I am absolutely, totally, incredibly in love with you."

"You are?"

He laughed. "Yes. How could I not be? You make me laugh—at myself and at my problems. You make me think—of possible futures and of different ways of seeing the world. You make me a better man.

"And you make me want to have you at my side, today and always."

"Oh Riley, I love you, too. I don't know how it's possible to love someone so much after knowing him only two weeks, but I think I fell in love with you the moment you stooped down beside me to help me up in the livery yard. It's like I've known you forever."

He squeezed her hands. "Then you'll marry me?"

She slipped her hands from his and threw her arms around his neck. "Yes!"

The kiss that they sealed their agreement with was the best one yet.

Epilogue

Riley gave the nail one final thwack, then stood back to study his work. It was coming along nicely. Within the next two days, he should have half the roomy attic walled off into two bedchambers, one for Pru and one for Noah.

It had been nearly a month since Guy had been arrested and just yesterday they'd learned that he'd been sentenced to life in prison. At last the children were safe and they could begin to set down roots again. Even Pru's nightmares had faded and she and Noah were thriving the way children were intended to.

The two were looking forward to having their own rooms. In fact, if they hadn't been in school right now they would probably be up here helping him. That the rooms were up in the attic was seen by them as an added bonus. Apparently the kids were looking at this as the tower from one of those fairy-tale stories Mrs. Flanagan liked to read to them.

The woman had become a surrogate grandmother to the two kids, and the affection ran both ways. As soon as Mrs. Flanagan had heard he and Cassie were getting married, she had insisted that they move in permanently with her. Riley had tried to protest, then tried to insist on paying rent, but the feisty widow was having none of it.

"I've realized over these past few weeks how empty this house has been since all my menfolk left me," she'd said. "And I've gotten used to having young people around me again. Not only used to it, but fond of it. In fact, I'd consider it just plain cruelty if you were to take those two children away from me."

The only thing she would allow was that they help with the groceries and the chores, which was fine by him.

"You look like you could use a glass of lemonade, Mr. Walker."

He turned to see that his lovely bride of two weeks had joined him. She was carrying a glass in one hand and what looked like a document of some sort in the other. "Why, thank you, Mrs. Walker, I don't mind if I do."

She smiled. "I don't think I'll ever grow tired of being called Mrs. Walker. "

"I sincerely hope not." Riley took the glass from her, then pulled her close, giving her a quick but oh-so-sweet kiss before releasing her.

She looked up at him with shining eyes. "That's something else I'll never tire of."

He tapped her nose affectionately, then indicated the paper she held. "What's that you have?"

"I stopped by Reggie's studio while I was out. Our wedding picture is ready."

He'd learned that Regina Barr was the town photographer, and he'd hired her to memorialize their special day.

Cassie handed the photograph to him and then nestled against him as he studied it.

Riley gazed at the photograph, a feeling of contentment settling in his chest. They were all pictured there—

he and Cassie in the center, Noah and Pru on the left and Mrs. Flanagan and Cassie's father on the right.

Riley had found a place to belong, and settling down had been no sacrifice at all.

In fact, with Cassie at his side, he was right where he wanted to be.

Cassie looked at the picture Riley held and couldn't believe what a beautiful life the Good Lord had planned for her. Two beautiful children, a wonderful, loving, God-fearing husband, a father she was now reconciled with and a woman who was as precious as a mother to her.

There was no richer life she could imagine. Like the Cinderella in the children's favorite story, she'd found her prince and her treasure, and she planned to live her very own happily ever after.

* * * * *

If you loved this story,
pick up the other books in the
TEXAS GROOMS *series*

Available now from Love Inspired Historical!

Find more great reads at www.LoveInspired.com

Dear Reader,

I hope you've enjoyed Cassie Lynn and Riley's story. I knew as soon as Cassie Lynn popped up as a secondary character in *The Holiday Courtship* that she needed to have a story of her own. She arrived on the scene and suddenly she was such a fully realized character in my mind. There was so much I knew about her that I couldn't show in that book. It took me a while to figure out who her hero would be, but I think Riley worked out perfectly to be her forever match.

Both of these characters had some tough issues to work through, issues where it wasn't easy to see what the "right" choice would be, issues that ultimately required them to take a hard stand, a stand they couldn't have made without this journey they took together.

And if you enjoyed this book, I hope you'll be on the lookout for the next in the series. For more information on this and other books set in Turnabout, please visit my website at winniegriggs.com or follow me on facebook at Facebook.com/WinnieGriggs.Author.

And as always, I love to hear from readers. Feel free to contact me at winnie@winniegriggs.com with your thoughts on this or any other of my books.

Wishing you a life abounding with love and grace,
Winnie Griggs

MONTANA COWBOY DADDY
Big Sky Country • by Linda Ford

With a little girl to raise, widowed single father Dawson Marshall could sure use some help—he just didn't expect it to come from city girl Isabelle Redfield. The secret heiress who volunteers to watch Dawson's daughter wants to be valued for more than her money, but will hiding the truth ruin her chance of earning Dawson's love?

THE SHERIFF'S CHRISTMAS TWINS
Smoky Mountain Matches • by Karen Kirst

After confirmed bachelor Sheriff Shane Timmons and his childhood friend Allison Ashworth discover orphaned twin babies, Shane offers to help Allison care for them—temporarily. But as Shane falls for Allison and the twins, can he become the permanent husband and father they need?

A FAMILY FOR THE HOLIDAYS
Prairie Courtships • by Sherri Shackelford

Hoping to earn money to buy a boardinghouse, Lily Winter accompanies two orphaned siblings to Nebraska. But when she discovers their grandfather is missing and the kids are in danger, she hires Jake Elder, a local gun-for-hire, for protection—and marries him for convenience.

THE RIGHTFUL HEIR
by Angel Moore

Mary Lou Ellison believes she inherited the local newspaper from her guardian...until Jared Ivy arrives with a will that says his grandfather left it to *him*. The sheriff's solution? They must work together until a judge comes to town and rules in favor of the rightful heir.

REQUEST YOUR FREE BOOKS!

2 FREE INSPIRATIONAL NOVELS
PLUS 2 FREE MYSTERY GIFTS

Love Inspired® HISTORICAL

YES! Please send me 2 FREE Love Inspired® Historical novels and my 2 FREE mystery gifts (gifts are worth about $10). After receiving them, if I don't wish to receive any more books, I can return the shipping statement marked "cancel." If I don't cancel, I will receive 4 brand-new novels every month and be billed just $4.99 per book in the U.S. or $5.49 per book in Canada. That's a saving of at least 17% off the cover price. It's quite a bargain! Shipping and handling is just 50¢ per book in the U.S. and 75¢ per book in Canada.* I understand that accepting the 2 free books and gifts places me under no obligation to buy anything. I can always return a shipment and cancel at any time. Even if I never buy another book, the two free books and gifts are mine to keep forever.

102/302 IDN GH6Z

Name	(PLEASE PRINT)	
Address		Apt. #
City	State/Prov.	Zip/Postal Code

Signature (if under 18, a parent or guardian must sign)

Mail to the **Reader Service:**
IN U.S.A.: P.O. Box 1867, Buffalo, NY 14240-1867
IN CANADA: P.O. Box 609, Fort Erie, Ontario L2A 5X3

Want to try two free books from another series?
Call 1-800-873-8635 or visit www.ReaderService.com.

* Terms and prices subject to change without notice. Prices do not include applicable taxes. Sales tax applicable in N.Y. Canadian residents will be charged applicable taxes. Offer not valid in Quebec. This offer is limited to one order per household. Not valid for current subscribers to Love Inspired Historical books. All orders subject to credit approval. Credit or debit balances in a customer's account(s) may be offset by any other outstanding balance owed by or to the customer. Please allow 4 to 6 weeks for delivery. Offer available while quantities last.

Your Privacy—The Reader Service is committed to protecting your privacy. Our Privacy Policy is available online at www.ReaderService.com or upon request from the Reader Service.

We make a portion of our mailing list available to reputable third parties that offer products we believe may interest you. If you prefer that we not exchange your name with third parties, or if you wish to clarify or modify your communication preferences, please visit us at www.ReaderService.com/consumerschoice or write to us at Reader Service Preference Service, P.O. Box 9062, Buffalo, NY 14240-9062. Include your complete name and address.

SPECIAL EXCERPT FROM

Love Inspired **HISTORICAL**

*Sheriff Shane Timmons just wants to be left alone,
but this Christmas he'll find that family is what he's
always been looking for.*

Read on for an excerpt from
THE SHERIFF'S CHRISTMAS TWINS,
the next heartwarming book in the
SMOKY MOUNTAIN MATCHES *series.*

"We have a situation at the mercantile, Sheriff."

Shane Timmons reached for his gun belt.

The banker held up his hand. "You won't be needing that. This matter requires finesse, not force."

"What's happened?"

"I suggest you come see for yourself."

Shane's curiosity grew as he followed Claude outside into the crisp December day and continued on to the mercantile. Half a dozen trunks were piled beside the entrance. Unease pulled his shoulder blades together. His visitors weren't due for three more days. He did a quick scan of the street, relieved there was no sign of the stagecoach.

Claude held the door and waited for him to enter first. The pungent stench of paint punched him in the chest. His gaze landed on a knot of men and women in the far corner.

"Why didn't you watch where you were going? Where are your parents?"

"I—I'm terribly sorry, ma'am" came the subdued reply. "My ma's at the café."

"This is what happens when children are allowed to roam through the town unsupervised."

Shane rounded the aisle and wove his way through the customers, stopping short at the sight of statuesque, matronly Gertrude Messinger, a longtime Gatlinburg resident and wife of one of the gristmill owners, doused in green liquid. While her upper half remained untouched, her full skirts and boots were streaked and splotched with paint. Beside her, ashen and bug-eyed, stood thirteen-year-old Eliza Smith.

"Quinn Darling." Gertrude's voice boomed with outrage. "I expect you to assign the cost of a new dress to the Smiths' account."

At that, Eliza's freckles stood out in stark contrast to her skin.

"One moment, if you will, Mr. Darling," a third person chimed in. "The fault is mine, not Eliza's."

The voice put him in mind of snow angels and piano recitals and cookies swiped from silver platters. But it couldn't belong to Allison Ashworth. She and her brother, George, wouldn't arrive until Friday. Seventy-two more hours until his past collided with his present.

He wasn't ready.

Don't miss
THE SHERIFF'S CHRISTMAS TWINS by Karen Kirst,
available wherever
Love Inspired® Historical books and ebooks are sold.

www.LoveInspired.com

SPECIAL EXCERPT FROM

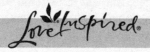

When Macy Swanson must suddenly raise her young nephew, help comes in the form of single rancher and boys ranch volunteer Tanner Barstow. Can he help her see she's mom—and rural Texas—material?

*Read on for a sneak preview of the first book in the **LONE STAR COWBOY LEAGUE: BOYS RANCH** miniseries, THE RANCHER'S TEXAS MATCH by Brenda Minton.*

She leaned back in the seat and covered her face with her hands. "I am angry. I'm mad because I don't know what to do for Colby. And the person I always went to for advice is gone. Grant is gone. I think Colby and I were both in a delusional state, thinking they would come home. But they're not. I'm not getting my brother, my best friend, back. Colby isn't getting his parents back. And it isn't fair. It isn't fair that I had to—"

Her eyes closed, and she shook her head.

"Macy?"

She pinched the bridge of her nose. "No. I'm not going to say that. I lost a job and gave up an apartment. Colby lost his parents. What I lost doesn't amount to anything. I lost things I don't miss."

"I think you're wrong. I think you miss your life. There's nothing wrong with that. Accept it, or it'll eat you up."

Tanner pulled up to her house.

"I miss my life." She said it on a sigh. "I wouldn't be anywhere else. But I have to admit, there are days I wonder if Colby would be better off with someone else, with anyone but me. But I'm his family. We have each other."

"Yes, and in the end, that matters."

"But…" She bit down on her lip and glanced away from him, not finishing.

"But what?"

"What if I'm not a mom? What if I can't do this?" She looked young sitting next to him, her green eyes troubled.

"I'm guessing that even a mom who planned on having a child would still question if she could do it."

She reached for the door. "Thank you for letting me talk about Colby."

"Anytime." He said it, and then he realized the door that had opened.

She laughed. "Don't worry. I won't be calling at midnight to talk about my feelings."

"If you did, I'd answer."

She stood on tiptoe and touched his cheek to bring it down to her level. When she kissed him, he felt floored by the unexpected gesture. Macy had soft hair, soft gestures and a soft heart. She was easy to like. He guessed if a man wasn't careful, he'd find himself falling a little in love with her.

Don't miss
THE RANCHER'S TEXAS MATCH by Brenda Minton,
available October 2016 wherever
Love Inspired® books and ebooks are sold.

www.LoveInspired.com